OUR FIFTH SEASON

…where murder derails love…

a novel

Josée Sigouin

Our Fifth Season
Copyright © 2025 Josée Sigouin
All rights reserved
Published by Blue Denim Press Inc.
First Edition
ISBN 978-1-998494-15-6

This is a work of fiction. Resemblances to persons living or dead, or to organizations, are unintended and purely coincidental.

Photo by iStock/Credit: imagedepotpro
Cover Design: Shane Joseph

Library and Archives Canada Cataloguing in Publication Title: Our fifth season : where murder derails love : a novel / Josée Sigouin. Names: Sigouin, Josée, author. Description: First edition. Identifiers: Canadiana (print) 20250230941 | Canadiana (ebook) 2025023095X | ISBN 9781998494156 (softcover) | ISBN 9781998494163 (Kindle) | ISBN 9781998494170 (EPUB) | ISBN 9781998494187 (IngramSpark EPUB) Subjects: LCGFT: Novels. Classification: LCC PS8637.I289 O97 2025 | DDC C813/.6—dc23

Dedication

To Jeffrey Hing Yin Tong, husband, partner, and best friend

One: January 16th to 24th, 2018 — Ithaca, New York

I haven't told anyone about Adam's arrest, not my sister Colleen, not my friend Emma at the Center, and certainly not my father. I don't believe he killed that woman. There has to be a mistake.

I know he feels like he has been trampled in the mud by a million boots, but how can he say he doesn't want me in his life anymore? A few days ago, he spoke as if I had already agreed to live with him in Korea.

Here, life marches on. I must collect Sean from the after-school program and dredge up enough energy to answer his questions.

"Adam calling tonight?" My sweet boy can't wait for Adam to finish the story he is reading to him on video calls.

"Sorry, honey, still busy with that emergency."

"Did he go in an ambulance?" His blue eyes widen with equal parts wonder and worry.

"No, sweetie. Don't worry." I push away images of Adam riding in an emergency vehicle, ambulance or any other kind. I read online that the police found his sweater and fingerprints in the dead woman's room. Maybe they needed to discuss a scene—director to lead actor— so he knocked on her door at the guesthouse? Then he drove home while she took a bath. And drowned.

If only he told me his side of the story, my head would stop spinning with all these scenarios.

The sidewalks are edged with towering snowbanks that Ithaca has just begun to clear. Syncopated *beeps* and blinking lights fill our street. Sean gapes at the yellow monster devouring the snow and spewing it into the bellies of dump trucks lined along the curb like elephants.

I tug his mittened hand. "Hey, buddy, let's move our feet. Almost dinner time."

"Mommy, look at our snow people." Sean saunters to the house with the Redbud tree that is inextricably linked to Adam. He loved how the branches fanned out, even in winter when it was bare.

Sheltering under the tree, Sean and I made three snow figures, one for him, one for Adam and one for me—our would-be family in front of the bungalow.

My co-worker Emma says I am lucky Sean likes Adam. She wouldn't call me lucky now.

The house is cold. Every light I turn on reveals chores I'm neglecting: a basket of laundry that needs folding, boxes of cereal in bags from Wegmans, a broken drawer blocking half the kitchen counter. Dinner is from a can—soft ravioli in a thick red sauce—a shortcut I haven't resorted to since Sean's father left.

I wash the dishes while Sean plays with the toy garage that Adam sent him for Christmas. He launches one car after another down the spiral ramp and watches them zoom across the kitchen floor, which does nothing to lessen my headache.

"Can Byron come over?" he asks.

"Not tonight, honey. Mommy's not feeling too well. This weekend, okay?"

He frowns and makes me promise that I will not change my mind. I promise myself that I will not fall apart.

It has been eight days since Adam said those awful words. I have tried his number so many times that it's embarrassing. I have left voicemails, emails, texts, long ones, short ones. He keeps ignoring me. I jump if either of my phones makes the slightest sound. I check them whenever I surface from sleep in the middle of the night, middle of the day in Korea.

I have tried to reach his manager, In-sung, but all I hear is a string of words I don't understand with no signal at the end for leaving a message.

To love someone from so far away means always being thirsty and seldom slaking that thirst. What I crave right now is his voice, his happy voice when he toured 'our renovated house' for the first time; his tired voice, his bedroom voice, his euphoric voice after he finished filming his last scene.

Actor turned director: that was his plan. And when it proved impossible to continue studying in Korea, he came to Cornell. We see all kinds at the Center, and what struck me when I met him was how comfortable in his skin he seemed. That was a year ago.

I introduced myself, "Joanne Rollins." I motioned to my visitor's chair, but he waited until I'd squeezed between the desk and the filing cabinets, and reached my chair. He bowed before sitting.

I can still picture him scanning the room, the nineteenth-century wainscoting and the wide baseboards, while I asked for his student number.

Dae-hyun (Adam) Ahn, I read from the student information system. "Did I pronounce it correctly?"

"Yes." I caught amusement in his eyes. "Adam is fine."

Home institution: Korea National University of Arts

Enrolled at Cornell: Winter term 2017

Date of Birth: 1986 11 16. He was thirty, like me. Same birthday.

His assignment was a screenplay, and I felt immediately gripped by the action. It took a construction from another language to bring me back to the task at hand. "Here," I showed him, "'She wants that it is morning already.' It's better to say, 'She can't wait until morning.' Even if she *does* wait until morning." I smiled and he smiled back.

He wore an off-white sweater buttoned along one shoulder, not like everybody else, not eye-catching either, not shouting "superstar."

The campus looks forlorn on this January morning: grey stones, grey pavement, grey sky. The water in Cascadilla Creek flows as if against its will, folding upon itself in sluggish eddies. The few people I encounter wear black. I wear black. My reflection in the doors of McGraw Hall, home to Cornell Student Services, shows a woman I barely recognize. Her face looks pinched, and her shoulders slump under the weight of her coat.

After the elevator ride to the Academic Writing Center, I pass by my coworkers' offices and catch snippets of conversation. Emma sits behind her desk and raises her head. Drab colours have no place in her wardrobe. She wears a teal sweater over a rust blouse and two-tone earrings to match. "Has Adam mentioned it snowed? A foot and a half in Seoul."

"Of course." I smile, maintaining the fiction that he is busy with post-production. I don't even know if he is in Seoul or at the house near Danyang.

"No new snow here, thank God."

Emma lives with two Siamese cats and keeps the Weather Channel on while she eats breakfast. At night, it's CNN. If the hosts mention Seoul, it is because the South Korean government has reported another nuclear test by North Korea, not because a Korean screen star stands accused of killing the star of his upcoming film.

In my office, I switch the computer on and check the Korean news sites, something I avoid doing at home in front of Sean. The *Chosun Ilbo* has nothing new on the case. It quotes the eulogies delivered at the actor's funeral:

Everyone is devastated by the loss of Baek Young-hee, the First Lady of Korea, as we affectionately called her. Among her many successes, no one will forget the role she played five years ago in Reunification. *We all believed in her character's power to achieve our country's most cherished dream: to live again as one nation, working hard but never starving, prosperous because of our ingenuity and openness to the world.*

Many speculations about why she died have surfaced on social media. True or false, none imply any wrongdoing on her part. Today, let us remember her as an honorable citizen of our country who won the respect of all nations in Asia. May she rest in peace.

I would like to check other sites, but it is time to see the first student of the day. The floorboards creak as I make my way to the waiting room, once a faculty lounge with a fireplace that hasn't been lit for decades. All the chairs are filled, and it is only nine in the morning. Essays due. Midterms coming.

A few hours later, I answer students' emails while eating my lunch. I steal a moment to check *The Orbiter*. It includes a quote from a fellow actor:

I was in Reunification *with Baek Young-hee and Ahn Dae-hyun. He was my role model, always humble and considerate to others, but that was all an act; I see that now. He is actually a vile and calculating man who thinks nothing of killing a woman to raise his film's profits. I am shocked.*

Emma opens her door across the hall and tells a boy to return whenever he needs help. She follows him a few steps and stops at my door, still smiling from the goodwill she showers on every student who visits the Center, a smile that vanishes as soon as she sees me. "What's wrong?"

"Nothing." I spring out of my chair to mask how hard the actor's words hit me. "Coffee? I'll bring you back a cup." I climb the narrow stairs to the lunchroom, clutching the ramp. Did the mild-mannered man I thought I knew hide a monster? Pain shoots between my temples. Liquids. I need liquids to soothe my parched throat and shake off the shivers that refuse to go away. I can't afford to stay in bed, not while the Center is this busy.

By the end of the day, my forehead burns. Stepping outside brings me a modicum of relief, however, helping Sean into his snowsuit takes more energy than I thought I had. "Not too fast," I say as we walk the two blocks to the house. As soon as we have crossed the last intersection, he races ahead. Runs back. "Our snow-people."

Someone has knocked them down, scattered a head here and a body there, broken the carrot noses and ground the button eyes in the snow.

Two: April 17th, 2018–Danyang, South Korea

Adam swings his axe up and brings it down on the first log of the day. A loud *crack* fills the yard and bounces from house to mountain and back again. He times his next stroke to match the echo, and his mind takes off. From blue sky to buds on trees to the day of the month.

He was released on bail one hundred days ago. Men give women a single rose when they have dated for that long.

In-sung, he thinks. If anyone knows about rituals, it is Kim In-sung. After the bail hearing, and once he had outmaneuvered the last television van tailing them on the highway, In-sung pulled behind one of those shacks that sells everything from eggs to instant ramen, and disappeared inside. No sooner was Adam alone than he started to shake. He put his head between his knees, waiting for it to subside.

By the time he straightened up, In-sung was back behind the wheel. "Here." He put a block of tofu in Adam's hand, the time-honoured ritual for anyone released from jail, white as a clean slate, bland and stripped of anything but nutrition. *Stay alive, Ahn Dae-hyun,* it said, *even if you don't feel like it.* Adam forced it all down before In-sung pulled the car back on the highway, took the Danyang exit, and drove to the house Adam still owns in the countryside.

He has come to rely on In-sung for so much: books to fill the hours when he cannot sleep, beer to drink when he comes from Seoul, and news of a world that sees him as a monster. "We'll pull you out of this, Dae-hyun-*ah*," he says every time—In-sung, his manager at the Star Shop Agency, his closest friend, and now a member of his legal team.

After three months, Adam has finally persuaded him to take a vacation, give back to his young family the attention they deserve. When In-sung returns, he will find Adam as he is now, checkered shirt sleeves rolled up, forearms grown thick and sinewy from chopping so much wood.

Under the midday sun, the *hanok*'s roof tiles blaze. Adam shades his eyes with a hand to view the rooftop's dragon-back silhouette. Mahogany beams anchor the house to the ground and mark where each room begins and ends. Latticed doors, a set for each room, let daylight filter through the mulberry paper and allow the house to breathe.

The narrow ledge running around the *hanok* is in deep shade, barely noticeable if not for Grandmother peeling potatoes by the kitchen door. She wears the same orange scarf as when she arrived with In-sung soon after Adam was released on bail. In-sung helped her out of the car and took her bags to a spare bedroom while Adam stood outside, axe in hand.

"Dae-hyun-*ah*," In-sung said after settling Grandmother in, "we can't have those rats from *The Orbiter* snap pictures of you with that thing in your hands."

"To hell with them." He chopped a few more logs and asked In-sung how long his grandmother intended to stay.

"You need a guarantor. Judge's order." In-sung nodded toward the police guard on duty at the *hanok* since Adam's return. "Temporary measure."

"Right," said Adam, who remembered no such detail. "Are you saying my father's okay with his mother staying with a potential murderer?"

In-sung gave him a look—*it's complicated*—and that is as far as the conversation went. He found a log to sit on, pulled a file from his briefcase and asked Adam the questions he had collected from the legal team.

In the days that followed, the idea that Han Dok-ku and his army of paparazzi at *The Orbiter* could demonize Adam even further by publishing a photo of him wielding an axe sank in. He moved his wood-chopping activities behind the house.

He has now chopped enough logs to keep the *hanok*'s floors heated for the next two years. *Thwack*, goes the first-degree murder charge against him. *Thwack*, the three nights he spent in jail after his arrest. *Thwack!* the men taunting him, "Pretty boy in trouble." *Thwack*, the tracker locked around his ankle.

He swings his axe up and brings it down, slicing the heart of every log, destroying its wholeness and reducing it to pieces that he throws on the woodpile. With them go the trappings of his life as an actor: the penthouse in Seoul, sold to cover the bail bond; the sports car he loved to drive, given to In-sung; the adoring fans, silent now that he is offline. None of these matters as much as losing friends, family, and the woman he loves.

On the first day of his new life on bail, long after the guard had dozed off on the *hanok*'s ledge, and Adam had reduced dozens of logs into kindling, he pulled his phone from his pocket and rang Joanne in America. He had ignored the reams of messages she'd left him; it was time he faced her questions. He would focus on the positive: Attorney Choi had convinced the authorities to redo the DNA test that incriminated him. Adam rehearsed his lines—*There's a good chance* – No. *There's every chance that the police will drop the charge*, and pressed on his number-one contact. "It's me."

"Thank God. I was so worried. What happened?"

He wanted to ask how much she knew.

She spoke first. "I read online. I can't believe it."

Neither can I, he wanted to say, but something stuck in his throat.

"Say something."

Words zigzagged on his tongue, too jumbled to come out.

"I love you, Adam"—an affirmation, a pledge they had exchanged a hundred times. What he heard that time was different. She wanted reassurance, and he couldn't give it. Love was for people who lived, truly lived. Even if the charge was dropped, the stain would cling to him forever.

But he couldn't tell her that either. She would try to convince him otherwise. *She* would help him.

"Forget me, Joanne-*ah*." He fell back on old movie lines. "Forget we ever met"—the hero letting go of his one true love with a lie. Hurtful in the short run; kinder in the end. "It wouldn't have worked. I would have messed up your life. Even without this."

"That's not true. You couldn't have been with that woman when she died."

"For Christ's sake, Joanne-*ah*. True or not, I'm finished. Whatever we had, it's over."

Go, he wanted to say, *Ka*, but Westerners need more than a monosyllabic dismissal. "Listen, I'm a jerk, okay? I. Don't. Want. You. In. My. Life. Anymore." His thumb squeezed End Call even though he heard her shout, "Wait."

He put the phone on his chopping block and slammed the blunt end of the axe on it. The blow travelled through his bones, and he let go. He landed on the ground with his legs stretched out in front of him. All night and all through the next day, his throat burned from the scream he uttered as he severed the last tie between them.

Over the next ninety-nine days, he has chopped countless logs and lain in bed, crushed by despair. His only balm is to think of her, the smile that curls the corners of her mouth, the blue-green eyes that shine in the dark, and the hair with the threads of gold that spiral over her shoulders.

Sleep eludes him again, and an idea takes shape, a ritual to mark his one-hundredth day: the petals of a single rose in an envelope with one word on a piece of paper, "Sorry." But where would he find a rose so late at night? And how would he mail it when every time he leaves the *hanok*, he needs permission from his bail officer? It is all so complicated. And he would be referencing a custom she doesn't even know.

Three: March 12th, 2017 — Ithaca, New York

Sean stood by the living room window, watching three students preparing for a film shoot outside our house. "What's that?" he asked, pointing at the equipment they were unloading from a car.

I sat on my heels and wrapped an arm around his waist as I explained the tripod with three legs to hold the camera steady, the microphone that catches the sounds the students want to record, and the funny furry cover that muffles the sounds they don't want, like the wind. "It's make-believe, see? Like when you play and mom records you on video."

"But you don't do *that*."

I laughed. "Listen, buddy, I'm going to change your bed. Want to help?"

He shook his head. "Who's that one?"

"Let's not point fingers at people, okay? The man near the camera? His name's Adam. And that's Jamie on the top step, and the woman is Maria."

I continued doing my Saturday morning tasks while Sean went from deep absorption to total boredom. "They're always doing the same thing."

Over a western omelet and toast, I said that to make real films, like the Harry Potters he likes, actors need to practice a few times, and then the camera records the scene a few times too.

"That guy runs down the stairs with no jacket on."

I told Sean that Jamie's character had to rush out of the house really fast.

"Then the other guy goes like that"—Sean mimed a "cut" motion—"and the first guy puts his coat on real fast."

"You think it's funny?"

"Yeah."

I am not in the habit of volunteering my house for student projects, but a sign on the bulletin board outside the food court in Kennedy Hall caught my eye:

Scouting for <u>Exterior</u> Location
Student Film Project
House with Front Steps

A few days later, Adam dropped by the Center for advice on an essay and, carried away by curiosity, I asked if the sign had anything to do with his screenplay.

He looked surprised, amused. "We just need steps that look like they're outside a house."

"I live in a house." Once the words were out, I couldn't take them back. "Would two weekends from now work?" I figured Sean would be with his father in Syracuse. Helping a few students work outside my house wouldn't entail much.

"Very kind." He dipped his head. "Hm, the project is due Thursday. But no worries, please."

Emma wouldn't have hesitated a second even if she had ten children to entertain at home. "Actually, this weekend's fine," I said. He thanked me. And shook my hand. And bowed again. And smiled.

And now he was so absorbed in his work that he had no idea I was behind the window, wondering why my eyes kept going to him. He was of medium height and medium weight, yet he moved with the agility of a cat. Mesmerizing. His hair was medium brown and medium length, yet here I was, itching to run my fingers through it. A line of stubble darkened his chin and upper lip, *à la* Don Johnson in Miami Vice. How did he do that? He neither slouched nor stood straight but somewhere in between, loose and comfortable. Confident without being arrogant. Patient. Polite.

It was like looking at an *objet d'art* kept behind glass in a gallery, knowing I would never own it but feeling stirred nonetheless, feeling alive. Feeling that I had found her again, the woman I lost when Charlie left me for a younger woman.

Adam's short film also dealt with a broken relationship, although it involved a woman who found the courage to leave her abuser. Jamie played the husband who raced to catch her before she disappeared into a cab.

Throughout the afternoon, between baking batches of muffins and doing crafts with Sean, I peeked through the front window. Maria's scene was next, similar to Jamie's, but wheeling a suitcase and casting worried glances back at the house. Whenever she stood on the sidewalk to discuss her role with Adam, Jamie joined her and huddled close.

The sun was casting long shadows when the third scene took shape, Maria hurrying to board a taxi driven by a cap-wearing Jamie. Whenever Adam wasn't looking through the viewfinder, he shifted his weight from foot to foot and blew warm breath into his hands.

The next time I checked, the students had started to pack. I opened the front door and called out, "Would you all like a cup of cocoa?"

"Yes, please!" Maria had frizzy hair that made a halo around her heart-shaped face.

Jamie followed her inside, and Adam came last, bringing in the camera, a boxy one-eyed head mounted on skinny legs. He levered out his black sneakers while Jamie and Maria settled on the loveseat.

Sean stood against the wall, too shy to join them. I motioned for him to follow me to the kitchen but he shook his head.

When I returned with steaming cups of hot chocolate and a plate of muffins, Adam was still standing, showing Sean how to swivel the camera and record what he saw.

"Look it, Mommy, I'm a camera boy." He made a goofy face.

"Careful, now," I cautioned, although Adam said it was fine. "I'll put the footage on a flash drive for you."

It was my turn to dip my head and smile. And hope that he saw me not only as a student counsellor and a mother, but also as a woman made of flesh and blood.

Four: March 16ᵗʰ to 18th, 2017 — Ithaca, New York

This is what freedom tastes like, marvelled Adam: sitting elbow-to-elbow with strangers at a counter in a busy sandwich shop, looking through a wide window in full view of anyone passing, and savouring good, honest food. His panini was done to perfection, crisp grill lines on the bread and smoky roasted vegetables with a burst of heat whenever he bit into a slice of jalapeño.

For three months, he had managed to slip under the radar: no screams piercing the hum of voices on the Quad, no crowd converging on him, no grainy proof of his whereabouts popping up on social media, not even a discreet autograph request from a middle-aged fan who swore she would not tell anyone.

In-sung was sure someone would blow his ordinary student cover. Adam was determined to prove him wrong. He texted him: *Just handed in our short. Another all-nighter. May rent a car this weekend.*

The caffeine from his cappuccino had yet to kick in. He gulped the rest and prepared to leave, parka zipped, knapsack on back.

Students entered and stamped their snowy boots on the mat at the door. Others exited while wrapping scarves around their necks. One of them looked familiar.

His first instinct was to lower his cap's visor and don his sunglasses, but he recognized the woman: the writing center counsellor with the wavy hair who allowed him and his classmates to film outside her house.

"Hello," he greeted her.

"Hey, Adam." Bright smile. "Class on Friday?"

"Yep." He practiced his American slang.

She carried two shopping bags in one hand and a Collegetown Bagel bag in the other. "Any plans for the weekend?" she asked.

"Maybe see the Finger Lakes, or even Niagara Falls."

"You can't miss the Falls. Spectacular in winter. And not crowded at all."

They were waiting for the traffic lights to change. There were no cars in sight and she asked if he was okay with 'jaywalking,' a term he had never heard, although the meaning was clear. They raced across Oak.

A weak sun lent a tinge of blue to Cascadilla Creek. Joanne—he may not have been Americanized enough to call a near stranger by her first name, but he could think of her that way—slowed down on the bridge. "It makes such nice sounds," she said. "Burble, gurgle, warble, bubble, giggle, babble."

Through the jumble of syllables, he heard a smile.

"My class is over there." He pointed to the far end of the Arts Quad.

"I was just thinking. I haven't *stopped* at Niagara Falls in winter, only passed by going to my sister's house."

"She lives near there?"

"Yep." Again, the smile in her voice. "Just wondering. Would you like some sort of local guide?"

They were in front of McGraw Hall, her destination, and he didn't know how to respond.

"Sorry. That was rather forward of me."

He waved his hands, no.

"In that case, what works best, Saturday or Sunday?"

They shook on Sunday, her hand cold but firm inside his.

The sun sulked behind a thick wad of clouds when Joanne's car stopped outside Adam's building, a six-story block facing Cascadilla Creek.

"No Sean?" he asked as he buckled in.

"With his dad."

Not "my husband," he noted. When he was preparing to leave for the U.S., he imagined taking weekend trips with a classmate or two, maybe a girl he would be interested in, not with someone who worked at Cornell. And not with the divorced mother of a young child.

Cayuga Lake, to their left, shone a dull silver. "What are the words you said the other day? On the bridge…"

She maneuvered past a truck before answering. "It's a tongue-twister my father taught me." She launched into what sounded like nonsense—rhythmic and rolling nonsense—ending in laughter. "Okay, one at a time: bur-ble, gur-gle, war-ble, bub-ble, gig-gle, bab-ble." She told him what each meant, the nuances between the pairs of words that sounded alike, and he took notes on his phone, the English spelling, the definitions, and the phonetic equivalents in Hangeul.

"Now you try," she said.

"Oh no." He waved both hands, laughing at what would come out of his mouth.

"Take it one step at a time."

"Then please teach me. Slowly."

"Okay, here goes: bur-ble,"

"No laughing, now," he warned before doing his best to reproduce the sounds, "*beu-reul-beul.*" "I mean, *'beu-reu-beul.*'" The distinction between the sounds for R and L was hard to master.

On they went, from word to word, while the trees and bare branches revealed glimpses of the lake, changing like the words he said, yet similar in how they felt.

They turned into the parking lot on Goat Island, an oblong piece of land that splits the Niagara River into two. The moment they opened the car doors, the sound of tumbling water engulfed them. Adam shouted. "What are the words for this?"

"'Roar' and 'Rumble.'"

All he could think of was "Danger" and "Excitement."

They crossed a park where ice coated every branch of every tree and every shrub. "Crystal." Adam found his camera and snapped picture after picture, first from a distance, then close-ups of crab apples sheathed in glass.

At the railing by the Horseshoe Falls, as close to the maelstrom as possible, Adam mounted his camera onto his tripod and filmed the wall of water rushing over the void. So much of it and so relentless.

Below, icicles clung to the cliff edge, defying the powers bent on breaking them.

"The sun's coming out," Joanne said.

The clouds thinned, more white than grey, and as soon as the sun broke free, a rainbow appeared through the mist downstream. Adam switched to his still camera, clicking, framing, zooming in and out, trying to capture the fleeting moment, although there was no end to it.

Joanne's hair, whipped by the wind, touched his hand without her noticing. "May I take a picture of you?" he asked.

His best shot had the unbroken rainbow framing Joanne. He showed her his screen, standing close, emboldened by the ambient sense of danger.

"I should have brought a proper camera," Joanne said. "All I have is this old phone." She held it at arm's length. "Take a few together?"

A thought occurred to him. What if Joanne knew who he was? All sorts of possibilities ran through his head, converging on the dreaded post that revealed his whereabouts.

"Alright. But not for sharing, yes?"

Her face turned serious as if she distrusted his need for secrecy.

"Just… hmm… cautious—is that the word—online?"

"Identity theft?"

He repeated the words, stumbling on 'theft' as he stood beside her. It was a tight squeeze, and not much of the Falls showed behind them, but her third shot caught them with eyes open, smiling. "I'm texting it to you," she said, thumbing on her screen.

Every few steps yielded a new sight that begged to be photographed. Now it was a woman in a multi-coloured coat who sat on a bench, surrounded by seagulls. The birds screamed as they jockeyed for the bread she tossed in their midst. At Adam and Joanne's approach, the birds skipped aside, flapped their wings and took off in slow motion.

Adam shot freehand from behind the woman, trying to juxtapose the rainbow and her coat, the birds so near yet so fearless, their curved beaks closed, and proud, or else open, and menacing.

In the Top of the Falls restaurant, only a dozen tables were occupied, mostly families with young children. A couple sat in a booth, fingers entwined, oblivious except to each other. Joanne led the way to a table by a tall window and deposited her tray. "Too bright?"

"Just fine." Adam tapped the sunglasses on his nose.

They ate and talked about what they had seen. A comfortable silence descended as they took in the view. The taller of the two towers on the other side beamed sunlight to their table. Joanne's eyes were closed, something he would never dare do in public. "Tired?" he asked.

"Relaxing." The corners of her lips curled up.

He wanted to try, just try to let go of the restrictions he had lived with for the past five years. First, he left one eye open enough to catch anything entering his field of vision. Nothing untoward happened, so he went all the way, laughing inwardly at his great daring and the strange circumstances that made it possible. "Nice."

"Mmm."

Her son must keep her busy at home, he surmised. These few moments of idleness must be rare for her too. "I'm happy."

On the drive home, Adam asked Joanne if clover grew in America. She laughed. "My front yard is covered with it. I get nasty looks from the neighbour across the street. He spends his summers mowing his lawn."

"One time," Adam said, "I was driving with the top down on my car. Hot day. Every car had windows closed and air conditioning on. There was a ramp like that one," he pointed backward with his thumb. "Cars and concrete."

She nodded, keeping her eyes on the road.

"A smell came to me." His hands made a floating gesture. "Clover. A field maybe? I could not see it. I felt … hmm … lonely. Nobody else noticed. Also … special; no, not special … blessed, chosen for something special; a gift."

She took a long breath as if savouring the story. "When Sean was three, we had a summer storm. The wind sounded like wild horses galloping between the houses. Thunder crashed and shook the foundations. Sean was so scared he couldn't eat. I held him on my knees and rocked him like a baby."

"Mmm."

"When the rain stopped, it was his bedtime, but I worried he'd have nightmares. I said, 'Let's go for a walk. Let's splash in the puddles with our rubber boots and chase the storm demons away.' We went to the park even though it was already dark. The breeze was so fresh, the scent of wet leaves and pine needles so sharp—It was like the best wine I've ever tasted. And with Sean's little hand in mine, it was the first time I forgot I was his mother. I was with a friend."

She turned into the visitors' parking at his building, and he slapped his forehead with the heel of his hand. "I forgot to bring the flash drive. Sean's film. Do you have a moment? I can make a pot of tea. Korean tea."

"Actually, I'm a bit late. Errands to run before the shops close."

"Fifteen minutes? I want to thank you for today."

"This is thanks enough. And I enjoyed myself. Honestly."

Maybe she was just being polite or maybe she felt a connection too. "Next weekend?"

"Next weekend, I'm sorry." She shook her head.

Rather than asking why and risk closing the door, Adam forged ahead. "Alright. Two weeks from now. Saturday. I'll barbecue something."

Five: April 1ˢᵗ, 2017 — Ithaca, New York

Parka on, purse hanging from shoulder, keys in one hand, bottle of wine in the other. I can always turn back, I told myself. It wasn't a fling, wasn't going to be a fling. It would be inappropriate. Frowned upon. Imagine if I were a male counsellor going to a female student's apartment on a Saturday night. Utterly unethical.

On the other hand, I had nothing to do with marking his work. Although, I did help him get better marks. Arguably, above and beyond the call of duty.

He must be lonely to ask me to his place on a Saturday night, a bit too old to hang out with college kids.

He might also be married.

He didn't want to be indebted to me. It could have been a cultural thing.

I still had time to change my mind. I hadn't entered his code on the intercom yet.

But I was curious to see how he lived, what he meant by "I'll barbecue something," and, if I was honest with myself, curious to see where this might lead.

"Hello!" he said through the intercom.

A security guard behind a marble counter checked my name and sent me on my way. "Have a pleasant evening, Ma'am."

"Ma'am." I smiled all the way to the sixth floor.

Cooking smells lingered in the hallway, and memories of my first apartment with Charlie surfaced. Trying to make ends meet on my part-timer's wages and his postdoc stipend. Waiting for him with dinner ready while he worked late in the lab. My pregnancy, and Charlie making it home later and later.

Adam's door was at the far end, painted forest green. By the time I lifted a hand to knock, he was already opening it. Smiled. Bowed (no handshake or casual hug). Relinquishing of the parka. Handing over of the gift bag with the wine. Taking off of boots.

"You can wear these." He pointed to rubber slippers similar to his, except for the colour—his navy blue, the other pair burgundy. I slipped my feet inside, wondering if he had ever worn them. Not minding.

His kitchen was separated from the rest by a breakfast counter that held containers covered with foil. All neat and tidy. The table in the dining room was set as in a restaurant, white tablecloth and candles.

In the living room, Adam insisted I take the deep armchair—pale-green leather—while he poured us each a glass of white wine and sat on a chintz sofa with a cabbage-rose pattern.

"Did the apartment come furnished?"

"A bit like, hmm, a woman's apartment?" He looked embarrassed.

I shook my head. "No, it looks … fresh." I meant new and of rather good quality for a student. Even his shirt, white and crisply ironed, must have been bought for this dinner.

"Happy you like it," he said, not answering my question.

I had more success probing his impressions of Cornell (favourable), his current workload (manageable), generalities like when he planned to return to Korea (third week in May) and whether he would have time to visit New York or L.A. (regrettably, no).

We made our way to the dining room and sat across the table from each other. Contrary to my expectations of a Korean meal, he served a mixed green salad with charred Bartlett pear slices and roasted pine nuts. He waited for me to give him my impression (delicious) before he started eating.

"How did you become a student counsellor?"

"By a rather convoluted route."

He professed interest, and I told him I came to Ithaca as the "trailing spouse" of a Canadian molecular biologist starting his postdoctoral training at Cornell. Since I wanted to work in the US, we had to get married.

"Ah." Adam nodded and rose to attend to the main course.

Not wanting to sit alone, I followed. "What can I do to help?"

He pointed to a magnetized timer on the fridge. "You can be the time-keeper?"

He tipped his head toward the containers covered in foil. "And carry one?"

Near the sliding glass door, a black towel served as a floor mat; cooking utensils were lined on a tea towel. He had prepared a footstool indoors for me and another outdoors, in front of a hibachi where briquettes glowed red.

The first container held baked potatoes that he finished cooking on the grill. The second was a chopping board with two T-bones. "Medium-rare?" he asked. Once he'd positioned them at the centre, he asked me to start the timer, set for three minutes.

He signalled for the third bowl, blanched broccoli florets that he caramelized on the grill. Our fingers touched and we acted nonchalantly. What went on under the surface was another matter altogether.

"Can you bring the plates from the oven?" he asked, and before long, we were back at the table with generous servings in front of us. Adam poured red wine into fresh glasses and raised his to mine. "To a fantastic tour guide."

"To a gracious host."

Everything tasted delicious and I said so several times, a compliment he accepted with a smile and a head bow. He cut a piece of meat, loaded potatoes on top with his knife and lifted his fork to his mouth. The backs of his hands were unblemished, whereas I had a nick on my right hand. His fingers were long and tapered. No ring, no watch, only white sleeves rolled up a few turns over smooth wrists. He noticed me noticing.

He spread his hands on the table. "Not married. Not now, not before. Not even a girlfriend in Korea."

I searched his eyes, and he held my gaze. Was he a seasoned liar, or was he telling the truth? My ex, Charlie, wasn't a good liar, but I so desperately wanted to believe him that I fooled myself into thinking he was telling the truth. Never again.

"Alright," I replied in as cool a tone as I could muster. (*Stamp on it, Joanne!*) I sliced a piece of broccoli and chewed it slowly.

I felt full. I ran the risk of offending, though it couldn't be helped. "Would you mind if I stopped eating? It's all so delicious (*that word again*), but it's more than I can eat. Much more."

He looked stricken, or I imagined he did. Maybe I spoke too fast, and he was not clear on what I'd said. I pushed my plate forward by half an inch.

He smiled and nodded.

Nice recovery.

We were now sipping the rest of the wine, and I asked what had led him to choose film-making.

"Ah." He took a moment to consider his answer. "I want to be *behind* the camera, not in front."

"Are you saying you've been in front?"

"Mmm." He nodded. "TV. Commercials."

"You don't like it?"

"It's other people's ideas."

I nodded.

"I'd like to try *my* ideas."

I sensed that he would expand if not for his limited English.

"Tea and dessert," he announced as he rose and lifted our plates from the table.

I carried the wine glasses and set them on the counter.

"This is the Korean tea I wanted to make last time." He measured a few scoops into a smallish teapot and waited for the kettle to boil.

"I nearly forgot." He raced to the bedroom and returned with a flash card in a blue holder. "Your son's film."

I promised to return it after downloading the film, reasoning that a flash card is not something a student can simply give away. He dismissed the notion. "It's nothing."

Truth or face-saving? Impossible to tell.

The kettle whistled and he transferred all the water to a measuring cup, topped it with cold water, and filled the teapot, all in easy, practiced motions.

"First, we wake the leaves," he said, pouring the barely infused tea into two small cups and the rest into the sink. More water went into the pot, and he loaded a tray with the tea implements, plates and a cardboard box from a cookie shop.

"This way." His chin lifted toward the living room.

As soon as he had placed the tray on the coffee table, he sat on his heels on the floor, emptied the contents of the cups into a collecting bowl and refilled them with infused tea.

"Please." He motioned to the armchair. He did not move to the sofa but sat cross-legged on the floor. He offered me a cup, one hand underneath and the other keeping the vessel steady, bowing his head.

I accepted it in the same manner, and our fingers brushed once more. As I knew they would. As he knew they would. The fleeting feeling of his fingers on mine.

He mimed drinking and nodded for me to taste.

(Focus, Joanne!). I sipped.

My first impression was "delicate." Refined. Mildly floral but mostly grassy. "It's fresh and sweet," I said.

He took a sip, and a smile bloomed on his face. "I was afraid I wouldn't do it right."

"And if you didn't?"

"It would taste bitter."

I leaned back and closed my eyes to fix the moment in my mind: sitting without a care in the world, tasting a delicious beverage and biting into an exquisite cookie from a local shop. I reopened my eyes to find Adam looking as relaxed as I was, two souls comfortable together without needing to talk.

"Music?" he asked.

"Mmm." I was still in a dreamy state, and it took me a while to realize that the piano notes filling the apartment were beyond familiar. "*The Köln Concert*," I said, "Keith Jarrett."

Adam's eyes widened, and I debated whether to tell him that dancing alone at home, stringing together ballet, jazz and mime to this and other pieces of music, was my way to reconnect with myself.

We listened, united in anticipating every intricacy of the piano improvisation. Intimate in our souls.

"I dance to this music," I said. "I mean, I invent my own dance."

"Show me." Not so much a demand as a dare.

"It's not for anyone to see."

"I'll keep my eyes closed. I promise." He chuckled while squeezing his lids together. "Go ahead." The piano beckoned and I rose. On the floor at Adam's back, I danced steps that expressed a fairyland feeling here, and quirky stomping there.

Jarrett reached his main motif and spun one variation after another. I did a sequence with an *arabesque*, a *plié*, a *glissade* into a turn while my leg did a *fouetté*.

Adam clapped. He was facing me, eyes wide open.

I wagged a finger. "You didn't keep your promise, Adam Ahn. Your penalty is that *you* must dance."

He shook his head, grinning. I sat cross-legged on the floor and motioned for him to rise. The piano notes rained furiously, defying choreography.

Adam stood on bare feet but had no idea what to do.

"Do the mad-marionette," I said.

"'*Madame*—' what?"

"Like a puppet with a crazy master."

He took a moment to process my instructions. He started to jump erratically and fling his arms about.

"Bravo!" I clapped while Jarrett segued again into his main motif. At the end of each variation the pianist cheered himself on, "Han!" and "Ho!" his ecstasy mounting as he pounded the keys, "Whoa!" and "Whoo!" and "Hoo!"

It subsided. Liquid notes. Tender notes. Adam reached for my hand, "You too, Joanne." We stood frozen, which suited the music as it had almost stopped, no rhythm, only a few high notes.

Jarrett plunged into the low range, hitting harder, heralding tragedy. I made my hand into a visor and "searched." Adam did the same. The musical storytelling continued. I twirled on my toes, and Adam twirled on a heel. I swept an arm out, and he did the same, albeit more stiffly.

The notes piled up, a crowd gathering, culminating into … an apparition: The Angel of Death.

Sorrow—miming tears falling.

Anger—punching the air, stomping.

Denial—squatting into tight balls, keeling sideways on the floor, fetal position, facing each other. Our eyes met. Was our clumsy *pas de deux* a figment of my imagination? Thinking, his eyes reminded me of a tiger.

The story continued. Signs of life appeared—wiggling fingers near the ground. Bells pealed—hand cupped around ear.

The main motif resurfaced, my signal to rise. Adam's fingers connected with mine, pulled me closer. Our lips met, parted, tasted grassy tea. My fingers felt his taut back, ran through his hair. I inhaled his scent, rubbed my cheek against his neck, my chin against his shoulder.

Far away, Jarrett went, "Ahh!" We pulled our tops over our heads, wriggled out of our pants, and lay heat to heat.

"Adam." The pleasure of saying his name.

"Joanne." A term of endearment.

We touched with lips and fingertips, nudged with noses, tasted with tongues. He was different and yet the same. "Adam."

His eyes turned serious. "Yes?"

"Yes."

His fingers circled inside me. I moaned. *More.* My eyes locked on his. *Yes.*

He entered me in a long slide, and for a moment, I felt whole. We both moaned, looking into each other's eyes, unable to change course. Unwilling.

Every time he went down, I tried to keep him there, but he escaped. He slowed the pace, took pleasure in teasing me. I let him. I smiled. He smiled. We smiled. His beautiful tiger eyes shone.

"Your blue-green eyes take my breath away," he said. We kissed. We joined at the mouth, the tongue, soft and hard and wet. I set the pace now, faster, twisting, rocking under him. Oh God, jolts of ecstasy, climbing, climbing. I gasped, and Adam froze. "Hurt?"

I shook my head. Climbing.

"Now?" he asked.

"Yes."

I exhaled and felt his release.

He lay on top of me, nose buried in my hair, heart racing against mine. His barely-there beard rasped against my cheek. Our eyes met and we laughed. Tears trickled from mine and he wiped them with the back of his hand. "Don't cry."

"I'm not crying," I said, although I was. Crying for how long it had been since I felt this way. Crying because this just began, and I already had to think about the end.

Six: April 15th, 2017 — Finger Lakes, New York

Flashes of silver ran left to right beyond the pine trees in front of Adam's building. It was Joanne's Civic, rounding the corner and stopping for him.

"Any hiccups?" he asked, a word she'd used on the phone last night.

"I was up early."

No strings attached, they'd agreed; fresh air and a chance for Adam to practice his English. Expand his vocabulary. The air was indeed fresh, verging on chilly. In the car, already warm from sunshine, it felt delicious.

A week before, they had met for lunch at Collegetown Bagel. They sat at the eating counter, backs to the Babel of voices, heads leaning together to hear each other speak. Through the window, their reflections floated in front of the empty benches lining the sidewalk, the bare tree limbs etched against the leaden sky, with a splash of red from a fire hydrant. Clumps of white swirled through the air, turning into a full-blown flurry of fat flakes that transformed the streetscape into a ghostly vision.

Sitting beside Joanne in the car, Adam smiled at the recollection, the connection he felt with her, the warmth in her voice, the pressure of her thigh against his, light yet easy. Familiar.

Trees were leafing out, tender greens and gaps in between, reddish buds ready to erupt, and the grassy banks of Seneca Lake dotted with yellow.

"Dandelions look so friendly when they're not on your lawn."

Adam nodded.

"Do you have a lawn?"

"No lawn."

"Indoor plants?"

Adam took a moment to think. "They must all be dead by now."

"No one waters them?"

Adam mentioned In-sung. "My friend's no plant expert." He spotted a bird perched in a tree. "*Wah*, did you see that … a hawk? I think it was a hawk. '*Meh*' in Korean."

"*Meh*," she repeated. "Did I say it right?"

"Hmm, and eagle is '*soori*.'"

"*Soori*. Sounds like French for 'mouse': '*souris*.' Or if I say, '*Souris, Adam*,' I mean that you should—"

"Catch a mouse?"

She laughed. "No, you should smile. From the verb '*sourire*.'"

"You know French?"

"My major."

"*Oui, merci*," Adam said. "That's all I know."

They drifted into a lesson in Korean. Ways of saying "yes": *neh* and the more formal *yeh*, and "thank you": *kamsa hamnida*.

"*Kamsa mida*," repeated Joanne, and Adam went one syllable at a time as she had done on the drive to Niagara Falls.

They stopped for supplies in Watkins Glen at the southern tip of Seneca Lake. Joanne had never been there so they scanned the main streets for possibilities until Adam pointed to a general store.

Inside, gleaming jars, filled with candies in all colours imaginable, lined the counter, drawing another "*Wah*," from Adam. Glass-fronted shelves displayed glistening fudge that ranged from ivory to deepest brown. Behind the counter, more shelves with jars: jams, chutneys and jellies with hand-written labels; loose teas, dried herbs and coffee beans packaged in brown paper.

The opposite wall was devoted to wooden toys arranged on square shelves. Joanne tapped on a four-note xylophone, nudged a miniature rocking horse that nodded to and fro, and tested the wheels of a one-seater car shaped like a cigar. "What do you think? The car or the xylophone for Sean?"

Adam was farther inside, trying on hats. "Indiana Jones, or"—he changed—"Charlie Chaplin?"

Delicious smells drew them deeper inside. A window poured daylight on a counter filled with cold cuts, terrines, cheeses and salads; to their left, a bakery corner with homemade breads, cakes, cookies and pies that all looked tempting. Beyond, the clink of flatware on china announcing a café. All tables save one were occupied.

A server wearing paint-splattered jeans and a matching T-shirt greeted them with a broad smile. She showed them to a pair of old student desks pushed together and low wooden chairs coated in an exuberant mix of colours. Outside the window, the ground dipped to the blue waters of the lake, framed by two willows covered in cascading yellow-green.

Adam's heart swelled. He reached across the desk for Joanne's hand and found her reaching for his. "Thank you for bringing me here," he said.

"I had no idea. *You* found this place."

Adam's filmmaker instincts told him to get his camera, but his connection with Joanne eclipsed all. Almost all. Behind him, a conversation caught his ears.

"He's holding her hand," a woman said in Korean to the man sitting at Adam's back.

"Not so loud!" the man whispered.

Adam had noticed the middle-aged couple as he and Joanne walked to their table. The burst of sights and sounds around them had scrambled his vigilance.

"It's him, I tell you," the woman muttered.

"It's not. What would he be doing in this small town at this time of year?" Even though the man did a better job of lowering his voice, he *was* sitting back-to-back with Adam.

Joanne mouthed, "What is going on?" and Adam conveyed by sign language that he would tell her in the car. Their food arrived while the wife insisted that her sister would never forgive her if she let the opportunity pass. The husband argued that even if the stranger was the actor, the last thing he would want was some nosy woman pestering him for an autograph. "Your sister's a nut case," he said. "Keep your mouth shut and she'll never know."

Adam struggled not to laugh, beaming a smile at Joanne and cutting a piece of quiche, intent on putting it in his mouth. Chair legs scraped against the floor. *Oh no, here she comes.*

But the husband sucked air through his teeth and, in English loud enough for everyone to hear, said, "Leave that poor man alone."

Forks hung in mid-air. The server in the paint-splattered jeans stood frozen, a bowl of soup in each hand, until the espresso machine hissed behind the counter and the tinkle of flatware resumed.

Seven: April 15th, 2017 — Finger Lakes, New York

My mind reeled as I drove to the cabin where we would spend the weekend. Adam was a famous actor in Asia. How could anyone so unpretentious have hundreds of thousands of fans as he just told me? He sat and watched the scenery go by. He must be acting every second he's with me. So much for thinking he was special. Or *I* was special. I was one of the many conquests he made everywhere he went. A single mom who would fade from his life the minute his plane home took off.

"The turning should be half a mile ahead," he said, the directions sent by my co-worker spread on his knees. My colleague's advice: "If you don't want to freeze at night, light the wood stove right away," flit into consciousness as the cabin came into view, an unpainted structure squatting under tall evergreens.

I killed the engine. "We don't have to stay," I said. "This place looks like a… It looks worse than I thought. Much worse."

"Let's have a look."

"There's no running water at this time of year, no electricity. I don't know what possessed me to think it made sense." If Adam heard the edge in my voice, all the better.

"The key?" He dangled a bronze object with one hand, smiling his dazzling smile.

I nodded, furious for leaving it in the cup holder.

Mr. Superstar jogged to the cabin, unlocked the padlock, and disappeared inside.

I didn't want to go through with this … dirty weekend—might as well call it by its name. And to think I worried I was in too deep. (*Grow up, Joanne!*).

He waved me over and flashed me another thousand-watt smile.

I stayed in the car. Home-field advantage. I opened the window and waved him back.

He raced over, opened the passenger door, and peered inside. "It's fine. The place will warm up in no time. There are oil lamps and candles—"

I patted the passenger seat. "We need to talk. Please."

He sat and waited while I debated where to begin. "Just tell me," he said.

"This is a mistake. For me. I'm sorry, Adam, but I want to go back." I took a sip of water. "I'll drive you home, of course. Or I can drop you anywhere you want. You can take all the food."

For a few heartbeats, he said nothing. "Alright, I'll lock the door first." Tone: neutral. Body language: hiding what he thought.

"I'm sorry," I said again once we reached the highway. "You worked so hard to clear your weekend, and now I'm getting cold feet."

"I *wanted* to work hard."

"You could have gone with a schoolmate—"

He didn't answer. He looked at the sun brushing the tips of evergreens.

I would have liked to turn on the radio, but what if it made things worse, me always calling the shots? I didn't want to be his "girl in every port," didn't want to be at a rich man's beck and call. Best to nip this infatuation in the bud.

He had closed his eyes. Was he sleeping?

Men look so innocent in slumber. Even superstars. I thought about the woman arguing with her husband, about her sister, the super-fan. If she knew I'd backpedalled on spending the night with the man of her dreams, she would think me crazy. I felt we had a connection, and it was worth finding where it led. Now I knew I'd imagined something that wasn't there at all.

As darkness fell, the red taillights gliding ahead had a hypnotic effect. I would have loved a cup of coffee, however, if I stopped, he'd wake up, and we would both feel uncomfortable. I made do with drinking from my water bottle to break the lulling rhythm. (*Stay awake, Joanne. Drink little sips, otherwise you'll have to stop for a bathroom.*)

Half an hour away from Ithaca, Adam began to stir. "Was I sleeping?" He rolled his shoulders and rummaged through his backpack. "I still have tea." He poured a portion into the thermos cup and handed it over, making sure it was safely in my grasp before taking his hand away. "Let me know when you want more."

He drank from the same cup. "Not as nice as freshly made."

Soon, he would leave the car, and I would never see him again. A brief brush with celebrity. "What's it like to be famous?"

"Which part? Having lots of money?"

"That, and having people recognize you?"

"The money is nice. You can buy what you always wanted, a car, a condo, a $2,000 bottle of wine. You can buy your friends expensive gifts. If you have any left, you can put it in the bank for when you're not famous anymore." He laughed. "You can give money to the charities you like, and your fans will give to the same charities. That's great."

The glaring lights of a car dealership turned night into day.

"Being recognized … hmm … not so nice. You try to eat at a restaurant with your friend. Someone comes to your table. For me, it's older women—long story." He pitched his voice higher. "'Ooh, Ahn Dae-hyun-*ssi*, I'm your greatest fan. Take a selfie together? Give me your … *sa-in?*' How do you say when …" he mimes scribbling in the air … "sign?"

"Autograph?"

"Autograph. More fans follow the first. You can't talk to your friend anymore. They take pictures from their tables while you have food in your mouth. They'll post them on social media. You're annoyed, but you have to act nice. Smile and find your signing pen again because these are the people who watch your series and buy the brands you endorse."

Eight: April 15th, 2017 — Ithaca, New York

"Music?" I asked as we took the ramp off the highway.

"Alright." His tone wasn't particularly enthusiastic; neither was it dejected. Good. He must think that I changed my mind at the cabin because I distrust all famous people; it was more complicated. I was drawn to him. Too much. Even in the days of Adam-the-hard-working-student, *something* shone through. His heart? His eye for beauty—and I didn't mean me. Poetry, light and dark, earth and sky, water and air.

Fame sounded like such a burden if every time he left his house, perfect strangers accosted him. A college town where nobody knew him made an ideal place to escape. Being part of his escape scared me. An escape is never real life, and sooner or later, I'd have to come to terms with real life. Still, being part of his escape had its moments.

"Great music," he said. We were listening to Cornell's student-run station. What had started as a dreamy instrumental shifted to pounding like waves washing ashore, each one stronger than the one before.

We stopped at a traffic light, and the musical waves kept on building until they crashed in a jangle of notes that shot straight to my heart.

"Did you feel that?" He pressed his hand to his chest.

The light turned green and I drove on while the instrumental morphed into a waltz that unspooled gaily and ended in a jazzy swirl of flute.

I had forgotten to turn onto Adam's street.

The radio host said that the piece of music represented a season outside the cycle of spring, summer, autumn, and winter; a fifth season.

"Did you hear the name of the piece?" Adam asked.

"Something like 'The Fifth Season?' Maybe the playlist's online. We could check at my place."

By the time we turned into the driveway it was full dark. My car's headlights beamed on the Redbud tree at the height of its spring glory, each limb covered with pink blooms.

"*Wah.*" Adam rummaged through his bag for his camera and shot the scene from multiple angles. That feline fluidity of motion. A beautiful man with what appeared to be a beautiful soul.

We set the food from the general store on the coffee table— tabbouleh, chickpea salad, and local cheeses—along with wine from a Seneca Lake winery.

Adam raised his glass. "To a lovely tree and a lovely song."

"You don't mind? About this afternoon?"

He gave it some thought. "A bit."

"I'm sorry." Trite words.

"I understand."

I spread pâté over a cracker and schooled my eyes to look neutral. "You seem like a decent man, Adam Ahn." A decent man for not pressuring me, contrary to what I expected from a star.

Nine: April 15th to 16th, 2017 — Ithaca, New York

"I should be going home." Adam stood and looked for his jacket.

"'The Fifth Season,'" Joanne reminded him. She opened her laptop, saying it would be faster than her phone. She made coffee, and he cleared the table.

The playlist had not been posted yet, and her search for "The Fifth Season" returned only a Hugo-awarded novel by Jemisin. "Maybe in French."

In next to no time, her eyes rounded. "Band's name: Harmonium. The French album title translates to: *If We Needed a Fifth Season*. Track, fifth and last, an imaginary season, 'Stories without Words.'"

"But in the language of music." Adam smiled.

Joanne clicked through and purchased two copies of the CD to be shipped to her address.

All is not lost.

"Dessert?" she asked, and soon they were sitting on the floor again, eating slices of chocolate cake from the general store.

There were many upscale *patisseries* near where he lived in Seoul's Gangnam district, prone to decorating similar confections with elaborate swirls of chocolate dusted with gold powder, but the basics were the same: the rich, creamy texture, the deep, earthy taste, the feel-good high.

"Stay?" Joanne's eyes beamed an apology. She leaned closer for a kiss that tasted rich and deep. And felt … amazing.

They took it slow. *Frisson*. The word popped into his head. *Oui, merci*. Joanne's hair was spread on the floor like a soft nest. "You're beautiful." He held in the words his heart longed to say: *Saranghae, I love you. You are perfect. You are perfect for me. Forget superstar Ahn Dae-hyun. I am ordinary exchange student, Adam Ahn.*

She brushed her hand over his chest. "Smooth." She felt the stubble on his chin. "Scratchy." She drew his lips into a kiss. "Soft."

She lay in his arms, a warm, silky presence. The curtains billowed and swayed, grazed the edge of her rattan dresser and subsided until the next breath of wind.

"Is that why you came to Cornell?" she asked. "Because you wouldn't be recognized?"

"Mmm." He kissed the top of her head. "At K-ARTS, people— other students, the media—left me alone at first." He told her about *Reunification* and the role that catapulted him to stardom in Asia, a role he accepted only as a favour to In-sung.

"The friend who's not good with plants?"

"But is a good manager."

Her head lifted from his chest. "Are you hard to manage?"

"Sometimes."

They made love again, teasing, play-acting, exaggerating, or pretending to exaggerate; it was hard to tell which, but it felt good. Adam's fear of not matching overblown expectations melted away. He was just a man, and she was just a woman he would like to know better. A thought knocked at his consciousness: you're leaving in five weeks.

Adam woke to curtains filled with light, sighing in the breeze. Joanne stood with her back to him and reached for a robe behind the door.

"Joanne-*ah*," he said.

"Good afternoon." She smiled.

Her skin bore the imprints of the twisted sheets, though his English was too limited to tell her. He said it in Korean, more to himself than her, while she disappeared in the bathroom.

After his turn showering, he found her at the stove in the kitchen, her back to the entrance. He cleared his throat to announce his presence and peeked over her shoulder. Pancakes.

Her hair was still damp, and the top of her robe showed a spread of wet. Adam found a towel and pressed it to her curls. He hugged her from behind, encircling her waist and moving his hands up.

She leaned back, kissed him, and tapped his hands away. "Shoo. Breakfast is ready."

The table was covered with a blue checkered tablecloth, and a fruit bowl at the centre held bananas, apples and clementines.

She pulled two plates from the oven, and they sat across from each other, drizzling maple syrup bought yesterday over their pancakes. The coffee she poured in his cup had chocolaty undertones. He asked why she said "shoe", and she asked why he called her "Joanna."

"How to explain?" He mimed two sections. "Your name, with 'ah' at the end. It means we know each other … mmm." The English words eluded him. "Like lovers." He winked.

Joanne ran her toes against his jean leg. "You were telling me why you came to America."

"Tourists." He paints the scene: putting his books away after a class on the top floor of the Film School at K-ARTS and taking a look from the window. "Huge flowers below." He uses his hands for emphasis. "Pale blue, pale pink, pale yellow, pale green. Raining hard. Umbrellas." He assumed the people sheltering from the elements were waiting to enter the auditorium next door.

"I thought it would make a great picture. Downstairs, students waited in front of the open doors for the rain to stop. I made it to the front and took wide shots. The people under the umbrellas were all women; they chanted something, a name ending in 'san.'"

"The tourists?"

Adam nodded. "My last series was shown on Japanese TV. They were chanting 'Ahn Dae-hyun-*san.*' Nice dresses. Same red and white hats, like sunhats children wear. Only one man, the tour guide."

Joanne looked perplexed.

"The man brought Japanese housewives to Seoul. To meet Korean stars."

"Housewives?"

"Strange, I know. They have more money than teenagers. More free time." Adam said the stalking incidents multiplied and soon exceeded K-ARTS's ability to contain them. His faculty Dean summoned him to her office. She was "concerned" by these "star-safaris" offered by Rising Sun Tours. Could he switch to online courses? Go overseas for his final term? Maybe a university where he would not be recognized? "So, not New York, not L.A."

Joanne refilled their coffee mugs, and Adam tried to catch her eye. She had turned inward, and all he could do was marvel anew at her irises, blue with flecks of yellow, shining like jewels. "You must think I come from another planet."

She sipped her coffee and continued to brush her toes against his jean legs. If not for that, he would have risen and left, a woman with a quiet life that a man afflicted with fame had no right to disturb. He was about to make his excuses when she put her hand on his arm.

"Not another planet, Adam. Another point of view."

Ten: May 1ˢᵗ-to-20ᵗʰ--Ithaca, New York

Fourteen thousand students buzzed around campus, scrambling to finish projects and cramming for exams. The Academic Writing Center ran extended hours. We had two more weeks of madness to go when I felt the dreaded symptoms of a cold, scratchy throat and pain whenever I swallowed. You won't beat me, I vowed. At home, I drank decoctions of lemon, ginger and honey, and threw myself into bed as early as possible as often as possible.

Thank heaven I had already registered Sean for day camps, or rather, profuse thanks to Byron's mother who did all the research so that the two friends could be together through most of the summer. For once, I was ahead of the game.

I spotted Adam sitting outside the library, soaking up sunshine and drinking coffee with other students. He rose to return inside and dipped his head in my direction.

I tried to convey, "How are you holding up?" and he nodded. That was Friday, a whole week ago.

My cold stalled at the sniffles stage. I lay on my side, exhausted by the day's work and the few hours at home with an energetic six-year-old, the useless entreaties to put his toys away, and the mounting chaos. I was waiting for the decongestant to kick in when my rheumy eyes landed on an unopened parcel peeking from under clothes piled on the chair in the corner. I could not muster the energy to rise and rip the sticky tape. My phone was on the pillow. I texted Adam to ask when he would be able to collect his CD.

I wanted to see him before he went, though I dreaded the end, the have-a-good-life-let's-keep-in-touch moment.

The phone rang. "Joanne-*ah*, hi. I'm..." The rest was drowned by voices in the background. Music. Carrie Underwood belting out "Before He Cheats."

"Find a place to talk." Sounds of footsteps. A greeting in midwest accent, "Adam, my man!" Creaks of a door; thud. "I am outside," he said. "Film school party. We had our last exam."

"Sounds wild."

"Yes, been a while. Hmm … would you like to come out for a beer? Somewhere quiet. Coffee?"

It was my weekend with Sean, I explained, along with my poor state of health. "Sunday?"

"Ah." A motorcycle growled through his phone. "Flying early Sunday. Two in the morning."

"From Syracuse?" Battling through brain fog, it occurred to me that he would have to leave tomorrow evening. "Can you come for lunch?"

The prospect of Adam's visit acted like a tonic. My feet carried me lightly from chore to chore, the bone tiredness, only an echo of what it had been over the past many days. My headache was gone, or kept at bay by painkillers. My voice croaked, but it wasn't painful. I managed to coax Sean into helping me put away all the toys he was not playing with *right now* when the doorbell rang. Adam had texted earlier that he would bring food.

He stood beyond the screen door in jeans and a matching shirt open over a black V-neck. He was clean-shaven and looked more like the pictures of Ahn Dae-hyun I'd found online, less like Adam.

He carried an insulated bag in each hand and lifted them for the benefit of Sean, peeking from behind me. Adam winked. "Roast chicken, salad and"—he pulled a tub of Häagen-Dazs—"Ta da!"

I handed the cold tub to Sean. "Hurry up, buddy. In the freezer."

Adam slipped off his canvas shoes and hesitated before taking a step forward. "Is it okay to—"

I pulled back. "Better not. You don't want to take this bug home with you."

At the table, Sean squirmed, round eyes fixed on Adam, while I cut his chicken. "Careful with that glass," I cautioned.

"Coke?" Adam asked. Hard to tell whether he would approve.

"Naw, prune juice," Sean replied.

"Nice?"

"Makes my poop come out."

Adam looked to me for clarification.

"Later."

The conversation turned to whether Sean liked kindergarten (yes), his favourite sport (soccer), favourite toy (Lego castle). Sean sat still, ate and behaved.

"Favourite ice cream?" Adam winked in my direction.

"Strawberry," my son replied in a smiling, giggling voice, knowing full well it was the flavour our visitor had brought, though not that I'd tipped him off.

Later, after Sean had crossed the street and been allowed inside Byron's house, we took our coffees to the backyard. The lilac bush in the corner was covered in deep plum clusters that released their scent into the air. I had dusted two reclining chairs, shabby models with aluminum frames and plastic straps, one green and one orange. I was past caring what Adam thought of sitting in them.

"Tired?" he asked. "Your voice—"

"Sounds worse than it feels."

"I wish I could hold you and make it all go away."

(I wish I could hold you tight so you wouldn't go away.)

We filled the void with stale air: whether he had finished packing, who would be waiting for him at the airport. We tiptoed around what was really on our minds. "We," "our." I could not vouch for what he thought, but why else would he have come?

At home, he would plunge into a film project right away. Acting, not directing. He had yet to study the script. Something to do on the plane.

"What's the film about?"

"I'll translate the tagline." He searched on his phone. "Two unlikely allies join forces to find a kidnapped student. Only one is the real father."

"Which one do you play?"

"You'll have to go and see the film." He grinned.

Only a third of the scenes would be shot in Korea. The rest in England. "Have you ever been to London?" he asked. "Any recommendations?"

I shook my head.

"You must come. We can see the sights together."

I laughed. "It might be easy for you. It's complicated for a single mom."

"Easy? Not really. Bodyguards, In-sung, and housewife-tourists from Japan. I'll make a rope with bedsheets and escape through the window. Let's make sure." He typed on his phone, reading the Korean as he went. He translated: "Please check if the hotel rooms' windows can open."

Was he joking, or did he send the text?

"See if In-sung replies." He laughed. "Three in the morning in Korea." He squeezed his eyes shut. "I must get used to the time difference." He reached over and took my hand. "Sleepy?"

"Mmm."

How much of that playfulness was genuine, uncensored; how much was nervousness?

"We sleep together."

How much was not knowing how to say goodbye to someone you have just started to love? Even though it was precarious. Impractical. Bound to fail. To hurt.

Love (noun): desire; a form of madness heightened by the presence of the cherished being.

We were lucky. We did not spend enough time together to go completely mad. The best way forward was to accept what had happened. He would return to his glamorous life. I would stay in my ordinary life with Sean. Wake, work, eat, sleep. Repeat.

I opened my eyes to find Adam gone. The first quarter of the moon floated overhead, a thin half-coin cloud in an otherwise blue sky. The shadows had lengthened, and the lilac's scent had diminished. Something was draped over me. A denim shirt.

Laughing voices came from the house, Sean's and Byron's. I jumped from my recliner and black nothingness descended over my eyes, scrambled my brain and turned my legs to jelly. I gripped the back of the chair, careful not to make it tip, until my vision cleared and everything fell into place again.

Inside, Adam sat at the kitchen table with the boys, finishing a bowl of ice cream. "There's more for you," he said.

Our lunch dishes dried on the drainboard rack. The counters were clear. The clock said 4:15. Adam's eyes followed mine.

"It's time?"

He nodded and rose—my tall, dark stranger. He pointed to the back door. "My shirt." He was still barefoot.

"Mom," Sean called me back to my duties, "can Byron stay for dinner? Please."

I was too choked up to say no. This morning's burst of energy was all adrenaline and I was crashing. Fast.

"I'm at the front," Adam called.

Each step I took was a step closer to him leaving. I would be strong. I would be stronger. I would accept "never again" and think, "we had Niagara, *The Köln Concert*, 'The Fifth Season,' and strawberry ice cream." I cried inwardly.

He put on his canvas shoes. He stood still, and I did the same. I filled my eyes with him, his tentative smile, his occasional nod to which I responded with a nod, the tiny scar forming a line on the side of his nose that I noticed for the first time. He made a "one" sign with his index finger, moved closer and wrapped his arms around me. He whispered, "Farewell, Joanne-*ah*," and kissed my forehead, lips light as butterfly wings.

The door handle clicked open, and he was gone. He did not turn, the man who could smell clover in the middle of a concrete desert. He kept going.

A minor dispute had erupted in the kitchen. Over a loose tooth. "Pull it," Sean coaxed.

"Not wiggly enough."

"Mom!"

"Coming." As I passed by my laptop, I noticed a cellophane-wrapped CD. "I'll just be a minute," I told the boys. "Don't pull the tooth." I stepped into flat shoes and, in blatant disregard for my parental responsibilities, hurried out.

Adam had disappeared. I ran and checked each turning in the direction of his apartment.

On Linn, I recognized his silhouette, his gait. "Adam." I lifted the disc in the air, and he stopped.

We were face to face again.

"I will…" He searched for the right words as he clasped the CD to his chest.

I nodded. "I will cherish it too."

Eleven: May 23ʳᵈ, 2017 — Seoul, South Korea

Adam swung his legs to the ground. Not three in the morning yet, but he could not lie still another second. Craving fresh air, he crossed the darkened living room and stepped onto the terrace. Seoul's multicoloured lights outshone the stars and planets, except for Jupiter, parts of Ursa Major and Ursa Minor, and the North Star, a faint pinprick straight ahead.

Joanne had sent him a text, and he replied that yes, he had made it home safely. *Are you feeling any better?* he typed, but reconsidered. A question would create an obligation to respond. He knew so little about her, what she wanted, how much space he occupied in her mind, her heart. *I hope you feel better,* he wrote instead.

In-sung's many texts were all reminders of what he had already told Adam on the drive from the airport: the stylist coming at eight, the prayer ceremony, concluding with *Rest well. It's going to be a long day!*

The Agency stylist and her assistant had just left Adam's apartment when In-sung called from the underground parking. Adam wore a printed suit, black and grey on white, with a matching shirt, straight from the Paris runway, including the laced patent leather high tops.

"Awesome," In-sung said when Adam joined him in the back of the limousine van.

"Yeah, yeah."

"Better you than me." In-sung winked. This obligation to conform to whatever designers decreed people must wear each season, no matter how outlandish, was a recurrent joke.

The driver took them across the Han River with plenty of time to spare. In-sung put a square box in Adam's hands. "From Takeshi-*san*."

They had visited the jeweller's studio in Tokyo the year before, after a fan event that filled all 30,000 seats of the Saitama Arena. The box held a Buddha bead bracelet with three gold heads of the

Transcendent Being interspersed with round, porous black stones. "Lava?" Adam rolled a bead between his thumb and finger.

"Mmm. Read the note."

Takeshi-*san* would be honoured if Adam accepted this bracelet designed especially for him. It felt heavy, twenty-four karats according to the note. Adam fastened it on his left wrist. "A Christian man wearing a Buddhist symbol to attend a shamanic ceremony." He grinned.

In-sung said he was receiving scripts for future films. One showed promise. "Do you want to see it?"

"Not now." Adam wanted to find his acting feet again. "Maybe when we're in England?"

"New development. I will not be going."

"A new K-pop act joined the Agency?"

In-sung snorted. "How insecure actors are."

"Trouble with existing talent?"

"Hee-jin—my *wife*, not the lead singer of Tara—is expecting." He sounded smug.

Adam elbowed him. "I'm so glad." He was about to say more, but the van turned onto Sheraton Grande Walkerhill Road.

The *gosa* ceremony was a semi-private affair, with cast, crew, and press. However, a hundred or so fans had come and held signs that proclaimed their love for the star.

Excitement and stage fright flooded Adam. Part of him clamoured to stay in the van until they all went away; another relished how he felt in those situations: invincible, on top of the world. He passed a hand over his hair to tame any unruly strands. A second later, the doors opened.

In-sung used his body as a shield so Adam could wave and flash his smile without being trampled by the mostly middle-aged women. They screamed like teenagers. The Rising Sun Tour group stood nearest the circular drive, recognizable by the Japanese-Flag sunhats and the presence of Nijima-*san*, who looked at Adam down the length of his nose. The other fans clustered near the entrance, keeping their distance from the stalkers, and waved flags from China, Singapore, the U.S, and Japan. "*Hwa-i-ting!*" or "Fighting!" they shouted, pumping their fists in the air.

An elderly woman wearing a burgundy kimono stood in the front row, cheeks flushed, posture straight and dignified, holding a bouquet. Adam stopped, bowed, let her release the flowers into his hands, and lifted them aloft.

Roar from the crowd. They loved him. He was a god, their god.

He did not want to enjoy the moment, but he did nonetheless. He shook hands and answered questions: "I'm well." "Glad to be back." "Stay healthy." He reached the doors and, as In-sung ushered him inside, turned around and surrendered to a surge of emotion, "I love you."

Was it love or a lie? Was it what they wanted to hear, what would make them flock to the theatres—greed—or was it a form of love? Love begetting love, theirs, overwhelming; his, sporadic yet heartfelt when it came? He couldn't tell.

Inside, the cooler air steadied his nerves. Paparazzi milled around the lobby, and he did what all actors do when they promote their work: play nice.

The Grand Hall was plunged in darkness except for lights shining over an altar at the far end. Pyramids of apples, pears, and oranges alternated with plates piled high with rainbow-coloured rice cakes. Candles and incense burned on either side of the ceremony's harbinger of good fortune, a pig's head holding pride of place at the centre. Hairless and pink, as if made of wax, its nostrils sniffed the air while its mouth gaped open with the hint of a smile made all the more realistic by eyes closed in apparent bliss.

Adam stood around the edges of the room, greeted the people he knew, was introduced to others, until a hush fell. *Swingtime*'s producer stepped forward on the bamboo mats and faced the pig while he unfolded a wide sheet of paper and read a prayer that called on blessings for the film they were preparing to shoot. The man knelt and set the paper on fire, holding one corner until the last possible moment, letting fiery fragments soar, and charred remains flutter to the mat.

The director went next, followed by Adam and the other actor in the film, a man he met that morning for the first time. They slipped off their shoes while shutters clicked like insects colliding in midair and emitted bright flashes. Adam received a cup in his two hands, one supporting the other, humility. Rice wine was poured in, and he swirled it clockwise, then counterclockwise, spilling a few drops for the gods in the process. After the other actor's turn, they stood side by side again, hands steepled in prayer. They knelt in unison, hands on the ground, left over right, lowered their foreheads to the mat and offered their prayers. They bowed two more times, pulled envelopes from their breast pockets, stepped closer to the altar, and placed their money offerings in the pig's mouth.

The ritual continued with the film's financial backers and the creative team leaders, soon filling the pig's ears, snout and mouth with money envelopes.

In-sung drew Adam aside. Someone wanted to see him. The person's name, whispered in his ear, made Adam's stomach lurch. How did he not recognize him when the man's turn came to make his offering?

In-sung led him to a corner guarded by two men with wires spiralling from ears to shirt collars. Behind a pillar, they found another man, short, with shoulders bulging from an expensive suit. He trained his eyes on the actor and dismissed In-sung with a flick of the eyebrow. Adam was alone with Han Dok-ku, whose media empire was among the many backers of *Swingtime*.

The man examined Adam from head to toes. "We meet again."

Adam bowed his head.

"I was against you in the lead. I don't think you've got what it takes. However, the director insisted. You'd better not disappoint me, Ahn Dae-hyun-*ssi*." His stress on the honorific dripped with disdain. "Understood?"

Who did Han Dok-ku take him for? Adam considered quitting *Swingtime* on the spot; let Han Dok-ku wrestle with the logistics. However, he had a duty toward people like the woman in the kimono. Against tradition, she had given flowers to a man; showed deference to a younger person. Despite being taught to despise Koreans while the peninsula was under Japan's colonial rule, she had paid respect to a Korean.

Adam held Han Dok-ku's gaze then bowed an overly polite bow infused with as much contempt as he could.

Twelve: June 1ˢ to 10ᵗʰ, 2017 — Seoul, South Korea

S hooting began for *Swingtime*.

One evening at the soundstage, Adam heard the usual call at the dressing room door, "Ready?" A woman he had not met before came to stand behind him and brushed his hair. Hers was short and cut asymmetrically across her forehead. She smiled at him in the mirror, and he recognized Yu-mi.

"*Oppa!*" Her eyes widened in mock-surprise. She must have bribed someone to come in. She seemed taller than he remembered until he spotted her high heels. Her hips swayed in her sequined shorts as she came to sit in the other chair.

"I can hardly recognize you," he said, noting the cherry-red lipstick and thick mascara.

"You like my new eyes?"

She'd had double-eyelid surgery.

They talked about her return from Australia until the director called Adam.

"Let's go clubbing afterwards," Yu-mi said.

"Sorry, it's an all-night shoot."

"Here." She found an eyeliner crayon and seized his hand, which Adam pulled away.

"Best not." He tipped his head toward the door and the role he was preparing to play.

"Alright." She proffered her hand, rosy-pink palm with slim, tapered fingers that matched his recollections. "Give me yours."

Yu-mi suggested they meet for mushroom stew at the cheap eatery of old. They wore caps, sunglasses and the plainest clothes they could find, and even fooled the *ajumma* who used to serve them.

"I followed your career," Yu-mi said. "Hard to miss, even in Kangaroo-land. I wrote on your forum. You never answered. I'm YouMe, by the way." She spelled it for him.

Adam shook his head and gave her an apologetic smile. In-sung read the posts and showed him only a few. "What did you write?"

"The usual drivel, how you had changed my life, although I never said 'for the better.' I wrote that I finished my exams and graduated *summa cum laude.*"

"Congratulations!"

"I'm working in a government lab and applying to American med schools."

Adam stirred the pot and tasted a spoonful. "Hmm, not as amazing as before."

"Your taste buds have changed. Truffles, caviar, foie gras, and triple-cream brie with figs."

"What makes you say that?" He laughed at how close to the truth she was.

"I can prove it."

This was how they found themselves in Adam's kitchen, checking the contents of his refrigerator, and in his bed not long after that. Yumi bit his earlobes a touch too hard, his nipples. She lay spread-eagled on the bed. "Do you have handcuffs?"

Adam shook his head. He entered her slowly, too slowly for her liking. She grabbed his buttocks and took control.

Sunday morning before daybreak, the street below was deserted. Two blocks away, the path running parallel to the Han River slumbered, clear of joggers and cyclists. It was a chance in a thousand, and Adam seized it, hastily dressing in shorts and slipping his feet in a pair of running shoes. Downstairs, he greeted the guard dozing behind the information desk and bounded out. The scent of ivory silk lilac, faint from his terrace, filled the air below. Adam adjusted his earbuds. On the long flight home three weeks ago, he'd had ample time to listen to *If We Needed a Fifth Season*, transfer a copy of the CD to his player, and read the liner notes, returning again and again to the final track, the one he and Joanne had heard while returning from Seneca Lake. Their weekend in April already felt like it belonged to another life. Adam was eager to test how well each of the five parts worked as soundtracks to his runs.

"The Isolation" began with sounds of nature, seagulls crying and waves washing ashore, a lonely island for the flute weaving in. Adam's feet found the rhythm, fast yet light, meandering like a man searching for something missing from his life.

Adam's life was so full of obligations—his role in *Swingtime*, going to London for the English scenes, shooting a few commercials—that finding time to miss something or someone would be a luxury.

The music carried him along as a leaf on a river, trembling as it began "The Call," where the guitarist plucked variations on six notes: "Where in the world are you?" The rhythm, anxious, *"Eodi-ae imnika?"* Desperate, "Where on earth can you be?" Insistent, *"Doh dae che eodiya?"* "Why have you gone from me?"

The calling notes drifted away; the rhythm dissolved. Adam felt as if he was treading water, uncertain what to do until a voice broke through, singing in no language at all and all languages at once. Running was easy again. Running away, running to her. "The Encounter." He should have had more time with Joanne, time to know her better, to explore whether it was love or simply an escape from loneliness.

The rhythm shifted, swung up and down and up again, rocked back and forth, climbed higher and higher until the lovers became one: "The Union." But he felt no jolt to the heart as he'd felt in Joanne's car.

And when the flute, so lonely in the beginning, became the twirling, dancing flute of "The Great Ball," he felt that he was watching revellers through shatterproof glass, forever separated from them, excluded.

For better or worse, he let Yu-mi in whenever she rang him on the intercom. He should have been reading the next day's script, getting in character, yet they stole a half hour together whenever she was free. He told himself it was research. The film's storyline became muddled with his strange relationship with Yu-mi. They were shooting scenes between his character and his boss's wife on a rooftop terrace high above the city, a closed set with a sex scene on the bench of a garden swing. The director explained the protagonists' motivation: "She wants something from you, and you want something in return."

Adam had a fair idea what Yu-mi wanted from him, but he did not know what he wanted from her. Closure? A proper ending to their story after the cease-and-desist order by her father all those years ago?

One afternoon, lying in a tumble of sheets, Yu-mi sprang up and sat on the edge of the bed, her back arched, the dip at her waist outlined by daylight. His apartment was so high up they did not even have to close the blinds. Just them and the sky.

She slipped her top on, a pale pink camisole shorter in the front than the back, so loose that a gust of wind could lift it past what it covered. Her pants were magenta, ripped by some clever designer in places that would make others blush. Not Yu-mi. She must have attracted catcalls that she ignored, Miss Too-Good-For-You, *aesaekki*!

The Buddha bead bracelet lay on his dresser. She ran a finger over the lava stones and tested the weight of the Buddha heads in her hand. "Twenty-four carats?" She put it on her wrist and moved her arm to test the effect. "Can I have it?"

"If you want," Adam said, although it was too large for her slim wrists.

"*Oppa*," she sounded tentative, "did you mean it when you asked my father?"

"Turn around," he said. "I want to see you." He had no idea what she was alluding to. The conversation with her father at the prayer ceremony was all one-sided, him talking and Adam itching to punch him in the face.

Yu-mi stood against the light, silhouetted like the collection of celadon pottery that lined his windowsill, her face in shadow.

"What did I ask?"

"In the middle of the road… Seven years ago…" Her tone implied that he should know without being told. "You said you loved me. And when I was old enough, and you could support me, we'd get married."

"Aren't you going to become a doctor? An independent woman?"

"Of course. That part doesn't matter to me." She looked him in the eyes. "I haven't stopped loving you, *Oppa*. Not for one minute."

What a monumental lie.

"We could marry. Secretly." Yu-mi twined her fingers through his. "When I'm in America, you can live with me between movies. I could go to UCLA, and you could give Hollywood a try. You'd be great."

Thirteen: June 11th, 2017 — Ithaca, New York

I knew full well that Adam would leave. I thought I'd move on, yet he was everywhere. I walked: Adam. I breathed: Adam. I said goodbye to Sean at school: Adam. I danced alone at home: Adam.

Not Ahn Dae-hyun, the actor, who went on with his life in Seoul, but the Adam I had known briefly in Ithaca. I was already thinking about him in the past tense.

We exchanged a few texts, and I even called twice. He said nothing about missing me. Neither did I. He was even busier than during exam time, he said, whereas the pace had finally eased for me. Daylight lingered into the evening. I had time to take Sean and his friend to their soccer games, sit in a folding chair with the other moms and dads, and chit-chat about nothing memorable. Thinking: Adam.

After each game, a parent passed thick wedges of watermelon around, and we took sweet, juicy bites, thinking that summer was finally here, life was wonderful, and our children would sleep well tonight. Thinking our secret thoughts. How I wished he were here.

One Sunday afternoon, I waited in the food court at the mall. The house was clean; the chores, done except for preparing lunches for tomorrow. Charlie came into view, steering a stroller with one hand and resting the other on Sean's head. Father and son looked alike, tousled auburn hair, piercing blue eyes and that easy, bouncing stride.

There was a time when Sean ran into my arms the moment he saw me, but he had come to terms with the new normal. His half-sister was ten months old, and Charlie liked to bring her along.

"You look well," he said.

Maybe I had come to terms with the new normal, found solace in a love affair, and was still basking in the afterglow.

"Can I ride the horse?" Sean asked.

I had a quarter ready, and we moved toward the electric menagerie, a court inhabited by ever-smiling creatures, a yellow duck the same size as a pink elephant and an orange chipmunk. Charlie's daughter looked on wide-eyed while I hoisted Sean in the saddle of a white horse and started the mechanism, back and forth, back and forth. The baby stretched her arms and would have tumbled out of the stroller if not for the straps that held her safe.

"I have news," Charlie said. "UC Irvine has offered me a job. Tenure-track. Awesome package to outfit my lab. Moving allowance. And loads more money."

"Sounds great. What does Lucie think?"

"They found something for Luce. Research associate in another department. She'll be able to publish a few more papers and, pretty soon, run her own lab. I'd be a fool not to accept."

The electric horse stopped, and Sean, resigned to only one turn, stretched his arms toward me. But Charlie asked if he would like another ride for being such a thoughtful brother to baby Amanda in the back of the car. The horse cantered again while the baby shook her arms and legs in time with the motion.

"So?"

"So I'm thinking Sean could spend the summers with us. We'll rent a place with a swimming pool to start with—"

"Starting when?"

"Listen, I know it's sudden, but I couldn't say anything before. It was all in limbo, whereas now—"

"Starting when?"

"Will you let me finish? We're all flying on July 14th."

"You can't spring something this major on me like that, Charlie. I emailed you Sean's camp dates. It's right smack dab in the middle of his softball camp. We've already paid for it."

"Joanne, listen. I'll reimburse you for all the camps you want—"

"As if it was only that."

"Hush. You're scaring the kids. Let's talk on the phone tonight. Nine-ish?"

I lifted Sean from the saddle and marched him through the parking lot.

"Mommy, you're pinching me."

The landline rang a good half-hour before Charlie said he would call.

"Sean has just gone to bed," I reminded him through clenched teeth.

"Is it a bad time? It's—"

"Who is speaking?" Not another charity wanting money I can't spare. I'm normally patient with these callers—volunteers or precariously employed people—but not tonight. "Sorry, I'm expecting a call."

"Can you text with OK time?"

"I'm sorry?" I was on the verge of saying, *I can't place your voice*, when the penny dropped. "Adam."

"Joanne-*ah*. You busy?"

"No. I mean, I'm not so busy I can't talk."

"I hope you're well."

We talked as near strangers do, the weather here and in Seoul, the campus so quiet in June. Adam was eating breakfast on the terrace of his condo.

"I'm making sandwiches for tomorrow."

"No Collegetown Bagel?" I heard a smile in his voice.

"I don't go there anymore. Students keep recognizing me. Then I have to take them to Niagara Falls; one thing leads to another..."

He laughed.

"How's your film going?"

"Lots of night shoots. I sleep during the day."

"Truly topsy turvy."

A pause. "A saying from your father?"

I smiled. "From me." How I wished I could see his smile.

"Teach me how to say and what it means."

I obliged, although I wondered if he was merely playing a role: Adam, the visiting student from Korea.

It was almost nine. "I have to say goodbye. I *am* expecting a call."

"Oh. And I should get ready." Through the phone I heard an emergency vehicle going *nee-eu, nee-eu*. "Great to hear your voice, Joanne-*ah*."

Charlie called a whole hour after nine. "The baby's teething. She wouldn't stop crying. I've been carrying her around for the last two hours."

I batted away the urge to say I had to deal with Sean's teething on my own. "Listen, Charlie. Six weeks in a new place—That's awfully difficult for a six-year-old. You'll be busy finding your feet. Not this year. I have summer camps all lined up for Sean here."

"But I won't see Sean until … I don't know when. Are you going to let him come for Christmas?"

"I haven't even thought that far." In fact, I had but couldn't find a solution. "You could fly east during the year, say, every other month?"

"Easy for you to say. Why don't *you* fly west with him once in a while? Spend a bit of time with that friend of yours who moved to L.A."

"Foisting our problems onto someone I've drifted away from, because it's convenient? That's awful."

"Alright. Let's mull this over. I agree it's not ideal to take him along in July."

I suspected "Luce" wasn't that keen either.

"Do you have a webcam?"

"Why do you ask? Isn't it expensive?"

"Not that much. You can pay for it with the alimony money I—"

"That's reserved for Sean, *our* son, who spends most of his time with me, not that I'm complaining." The landline's receiver was wedged between my ear and shoulder. I fidgeted with my cell phone, scrolling through my pictures: my father with Sean on his lap, both beaming. Niagara Falls, me, and Adam. I zoomed in on Adam, his tiger eyes, his smile, his pink lips, and the white teeth behind.

"Sorry, what was that?" I asked Charlie.

He pitched his voice louder. "I said that the webcam is for video calls with Sean. Although your cell phone might do."

Fourteen: June 11th, 2017 — Seoul, South Korea

Sunday. One contingent of Rising Sun tourists was flying home while another was packing their bags for an early start the next day. No one waited to snap Adam's picture and blow him kisses outside his building. He could drive his Mercedes SL55 AMG roadster through the garage door without attracting attention. He could even join the throng of luxury cars cruising the streets in Gangnam amid the money-to-burn crowd.

On this June Sunday, a week before he would fly to London, he texted Yu-mi.

She waited on Garosu-gil, a floppy green hat hiding her face, and half a dozen bags—Hermès, Dior, Louboutin—beached at her feet. He opened the door, and she slid in, all legs and mint chiffon.

He crossed the nearest bridge and took the road climbing behind Changdeokgung Palace, the car roaring uphill and hugging the pavement through the sharp turns. At a traffic light, he pressed a button for the hard-top to lift over their heads and disappear inside a special compartment. Yu-mi held on to her hat and talked about the weather, which was nice, her co-workers, who were not, her mother, who was asking too many questions, and her father, who masterminded the demise of a minister by linking him to a real estate scam.

Adam parked the car, and they continued on foot, ascending a winding track still muddy from rain the night before. Yu-mi wore high heels; she asked Adam to carry her on his back. He should have anticipated this, chosen a drier path for the quiet walk he had in mind. Instead, she wrapped her arms around his neck and hitched herself up, leaving him no choice but to hold on to her thighs and trudge uphill.

"I like a strong man," she whispered in his ear. He felt every inch of her body hugging his, and she knew it. There was a bench a hundred metres away and another twice that distance ahead. He started depositing her on the first, however, she clung to him and whined like a puppy stuck under a fence. Adam gritted his teeth and continued the piggy-back ride.

Once they had settled on the second bench, he mentioned his upcoming departure for England.

"I may be able to take a week off and join you."

"Yu-mi-*ssi*, I'm sorry." He braced for her reaction. "This isn't working. We should—"

"What do you mean, this isn't working?"

"I mean, *we* are not working. You and I."

She sprang to her feet and stood before him, arms crossed over her waist. "You can't mean that. We just found each other again."

He gave her his most serious look.

"*Oppa!*" Two creases dug in her forehead. "You'll never find anyone as suitable as me. Think about it."

He had thought about it. A lot.

"I'm the perfect woman to walk on the red carpet beside you: someone who brings her own money and her own smarts to the glamour deal, not some floozy actress who'll divorce you the moment someone better comes along. Or a mousy Miss-Nobody who won't be able to take the heat."

"Walking on the red carpet means nothing to me, Yu-mi-*ssi*."

"I know that. I mean, I understand what it's like to be an actor. I'll have my own career, and when we have time together, we'll have a ball. I know how to run a house, not like a cheap housewife, but with a staff. You won't have to worry about a thing."

"That doesn't matter to me, Yu-mi-*ssi*." How to explain that he was looking for more and less at the same time? Not a society wife. A woman he could grow old with. "I met someone," he said.

"I'm sure you've met a hundred someones."

"In America."

Yu-mi's skirt fluttered in the wind and the matching hat nearly blew away but she caught it in time. "JinA, Lee Jin-ah, who snared you the moment I boarded the plane for Australia seven years ago. And now this new woman. Another whore?"

"That will do."

"Sure. Whatever works for you, *Oppa*. You cried for that actress. You crumbled at her funeral as if you'd lost the love of your life. My dad's chauffeur saw you."

His knees indeed had buckled under him after JinA's burial, and he crouched behind his car, head between his knees.

"That was a long time ago." Adam felt exhausted. He wanted to go home. Alone. "We had what we had, Yu-mi-*ssi*, but it's over. If you want to think I'm fickle, go ahead. But let's stop torturing each other."

Fifteen: June 19th to August 3rd, 2017 — Ithaca, New York

Adam phoned me every few days around seven p.m. here, midnight in London. I pictured him freshly showered, a towel around his hips, unwinding after a frantic day. Sean tugged at my t-shirt, "Mom, let's go!"

I had promised to take him and his friend to the park and watch them hang upside down from the monkey bars.

The next time Adam called, he floated the idea of my joining him in London. "Come for the weekend. I'll send you a ticket."

I laughed. "I'm a full-time single mom nowadays. No free weekends."

"I'm sorry. Hmm." He pondered at his end, and I pondered how to end the conversation.

"Could you hire a babysitter? Or, could Sean stay with your sister?"

"I don't think so." I could rationalize seeing each other while he masqueraded as a student, but not accepting plane tickets from a rich actor. "For you, it's only about having fun." Sean played with his building-block castle at the kitchen table, not interrupting for once.

"Do you think so poorly of me?"

Sean was so wrapped up in his game, he failed to see his prune juice, served in a real glass. One wrong move and it keeled over the toy castle, spilling everywhere. The glass rolled off the table and onto the ceramic tiles. It shattered into a thousand pieces.

"Don't move," I yelled.

"It's nothing," I hastened to tell Adam. "Sorry, have to go."

But it was not nothing.

"Come here," I ordered Sean. "Watch where you're walking. Now take off those pants." The urge to spank him rose in me while Sean's eyes filled with fear. "Put this towel 'round you. Hurry. Wait for me in the bathroom."

I sat on the floor and beat my fists against the tiles. I wanted to walk out of the house. Let someone else deal with the mess. Someone like Adam, who wouldn't have a clue what to do. As if that wasn't enough, I'd agreed for Sean to spend the first half of August with his father. He was leaving the next day.

Our evening stretched on with packing Sean's suitcase, trying to convince him that he would be fine without Big Teddy—an argument I was tempted to solve by plucking out both of Teddy's glass eyes— and rescuing the toy castle by soaking every brick in a pail of hot water and promising Sean that we would rebuild it together when he returned.

Charlie met us at a family restaurant in Syracuse's Hancock International. The West Coast pace agreed with him. He looked fresh after his overnight flight, ready to turn around and do it all over again, child in tow. He and Sean ordered a full breakfast, ham and eggs, hash browns, toast and jam. I had coffee, which was stale. Stale, bitter and cold.

At home, I started on one task and hopped onto another. I put something in the microwave, sat on the sofa and fell asleep. The phone woke me. It was Adam asking about the commotion last night.

"Just a spill." The clock on the microwave said 3 pm.

"How's Sean? Is he hurt?"

"He's fine."

"I have an idea. The two of you should come. See London together for a few days. A week."

I heard voices around Adam, the vastness of the outdoors.

"There's a Peter Pan playground. He'd love it."

"We can't. I'm sorry. Actually, I'm busy, Adam." The sooner I stopped these calls, the sooner I could smother my yearning for him.

With Sean away, I filled the house with music—classical pieces like Tchaikovsky's "Waltz of the Flowers," more of Keith Jarrett's piano improvisations, and Astor Piazzolla's tangos. The old moves returned like a language, hesitant at first but gaining confidence with time. There was no one to please, no one to criticize, no one to make demands, except me. And I was pleased, I was happy. I was transported into other worlds.

This is what lay buried inside, I thought, summoned into the light by the skills of these composers, by players melding the sounds of their instruments into a stream with twists and turns; rushing rhythms, swaying rhythms, quieting rhythms; with notes so clear they pierced the heart.

I did not need this new Adam, although I continued to miss the old one. I danced to "Oblivion," the ballet-like tango by Piazzola: I twirled, spun, swept my arms above my head. I heard notes that did not belong. Again. And again. The telephone. Him.

There was music in his life as well. Opera. He went to a performance of *Tristan and Isolde* with his bodyguard at the Royal Opera House. "You should have seen this strong man wiping tears from his eyes when he thought I wasn't looking." Adam laughed, yet I heard loneliness. Who would go to the opera with a bodyguard rather than a friend, rather than a lover or a spouse?

I had not realized how lonely Adam felt. I told myself he would be fine in Korea, but tonight's conversation brought me a new insight. Even when Adam was surrounded by people, he was still alone. He had no friend to confide in and no friend who would confide in him.

I told him about Charlie's move, missing Sean when he was away and craving a break when he was home. Adam listened. It was late for him, but he listened until I had kept him on the line for an hour. "Not terribly uplifting. I'm sorry."

"I am glad you told me."

I did not know how to respond. "That's what friends are for," I said. Glib and not really how I felt. Still, friendship was all I could offer.

"I sent you a link," he told me the following night. "Open it."

It was for a flight, not to London but to Paris. It left in less than twenty-four hours. "I can't."

"Please? Do this for me? As a friend?"

Sixteen: August 5th, 2017 — Paris, France

This is how it feels to wait for someone at the airport, thought Adam, to know they will, they must exit through the frosted doors, yet still fear the worst, a hostage-taking, a mechanical failure that forced the plane to land elsewhere. A crash.

He stood in the Arrival Hall at Charles de Gaulle's Terminal 1, checking the board to confirm, again, that Joanne's plane from New York was not a figment of his imagination. It would land *A l'heure* in fifteen minutes. He had ample time to explore the offerings at the newspaper stand, sit at the bar and order a beer. He could study his upcoming scenes, but he couldn't focus on anything except the woman hurtling through the air to meet him. Her last text read: "Boarding."

In-sung's latest: "Enjoy Scotland!"

A few hours ago, Adam walked with his bodyguard through the Edinburgh airport, ostensibly following a weekend itinerary packed with the top attractions, though bent on a different plan. A dash of deception, a bit of bonus pay, in cash, to his bodyguard, who walked away into the Scottish mist for a solo vacation while Adam turned around to board a plane for Paris.

Less than half an hour earlier, he had come through another set of frosted doors, blending with other passengers, subdued after his early morning flight, though inwardly jubilant.

His black cap sat low on his forehead, shading his face, and he wore non-designer clothes, the same jeans and dark V-neck as when he last saw Joanne.

A sporadic flow of humanity kept emerging, pushing trolleys or wheeling cases of all sizes and colours. Adam watched for anyone wearing a Japanese-Flag sunhat—there was always a contingent staying at his London hotel, turning simple elevator trips into complex logistical maneuvers. Thankfully, no one fit that bill.

Joanne's flight rose on the board. *Arrivé*. Adam dashed into the nearest shop, bought two Perriers, and found a spot near the right exit.

A man with silver hair emerged from the frosted doors, changed his glasses while pushing his trolley and squinted at the waiting mass. A woman in a green dress peeled away from the crowd, flowery scarf streaming behind her, and stepped into the open area. "Claude, *ici*."

They hugged, their cheeks grazing one side then the other. They scrutinized each other's face and beamed in delight before walking away, his arm around her shoulders, hers encircling his waist, oblivious to anything else happening around them.

That's what I want, lodged into Adam's head.

Each time the arrival board updated, he dreaded that the status would change to *Délais*. Problems opening the door. Discovery of a dead passenger—surely not *her*, Dear God!—and the need to interrogate everyone on board.

People kept coming. Did they look American, Adam wondered. He eavesdropped on conversations. Was that a New York accent?

Six tall women emerged: athletic, sun-bleached hair pulled into identical ponytails. They paused, confronted by the wall of faces, then lifted a hand in unison, wide smiles brightening their expressions, and made for the opposite exit. Behind the group, a shorter woman with honey-blond hair hesitated as she scanned the crowd and followed in their wake, her back to Adam, wheeling a carry-on.

"Joanne-*ah*," he called. "Over here." His words drowned in the sea of voices, leaving him only one option. He skirted the back of the crowd and spotted the tall women laughing and exchanging *la bise* with a group of look-alikes.

Joanne squeezed through until she was in their midst. Adam stepped forward. He and Joanne were now as private as any two people could be in a crowd. Her face lit with delight, and they walked into each other's arms. They kissed—not the light peck of the older couple but the hungry kiss of lovers after months apart. Adam held on until Joanne pulled away, breathless. "Hungry, are we?" Her jewel eyes smiled.

The Hidden Hotel's entrance was as discreet as the name implied, opening onto a narrow street filled with shade. At reception, only one guest stood ahead of them, and it took the manager mere moments to deal with her query. He turned his attention to the newcomers, consulted his computer and asked stock questions—"Is this your first time in Paris?"—while waiting for his screen to refresh. "Here we are. Two nights in the Emotion Terrace Room. It is unique, *Madame, Monsieur,* our best, *absolument.*"

"And early check-in." Adam referred the manager to his printout.

However, the current occupants had recently asked for a late check-out. "You understand? Another room is available, a Sensation Room, with beautiful slanted ceilings. Like an artist's studio." In a mollifying tone, he offered them the option of switching altogether or using the other room to rest until their original choice was ready.

Adam could not keep his irritation in check. "When will that be?"

"No later than four o'clock."

He had not slept for twenty-four hours, and watching his back in unpredictable crowds had taken its toll. Joanne was tired. And he had set his heart on them being alone before they ventured in the city.

"What do you think, Joanne-*ah*?"

She smiled. "I saw a bistro around the corner. We could go for coffee and see how we feel?"

A broad avenue opened a few hundred paces away. Sunshine flooded the tall facades; delivery trucks rumbled past mopeds; people walked fast and with purpose. A flower shop display stopped Joanne in her tracks. "Did you see this?" She pointed to an arrangement of pale green orchids over black pebbles inside a glass cylinder. Roses at the peak of perfection rested on a cushion of greenery inside a trifle bowl. Each discovery brought wonder to her eyes.

Adam had an idea. "Imagine you're judging a contest: the best arrangement. Which one would win first place?"

A difficult choice punctuated by many changes of heart on Joanne's part, and delight in watching her on Adam's. She chose a bowl filled with white calla lilies, their stems snaking around the bottom, crisscrossing as the flowers strained to escape.

"I'll be a moment." Adam stepped inside the shop with a glint in his eyes. The florist spoke fluent English. The arrangement would be delivered to their hotel within the hour.

"What was all that about?" Joanne asked.

"Only saying how much we enjoyed the display." He could not tell whether she was pretending to ignore he bought the flowers, or whether he had genuinely fooled her.

Soon they were sitting at a table for two under a deep blue awning, waiting for coffee and *pains au chocolat*. Joanne stretched her arms and legs. "This feels wonderful. You have no idea how hard it is for single moms to find time to do anything. Thank you."

Adam could say the life of a film star was just as constrained, however, he did not want to spoil the moment. The espresso machine hissed in the background; a cyclist rang her bell and waved at an elderly gentleman shuffling in front of the bistro. The server brought their order, "*M'sieur, 'dame, bon appétit.*"

The coffee tasted deep and earthy, without any bitter undertones, and the croissants were by turns flaky, buttery, and chocolatey, in just the right combination.

"I…" She pressed her lips together. "I nearly turned around in New York. I don't like to feel that I'm being bought, Adam, that someone else is paying for me to enjoy things I could never afford on my own. I used your plane ticket, and you're paying for the hotel. That doesn't mean I feel a hundred percent right about it."

"Don't think of it that way. Please. Seeing Paris alone—" He punched his heart with a fist. "There would be a major piece missing."

"That's why I didn't turn around."

"And? How has it been so far?"

"Let me pay for this."

They found the Arc de Triomphe and watched cars headed for the giant roundabout at the Place de l'Étoile, drivers carving a path with sharp turns, sudden surges, and abrupt slamming of brakes. Horns blared and whistles blew.

"Keep going?" Adam asked.

They followed the Avenue des Champs-Élysées, seeking shade under the double row of chestnut trees pruned like an enormous hedge supported by living columns. Joanne snapped pictures. "Look at those balconies." She pointed to ornate wrought iron railings running along the upper windows of buildings that housed Mont Blanc, Zara, and the like on the ground floor. "It's a bit disappointing, though. Same shops we have at home, even McDonald's."

Adam reached for her hand, drawing comfort from feeling her by his side. He spotted the Houses of Louis Vuitton and Lacoste, and was tempted to browse inside with her for something she might like. It was a tendency he did not know he had, meant to express gratitude, not buy someone's affection.

They came to an expanse of green, the Jardins des Champs-Elysées, and followed a path to a fountain surrounded by sunflowers. "Now *this*, I like," Joanne said.

Few people passed by, absorbed in their own pursuits. Two grey-haired men dozed side-by-side on a park bench, and the tall flowers shielded him and Joanne from the other side. No one stopped and gawked. No one took pictures.

"Let's sit for a while." Joanne indicated an empty bench.

He lay on his back and rested his head on her lap. *How wonderful.* He closed his eyes.

She ran her fingers through his hair, and he managed a slurred "thank you" before drifting to sleep.

Seventeen: August 5th to 7th, 2017 — Paris, France

The first thing I saw upon entering our room at the Hidden Hotel was the flower arrangement from this morning, the calla lilies trapped in the fishbowl, their stems hopelessly tangled together. It sat on the dresser and caught the light streaming from the terrace doors.

Adam played innocent. "Champagne." He lifted a bottle from an ice bucket and read a card. "Compliments of the house."

Common for him, I was sure. And on that thought came tears: weak, stupid tears. The bathroom had no door, one of those intimate concepts some hotels have. Nowhere to hide. My vision blurred. I felt my way to the terrace and lay on a reclining chair, eyes shut. I shouldn't have come. In fact, I should leave. Go to the airport while my bags were still packed. Exchange my ticket for the first flight home. I would be so exhausted that I'd fall asleep in no time in one of those awful airplane seats.

Adam looked so peaceful when he slept on my lap, so trusting. He may have trusted me, but I didn't trust him fully. One deep breath, Joanne, two deep breaths, three: open your eyes and *go*.

He was standing right in front of me, leaning back against the railing.

"How long have you been there?" I blurted out.

He let himself slide down until he sat cross-legged on the floor. "The flowers are gone." He hung his head. "I'm sorry."

I wiped my cheeks with the backs of my hands.

"You want to be alone? For a while?"

I did not know what I wanted.

"You rest and I'll go for a walk. After that, we can talk."

The room was in twilight when I awoke. Morning? Evening? The curtains around the bed were pulled shut. It was the last thing I remembered doing after I showered. The clock said 8. It must be night. Was he back? "Adam?"

"I'm outside."

I parted the curtains, and his face appeared against an orange sky.

"I have a picnic." He lifted a bag in the air. "I only spent ten euros."

I joined him. He had plates and flatware. "From the hotel," he said, striking a match and lighting two candles. He opened take-out containers of tomatoes with bocconcini and basil, carrot salad, pâté, prosciutto, and devilled eggs.

The terrace looked out over windows open to the evening air. A man cradled a baby and walked the length of an apartment back and forth. After a while, he lingered in a barely lit room and exited without the baby. He joined a woman sitting at a table, put a hand on her shoulder, and she stopped typing. She tilted her head back, and they kissed. He disappeared, and she resumed typing.

"Beautiful," Adam said. We had eaten all the food, including six tiny pieces of cake with different layers and toppings.

"Now tell me everything," he said. "Anything."

I suggested we turn our chairs around to minimize distractions.

"Here goes." I took a steadying breath. "Do I like you? Yes. A lot? Yes. Is this going anywhere? Frankly, I doubt it." The wind rustled the leaves in the trees and snuffed out one candle. "You're a movie star who lives far away in a culture I know hardly anything about. I've already been in a much more 'ordinary' relationship, with the results that you know." I paused.

"That couple we saw with the baby? Reverse the roles, and that was Charlie and me when Sean was that age." The other candle suffered the same fate as the first, and all we saw was the bed beyond the open doors.

Adam spoke in his velvety voice. "I did a lot of thinking this afternoon. Why am I attracted to her? Why is she so special to me? These feelings, can they last for a year? For five? For a lifetime? What does that mean? For me? For her?"

He pivoted towards me, and I did the same.

"Okay, I'm not trying to boast, but many fans would do almost anything to sit in front of me like this." He rubbed a foot against my leg. "But what they want is not me. They want the man they saw on TV: strong, determined, caring; noble even."

I smiled. I would have added: attractive, fun to be with; sensual.

"Or maybe they want people to notice them, be jealous of them. To wear designer clothes and stay in five-star hotels." He rubbed his fingers in the universal sign for money. "But you're different. You didn't come to spend the weekend with a man from a TV show, or because you hoped he would buy you an expensive pair of shoes. You came because you know me outside of fame and money."

"I wouldn't say I know you that well."

Then what are we waiting for? his smile asked. I told him everything, anything, through touch, taste, looks, sounds, and he did the same until we lay breathless on the bed, spent and renewed at the same time. As sleep beckoned, he cuddled close, his chest against my back, his mouth close to my ear. "You know me better than anyone," he whispered.

At the Eiffel Tower, the next day, Adam was walking ahead of me, holding on to my hand, then he wasn't. He'd disappeared—escaping fans, I learned later--while I became more frantic by the minute. Was he always ten steps ahead, hence missing each other at every turn? In retrospect, what followed was a classic comedy of error. Needless to say, I was in no mood to laugh.

I kept a hand on my money belt, loath to deal with stolen credit cards. Pickpockets often worked in teams, one to distract the hapless tourist and the other to do the actual robbing. A hand reached around my waist from behind, an arm hooking me.

I slapped it hard and rushed between slow-moving bodies, dodging left and right until my back pressed against a safety net. How dare you, I thought, ready to knee the man if he tried again.

People pointed at landmarks in excited voices, snapping pictures, while my eyes remained fixed in the other direction. I saw a mirage, except he was no mirage. He looked like a cocker spaniel who'd like to say, "But you don't understand." I wrapped my arms around him, beyond ecstatic.

He froze for a moment, then held me in a big bear hug, "so worried," "so happy," tumbling from our mouths. Smiles of relief and delight. Whatever happened was in the past. It was time to continue from where we'd left off. His lips crushed mine, his tongue tasted mine, and that was all that mattered.

The taxi driver raced through one narrow street after another. Adam mouthed *faster* and grinned. Since finding each other, we had done everything tourists do at the Eiffel Tower: admired the views in all directions; lunched at one of the restaurants; and bought souvenirs at the gift shop.

In the back seat of the taxi, Adam squeezed my hand three times. *"Sa-rang-hae."*

I repeated after him and gave him the same signal.

"I love you," he said, eyes shining.

Inside the hotel, we scrambled up the stairs and fumbled to open the door with the key card, laughing and crying. On the other side, we tumbled to the floor.

"Are you all right?" he asked, worried I'd hit my head.

"You?"

I surrendered. To him, to my own desires, to all that made me a woman beyond motherhood and responsibilities. I surrendered my fear of being pushed aside. Maybe one day, but not today. Today was for joy, for embracing all he brought and all I brought to what made "us." He was warm and smooth, and his eyes penetrated mine while he danced inside me.

We slept, we woke, we dressed and went out. It was past eleven. "I feel free," I told Adam.

He wore beige pants with a crisp white shirt, rather chic even with the sleeves rolled to the elbows. My summer dress was blue with white polka dots and felt like wearing nothing at all. The evening air caressed my arms and legs, and I hung on to the illusion that summer would go on forever, Paris would go on forever.

"Listen," he said. Music spilled between two buildings.

We followed it to a courtyard café where a trio—guitar, upright bass and saxophone—played. A server motioned us to an empty table, a gracious gesture, inviting, as if the table had been waiting for us. We ordered wine and finger food.

"You know," he said, "I'd reserved a table at an expensive restaurant. I cancelled. I didn't want you to—"

"Get upset like yesterday?"

"To feel sad." He drank a sip of wine. "I only want to be happy with you. This is better than any expensive restaurant. This place is real."

The floor was paved with cobblestones and the walls were painted green, accented in yellow. Hanging baskets overflowed with blooms and trailing leaves. The band played numbers I had never heard before. The musicians moved with the beat—heads, torsos, hips and feet. They were building a story, inventing a phrase, repeating it, trying it another way, and another way, until they'd explored all the facets.

Adam lifted his glass. "To love."

Returning to the hotel on a brightly lit boulevard, we kissed, wanting to hold on to the moment for a while longer.

Upstairs, we showered and donned the cotton bathrobes hanging in the closet. I followed him to the terrace. We had a clear view of the Eiffel Tower's upper deck. He waved at tourists who might see us as stick figures through telescopes. I did the same.

"Let's sit for a while," he said. "There's something I'd like to see."

We gazed upward at the few stars bright enough to shine through the city lights. The high-low, high-low siren of an ambulance drifted from another world. A moth landed on my toe and beat its wings: tiny tickles.

"Look!" Adam pointed to a dot of light zooming across the sky. I remembered something Emma said a few days ago. The Perseids, the meteor showers that peak at this time. I made a wish: *May this last.* I pressed his hand three times, and he reciprocated.

His silence was comfortable. Comforting. His stomach growled, and he laughed. "Maybe finger food wasn't enough."

The mini-bar yielded a box of liqueur-filled chocolates that we took to the terrace.

I sat on his lap and fed him one. He held it between his teeth and pulled me closer to share. The chocolate shell cracked, and gravity did what gravity must. We were sticky and sweet everywhere, licking, kissing and laughing—but not too loud—on our terrace in the middle of Paris.

Eighteen: November 20ᵗʰ to December 1ˢᵗ, 2017 — Upper State New York

I was raking leaves in the front yard with Sean and Byron, who were more interested in jumping in the piles than filling bags, when my sister called, the type of call everyone dreads. Dad was in the hospital. A worsening cold; 911 call, ambulance; emergency room not too busy, thank God; x-rays: pneumonia with fluid accumulating in one lung. He had a tube installed to drain it.

"I'll ask for the week off," I said. "Maybe we can drive tomorrow." It was a short work week, Monday through Wednesday, then Thanksgiving, when Sean and I were due to visit the family. However Colleen and Jeremy had to juggle the hospital and the winery, and my coming with Sean would only add more chaos.

"I want to be there for him, Colleen. Don't worry about the house. I'll pitch in."

"I understand, Joanie. The thing is, kids aren't allowed to visit patients in intensive care."

If only Sean's father had not moved so far away, I could have dropped him off at his house and driven to Niagara. I was about to suggest that my brother-in-law, Jeremy, could watch over Sean while I went to the hospital when Colleen said, "In fact, it would be best if you cancelled your visit altogether."

"I want to see him, Colleen."

"I know. But visits exhaust him," she said. "Try not to worry too much. I'll keep you posted."

I supposed she was forgetting I had booked a flight to South Korea, leaving in less than two weeks.

At night, Adam entered our world via video calls. This time, he was early enough to read Sean a story he translated from an illustrated book that he angled toward the camera. He did each voice differently and even altered his facial expression to match the characters: the woodcutter who lost his rusty axe in a deep, dark lake; the wizard who offered him a golden axe, a silver one, though the man insisted they were not his. The sorcerer rewarded the woodcutter's honesty with the two precious axes plus his own. Rumours of his amazing luck spread in the village, and another woodcutter threw his old axe in the lake and waited. The wizard never appeared, and the greedy man was left poorer than he'd started with, without the means to earn a living.

This was not the first time Sean had heard the story. He followed along with his Lego characters, making the honest woodcutter skip happily after receiving the wizard's gifts, and the greedy woodcutter fall face down in despair.

Adam winked at me and took a sip of his morning coffee.

"Where are you shooting today?" I asked, following his progress as first-time director for his film, *An Affair of the Heart*.

"We're starting the hospital scenes."

His world became part of mine. I no longer mixed the lead actress's name, Baek Young-hee, with that of the screenwriter, Kang Min-chae.

Sean's game with the Lego characters carried him away to the living room and I mentioned my father's illness.

"Oh." Adam looked so sad I wished I had kept my worries to myself. Cancelling, or even postponing my trip to Seoul, would mean missing his film's premiere, for which I had yet to find a gown. And, he was keen to show me the house he had bought in the countryside.

"Let's hope the antibiotics work," I said. We joked about jumping through the screen to be together. He wished me a restful night, and I wished him an awesome day, words that seldom varied; words that left me feeling strong and calm, except for tonight when worries about my dad overrode any sense of peace I might have had.

I texted Colleen for a phone number to reach him. However, his bed was in a hallway until a proper room became available.

On Thanksgiving Sunday, I brought Sean to the outlet malls in Syracuse, where I tried over a dozen gowns, designer or otherwise. My father was now in a proper hospital room with three other patients. In our video call last night, he looked drained of energy. Poor, dear dad. I felt guilty planning a trip to see Adam yet not to visit him. And double guilt because I would leave Sean in Emma's care for a week while I indulged in pursuing my love life.

I spotted a Saks OFF Fifth outlet. "Okay, sweetie, one more shop then we go home."

The dresses that had not sold during last year's holiday season in New York adorned mannequins in the display window and hung on racks farther in. None looked promising and I was turning around when a sales associate found me. Middle-aged, chestnut hair carefully coiffed, great posture.

"What is the occasion?" she asked.

"An opening. Art exhibition," I lied. It was bad enough that I told Colleen about Adam a few months ago and faced her interrogation. "How do you know this guy?" "You flew to Paris to see a student! A Korean student?" "An actor?"

The sales associate sized me up and down as she conducted her questioning. "You're the artist? In New York?"

"Local."

"First rule: don't compete with your work. Do you have photos? It helps to complement the lines. Straight or curved?"

"I'm sorry. I should have made it clear. I'm not the artist."

"Then black. Straight lines, at least for above the knees. Here." She showed me a strapless mermaid gown made from a rubbery fabric reminiscent of a diving suit. "Or this one." Same style, but the flounces at the bottom were tiered and would force me to stand half an arm's length from Adam. And the cost … out of my league.

Sean was slumped on the carpeted floor, turning the pages of a book he'd already read a dozen times. "Hey buddy." I pulled him to his feet. "Let's go."

What a selfish mother I was, I admonished myself in the car. Depriving my child of fresh air and a whole day of play to come home empty-handed. I glanced at him in the rear-view mirror, head lolling, eyes half-closed. "Let's check on Grandpa."

I put the call through on the hands-free system, and Colleen answered. "He's awake."

Soft plopping sounds as she transferred the phone into Dad's hand. He greeted us in a voice even weaker than yesterday's. I told him only simple things to ease his mind before calling on Sean to say a few words. "Ask Grandpa if he ate any Jell-o," I prompted in a loud whisper.

My father took a raspy breath. "Giggly, jiggly Jell-o," he managed before coughing as if his lungs would rip apart.

Colleen ended the conversation, leaving Sean with a bewildered look on his face.

"Giggly, jiggly Jell-o." I winked through the rear-view mirror. "In red, green and yellow. And on Thanksgiving Day-o, what else but pumpkin Jell-o?"

"Pumpkin Jello? Eurk!" Sean said. At any rate, I'd brought us back to levity after hearing such painful sounds from Dad. He is such a remarkable man to have raised two girls on his own after Mom died. Colleen was twelve, and I was barely three. I owe her most of what I know about my mother and the brief time she was in my life.

One winter day, we were all trimming the Christmas tree, making popcorn garlands. My job was to supply Mom with a piece at a time so she could pass it through her sewing needle and slide onto a thread. But I kept gobbling up the popcorn, leaving us only enough for the top half of the tree. It lived briefly as a family joke, the half-finished tree and the little helper with the big appetite. Everything changed on New Year's morning when Dad hugged Collen and me, and said we would have to be brave.

Monday, Tuesday, Wednesday, I spent my lunch hours in second-hand stores finding nothing suitable, or disappointed that the only promising dress was too tight, too loose, or had other defects that couldn't be fixed. With less than thirty-six hours before departure, I changed strategy. I worked through lunch and left work early, bound for a boutique on the edge of town that sold designer clothes on consignment. I phoned ahead, and the shopkeeper, a woman who studied fashion design, was eager to show me the dresses most likely to fit my requirements. I told her as close to the truth as I felt necessary, the need to shine but not so much as to eclipse the lead female actor. I brought pictures of her that I printed from the web, including one taken at an award ceremony. She looked like a confident woman with curly brown hair, at ease in a slinky, off-the-shoulder dress.

"And the man you're going with?" the shopkeeper asked. "Any pictures of him?"

"I didn't think to bring one."

"Is he tall, slim, or not so slim? Does he have a dimpled chin?" She laughed at her joke and I remembered that I had the Paris photos on my phone.

"Hmm," she said as she swiped from one to the next. "He likes sunglasses. Nice smile." She backtracked and enlarged a portion of Adam's face. "Pierced ears?"

I took a look, certain I would have noticed. "It must be a tiny mole," I replied, strangely aroused from learning a new detail about him.

One dress drew my attention. "Versace," the shopkeeper said.

Simple lines and a pearly grey colour that seemed simple until I touched it. The satin shimmered, heavy, fluid and cool. It looked even better once I tried it on. The fabric created light and shadows that shifted as I threw back my shoulders and sucked in my tummy.

"Perfect," I heard. I imagined Adam's arm linked through this new vision of myself, a woman exuding poise and confidence, bowing like him at just the right time, just the right angle, and making him proud in front of his peers. I whispered a private word in his ear, the one with the pinhole mole on it, that I was nervous in front of all these people. And he beamed me his dazzling smile while he squeezed my hand three times, *I'm right here; I love you.*

Nineteen: December 4th, 2017 — Seoul, South Korea

For the second time in four months, I walked towards a door in an airport, wondering what would happen on the other side. Where was he? I searched for a man concealing himself under a baseball cap, a discreet wave of a hand. I told myself to carry on walking, he would appear out of nowhere like in Paris. Instead, I saw a sign bearing my name held by a man I presumed to be a chauffeur—tall, straight-backed and impersonal—until he introduced himself: Kim In-sung, Adam's manager and close friend.

I hid my disappointment and extended my hand.

Rather than breaking into a welcoming smile, his eyes looked above my head as he shook my hand. "Mr. Ahn could not come." He took the handle of my larger suitcase while I followed with the carry-on, the sights speeding by: people waiting for loved ones, lining up at counters to rent cars and book hotels; a bronze sun touching the horizon behind tall windows; announcements in a language I couldn't understand and signs in characters I couldn't decipher.

Adam would attract attention here, I reasoned. He could still be waiting inside a car in the parking lot. In-sung would open the door in his obsequious way, let me in and take the wheel to give us time to reconnect.

But In-sung remained cold and the car was empty.

Riding in the dark was like being on the plane, as if the fourteen-hour flight wasn't enough to reflect on what my visit meant. He had bought an old house in the countryside, Adam announced a month ago. Would I come to help him decide how to renovate it? He needed a woman's eyes to make it work like a modern home, yet retain its traditional charm. I was curious and I was flattered. I missed him. Still, I harboured no illusions that this trip would be like Paris. I had come to explore entering his life, seeing how well I fit, or not. The implications were complex. For him, for me, for Sean.

The car slowed at a tollgate, and In-sung pulled a box from a bag and handed it to me. It contained a phone I could use in Korea. "Press 1," he said.

The call went through, and here was Adam, thrilled that I'd arrived safe and sound, apologizing for still being behind the camera. "Soon we'll have a whole week," he said. In-sung would take me to his apartment and explain the arrangements for the premiere of the film shot in England.

The car glided among neon signs in all colours imaginable, lines of cars waiting for lights to change, skyscrapers with names like Gangnam Finance Center, Samsung Electronics and many more I could not read, decorated with masses of Christmas lights.

Only in the elevator, with my suitcases between us, did In-sung speak again. I needed to be ready by 2 p.m. on the afternoon of the premiere. Someone whose name I didn't recognize would bring me to the event. I wanted to ask where Adam would be during that time, however, In-sung had moved on to his next instruction: I must not call Ahn Dae-hyun at all that day.

The elevator doors opened. We had reached the top floor.

In case of emergency, I should call him, number 2 on speed dial, he said as we manoeuvred the suitcases into the hall.

We stopped at the only door in sight. "You will please dress in dark clothing; not draw attention."

How could I not draw attention if I attended as Adam's guest? My sleep-deprived brain could make no sense of what In-sung meant. He shielded his fingers and keyed in the entry code. He held the door open and bowed. "Please feel like home. Mr. Ahn here soon."

Once inside, I was a prisoner, unable to go for a walk around the block unless I left the door unlocked. I took my shoes off and donned the smaller of two pairs of slippers in the vestibule while taking in the room in front of me, the pale hardwood floors and the windows at the far end with nothing beyond but the dark blue night. A lamp shed subdued light, and I switched a few more on before sinking in a red armchair. I'd made it. I was both exhausted and elated.

I only had time to catch a few deep breaths before the door clicked open. "Joanne-*ah*." We embraced. In a way I could not explain, he smelled like home. Not my home. A different home. His mouth tasted like green tea, with the same grassy aftertaste.

In retrospect, I saw how In-sung's lack of fluency in English misled me. Before we moved farther inside the apartment, Adam showed me the entry code, 1333, the time I was born, something I mentioned in passing when we talked about our shared birthday.

In-sung's secrecy may have had an explanation, however, his coldness still rankled. "Your friend doesn't like me very much."

"It's not you. He's still mad at me for Paris."

"That was months ago."

He winked. "Let's forget In-sung."

My first impression of his apartment was of vastness; sparseness; well-chosen pieces. He suggested I unpack while he put a few things together to eat.

His closets were meticulously organized, not like the cramped spaces in my bungalow. Emptying my luggage and putting everything into drawers brought me a measure of peace after the stress of travelling. What In-sung meant by not attracting attention at the premiere began to make sense. I was Adam's guest, though I would neither enter with, nor sit beside him.

He came to ask if I needed anything more and lifted an item from its tissue paper wrapping. The pearly grey satin shimmered in his hands, heavy and fluid.

"Sexy nightgown," he said, eyes filled with anticipation.

I opened my mouth to set the record straight, but he spoke again. "I have to see you in this." He meant right away, before I joined him for dinner.

After taking a shower, I slipped the dress over my head and studied the effect in the mirror. It moulded every curve it could find, flattering or not. An organza trim let an inch of cleavage show, something I was less than comfortable with in the context of a public outing. A part of me was relieved I would not have to be in the limelight.

Adam whistled when I entered the kitchen. "*Bellissima.*" He took my hand and led me to the living room where candlelight and food awaited.

"Eat, it will do you good." He fed me a rice roll, soft and crunchy at the same time. Everything was bite-sized: mushrooms stuffed with crabmeat, mini quiches and fruits. Tiny cakes. He was right. The guilty goodbyes to Sean, the long flight, In-sung's coldness, all receded with eating, with hearing his voice live, not through a phone or a computer, with the heat of his body next to mine on the soft leather sofa.

Love. The act of love. It can be devoured like an ice cream cone that melts too fast, missing half the pleasure in the rush to eat it all. It can be savoured one lick at a time, one slow, lingering touch at a time. With eyes closed. Open. Closed again. Deep intakes of breath, deep exhales that say *More* and *Yes* and *Do that again, please!* Moans. Cries as the flavours build to piercing delight or shift into startling new ones. Colours like red berries, sweet and tart. Sounds like plucked strings that echo in the ears, clear and sharp, that quicken as the heart races and the senses overload.

We took the full tour. Between each round, we lay entwined as if letting go would mean death.

Twenty: December 5th to 6th, 2017 — Seoul, South Korea

I woke up in Adam's bed with the drowsy recollection of him rising earlier and telling me to sleep longer; of his lips brushing mine.

A bar of sunshine sliced through dark curtains and shone on a lacquered armoire inlaid with mother-of-pearl flowers, vines, trees, and fruits. All the furniture matched, a dresser, bedside tables, and even a mirror frame.

I found Adam working out in a room I had not seen yet, with banana trees and palm trees rising between gym equipment. On one side, glass panes angled from a peaked ceiling. On the other side, a climbing wall soared to meet the glass. Adam moved sideways from rock to rock, close to the ground, as if practicing a slow dance. "Espresso? Cappuccino? Latte? I can stop doing this anytime."

"No rush," I said. I tried to reach my dad at the hospital but learned that he was resting. I would try again later. Same for Sean. For once, I could take it slow. Serene music played. The instrument sounded like a violin with a sensuous twang.

As great as Paris had been once we understood each other, this first morning in Seoul was better. No need to fill the silence, hurry out and see the sights.

I would ignore In-sung's coldness. The Paris escapade without Adam's bodyguard could have led to complications. My presence here brought additional complications.

Adam wanted to show me the designs for the house he had bought in the countryside. We would drive there the day after the premiere, but he was eager for my opinion. He laid the blueprints on a coffee table in "The Den." I would have christened this room "The Prow" for the tall windows that jutted out, ship-like, in one corner.

He flipped through the pages until he found the kitchen. "What do you think about a dishwasher? Imagine you're staying in a house like that. Wouldn't it make life easier?"

The assumption that I would come for a longer visit.

"I see a playground here. Swings and monkey bars. How about a trampoline?"

That I would bring Sean. That he and I would move to Korea one day.

Part of me wanted to believe in his vision, even though I had been hurt before in what any reasonable person would consider a less risky situation. Adam's earnestness, his kindness, so unlike Charlie's selfishness, drew me in. I reasoned Sean had been uprooted often enough in his short life without me compounding the problem. In-sung also loomed large, In-sung who saw me as a complication—a movie star's plaything—rather than a new direction in Adam's life. How many playthings had he taken, then discarded for In-sung to think I was just one more?

Adam changed the music to the piece we had heard driving home from Seneca Lake. "Look at this." His eyes crinkled with glee as he pulled a drawing from the bottom of the pile. It showed a gate with a name carved in the cross-beam: *Our Fifth Season.*

Such enthusiasm. I smiled.

"Tired?" He checked an app on his phone, a closed-circuit television feed of the street below, I later learned. "Nothing like fresh air to cure jetlag." He opened the terrace doors. The December sun held the cold at bay as we stood near a smoked glass barrier. A modern city, with block upon block of white apartment buildings, spread into the distance. The Han River curved in a sweeping S, bordered by trails where people in bright gear cycled, jogged, and walked. The street below was deserted, a sleepy interlude on a Sunday morning. Across the water, atop a hill, N Seoul Tower glinted in the bright sunlight.

I waved at imaginary tourists.

Adam grabbed my arm and pulled me away from the barrier. "Don't do that!"

"But in Paris—"

"What if someone saw you?" Anger flashed in his eyes. "Here." He pulled a chair for me at a round table. "It's safer; your head is lower." Without another word, he went inside.

What was he saying? Did people with oversized telephoto lenses wait to snap photos of him and his guests? Was he ashamed of me? Was I such a plain Jane? And what was he doing inside? Sulking?

Wishing he had never invited me? I was tempted to pack my bags and leave. I stewed outside as long as I could, then went in.

He was in the kitchen, whisking eggs. "Here you are." Bright smile.

Two place settings at the eating counter; sliced fruit, golden-brown croissants and a selection of jams; a vase of blush roses.

He poured the egg mixture into a frypan. "Wine?"

I declined. A long-ago quote slipped from my mouth: "They are not long, the days of wine and roses."

He focused on his cooking, sprinkling chives and parsley before folding the omelet and dividing it into two. We sat side-by-side, and he brought my hand to his lips. "Thank you for coming, Joanne-*ah*. I'm so happy, I... I'm sorry about earlier. Paris was Freedom, *Liberté*. Here, I have to watch... I should have told you."

I hugged him, my lovely, lonely, caring man.

He left early the next morning for a series of interviews, and I reached both my dad, who was in stable condition, and Sean, who told me one of Emma's cats had slept at his feet all night.

I had a slice of time when nothing was expected of me. I read, ate on the terrace and watched a documentary on *hanji* paper made with the inner bark of mulberry trees on Arirang TV.

Even though I would wear a black skirt and grey turtleneck, I still needed to apply make-up and style my hair. I was ten minutes late to meet the woman who would take me to the premiere. She sat at the back of a taxi and beckoned me inside. She introduced herself as Kang Min-chae, enunciating her name slowly so it would not run all together the way In-sung had said it. Kang Min-chae. Of course, the screenwriter for Adam's directorial debut, *An Affair of the Heart*. She had studied her craft in California in the 1970s, hence her fluency in English.

She smiled and pointed out the landmarks—the 63 Building, the Lotte Department Store, Galleria. The names meant little, a world spinning on its own axis. There were familiar sights: women pushing strollers, teenagers hanging outside a 7-Eleven and, incongruously, a man in a beret emerging from a shop called Paris Baguette. For every sign in English—or French—there were twenty in Korean.

The theatre was inside a multiplex similar to those in America, same bright lights and popcorn smells, except that we were ushered to our seats by a teenager wearing a uniform.

"Dae-hyun mentions you often," I told Kang Min-chae, feeling strange about using Adam's Korean name. I hoped she would share her views, whether he was easy to work with or demanding, reliable or not.

"He truly loves you." She patted my hand like she was my dearest aunt.

An interview Adam had given in the morning played on-screen while the audience filed in. Kang Min-chae translated: "The location shoots in England were hard, yes. I'm grateful for my fans' support while I was there." Adam addressed the viewers directly: "Please give this film all your love. Stay warm in the winter months." It sounded like stock phrases, yet the audience erupted with cheers and applause. "Fans," Kang Min-chae whispered in my ear. "They won tickets through a lottery."

She detected Mandarin spoken on her left, and I heard English in the row ahead. A woman squeezed into a strapless pink dress spoke English with a Southern drawl. Another had a British-inflected voice: sequin-studded sari, bangles flashing on her arms, hair pulled in a cascading do, sparkling with glitter.

The screen switched to the arrivals on the red carpet. Cheers rose outside the theatre and inside. Despite the noise, my eyes closed a few times as Kang Min-chae fed me the names of people emerging from the limousines.

"Baek Young-hee-*ssi*," I heard. The actor walked alone, regal in a short-sleeved gown. The red-carpet host asked her the name of the designer. Dior.

"Such a graceful woman." Kang Min-chae said. "We're lucky she agreed to be in Dae-hyun's film."

On the phone a week earlier, Adam told me she might even win the Palme d'Or at Cannes if *An Affair of the Heart* was selected.

"Her husband's not here?" I asked.

"He's not an actor."

Even a spouse wasn't worthy. I failed to grasp what I have learned since: ordinary people who enter the inner circle of celebrities risk being devoured by the public. Best to stay hidden.

The other *Swingtime* actors and the director had taken their seats in the front row, and the red carpet was empty. The camera caught In-sung waiting at the curb, still as a guard, until he lunged forward and opened a limousine door.

The theatre erupted. The host approached with her microphone and said something. "A Prince Charming," Kang Min-chae interpreted.

The camera remained on him all the way to the auditorium. Deafening cheers. He bowed deeply while a thousand flashes went off. Electrifying.

Adam had told me about *Swingtime*'s opening scene, the garden swing where his character has sex with his boss's wife, high above Seoul on a rooftop terrace. It gave rise to the story's central premise: an illegitimate child and a secret that returns to haunt both men two decades later. The grown son is studying filmmaking in his biological father's class in England. The young man disappears after inadvertently catching a shady deal between mobsters in the background of a video he shot at random in London. The English dialogue in roughly a third of the film was subtitled in Korean, but the Korean dialogue was not. Even with Kang Min-chae's interpretation in my ear, I missed many nuances. My eyes wandered to the front row where Adam's head pointed straight ahead, occasionally bending toward the director to exchange a few words, never turning back. The film ended with a convoluted action sequence where both fathers competed to rescue their son.

The end credits rolled and the people in the front row climbed on stage for a Question-and-Answer session. The MC praised the film at length in Korean before turning to the group. His first question concerned the action scenes.

The director replied that Adam had worked with a movement coach on a climbing wall. Adam added that he enjoyed the training so much, he continued to do it whenever possible.

The woman in the sari was first in line for questions from the audience. She introduced herself in English, saying that she lived in Singapore. The MC looked impressed by how far she had travelled. He translated in Korean for the benefit of the audience.

"What many of us would like to know, Ahn Dae-hyun-*ssi*," she said, "is how it was to … mmm … act on that swing?"

Laughter burst from the row ahead of ours, and an impish smile crept into Adam's eyes while the MC repeated the question in Korean.

"Precarious," he answered in English, launching chuckles from anyone who understood. The MC translated and delayed laughter rippled through the crowd. A spotlight followed the woman to her seat and caught me in its beam. His eyes locked on mine for a heartbeat before returning to the MC. I waited for him to look again, but he did not.

Kang Min-chae held on to my arm so we would stay together while leaving the theatre. A cacophony of hen clucks echoed off the walls. Were Adam to appear among us at that moment, these women would have pecked him to death.

"Did you see how he looked at me?" the Singaporean asked her friends.

I smiled inwardly.

The fans went on their merry way while Kang Min-chae hailed a cab. Adam had told me what would happen next: "I have to go to a boring party. Kang Min-chae will feed you a nice dinner at her house."

In the taxi, I nodded at what she said though I didn't absorb much. I could not block the images colliding in my head, this other Adam I had envisioned based on my first impressions, a quiet, self-possessed student. I was angry with myself for doing only minimal research online. Perhaps it was misplaced discretion, or skepticism over how popular his website claimed he was or, more to the point, putting my head in the sand. No still photo could have prepared me for what I witnessed that afternoon, the charisma he could turn on whenever the occasion warranted; everyone spellbound. I had watched a few episodes of his series, *Reunification*; I should have looked at videos of his public appearances.

A familiar flag caught my eye, red and white with a maple leaf in the centre. "Embassy of Canada," I read. The taxi took a sharp turn and stopped in front of a gate with 19-90 written in gold numerals—the land where I was born juxtaposed with the year my mother died.

Kang Min-chae had been tremendously kind throughout the afternoon, however the prospect of making small talk for God knew how many hours felt beyond me. "I'm sorry," I said. "I have a terrible case of jet lag."

She protested but eventually gave in and instructed the driver on where to drop me off.

I changed into my thrift shop gown and went to bed. How foolish I'd been to imagine walking beside Adam in that dress, a "Versace Fashion," the label said, not the real brand after all. The sheets hissed over the satin as I tossed and turned.

A few weeks earlier, I'd told my sister I was seeing a man who lived in Korea.

"You can't be serious," she said. "It's so far away."

I let it pass but here I was, so far away. Dead tired and wide awake. I wandered through the apartment and stared at the tops of buildings through the ship-prow windows. It gave the eerie feeling of sailing into the sky.

Adam's books and DVDs lined one wall. A spine caught my eye: his television series with Baek Young-hee. The box cover differed from the copy I'd bought. Adam was pressing Baek Young-hee against a wall and kissing her as if the world could collapse around them, and they wouldn't notice. It was just a role with no basis in reality. Still, alone in his apartment, I could not shake the notion that the hours were passing and the two actors were at the same party.

By the time he returned, I was back in bed. Sounds of crockery, of taking a shower. At last, he slipped under the duvet. I pretended to sleep, my back to him. He cuddled close, and I thought: no, not tonight, Mr. Superstar.

He fell asleep in minutes.

Twenty-One: December 7th to 11th, 2017 — Danyang, South Korea

Joanne hardly said a word during the two-hour drive from Seoul. Was she upset with him, he wondered? She kept her head turned toward the unfolding landscape yet gave no sign of hearing him point out a quaint guesthouse, farmers picking sweet potatoes, or ducks floating on muddy ponds. Was she sleeping?

By the time Adam stopped the SL55, the *hanok* already sat in shade, dark, though not dark enough to hide the broken fretwork on the doors and the cracked tiles on the roof. "It's not much to look at. For now." He hoped Joanne was not too disappointed. "But first things first." He ran around to the kitchen and lit the woodfire that would heat the floors.

She helped him unload the bags and supplies, asking where each item went, sounding resigned to follow his plan, though her heart was not in it.

"I have an idea," he said. "Let's put everything in this room." He unlocked the widest set of doors. "And take a walk before it's too dark. Stretch our legs." He took her hand and led her through the gate along the perimeter wall.

At the back of the *hanok*, the path veered into an aspen grove, the tall silver trunks straight as columns. Twigs buried under fallen leaves snapped as they passed. Bare branches chattered in the wind.

The trees made way for wild grasses that towered above their heads. The path narrowed, allowing them to pass only in a single file. Adam brushed the Eulalias' crinkled heads with his fingers.

"Woolly," Joanne said behind him.

The field of grasses ended where the ground turned to rock. A few more steps and the hilltop appeared, awash with sunshine. Joanne quickened her steps and overtook Adam, her skin gilded by the light, wonder suffusing her features. On the other side, the Namhan River made a molten lava ring from which the town of Danyang rose. A dragon might have been circling overhead, so surreal was the view.

They stood still as the red orb dissolved between two mountain peaks.

"Let's—"

"There's—"

Adam insisted that Joanne speak first.

"There's a lot to take in, Adam. It's one thing to know you're famous, to imagine what it feels like. But to see you in a room full of people, women, who worship you. . . To see. . . I don't even know how to put it into words. All that energy seemed to flow through you. You smiled, perfectly at ease. Calm. Accustomed to it." She paused. "It scared me."

He took her hand. "It used to scare me too, Joanne-*ah*. A lot. What if all these people decided to rush to the stage and hug me at the same time? What if they turned on me?" He motioned for them to sit on a boulder. "But they did not."

"They still keep watch outside your building."

"I'm used to it by now," he lied, afraid to scare her away. "And now we have this place." He swept his arm toward the *hanok*. "Wait till you see the house after the work's finished. Everything broken will be carted away. I'll send you photos. It will make all the difference. See over there? That's the playground for Sean. And any friend he wants to have over. That boy on your street. I'll pay for his flight. His mother can come too if you want." The plans had been percolating in his head for weeks. "You won't have to work unless you want to. We can hire someone to cook and clean. Haven't you ever dreamed of doing something completely different, something you truly enjoy? We can make that happen."

She smiled. "Sounds too good to be true." She rose, and they headed home. They had another four days to explore the idea of living here. The air was still through the tall grasses, the sky silver.

"It's snowing," Joanne said.

Fat flakes drifted overhead and alighted on the crinkled seed heads, coating, amplifying.

At the edge of the woods, woolly white dots hung in the air and transformed the aspen grove into an Impressionist painting. They stopped between the two sights. Adam would have liked to immortalize each with his camera, though he had left it at the *hanok*.

Their eyes would have to suffice. Joanne moved closer and slipped an arm through his. "Remember the flurries at Collegetown Bagel?"

He smiled and she raced away, zigzagging off the trail, hiding behind tree trunks, until he caught her and they collapsed on the ground, laughing.

Snow continued to fall throughout the night, muffling the sounds outside and cocooning the *hanok*. The heat radiating from the floor kept them warm behind their paper doors and windows.

In the days that followed, they cooked for each other. They danced to Leonard Cohen's "Dance Me to the End of Love" and many more songs. They cleared the snow around the house with brooms and their hands. They lit bonfires outside after dark. They listened to "The Fifth Season." They could not replicate the jolt to the heart they had felt the first time. It didn't matter. They made love. They sang the songs they both knew, "Row, row, row your boat," "Both Sides Now" by Joni Mitchell. His whole being overflowed with love. Nothing could hurt him, nothing except losing her.

Twenty-Two: December 11ᵗʰ, 2017 — Seoul, South Korea

Away from the risk of being mobbed, Adam blossomed again. We laughed, hiked, danced, and surrendered to passion: our own brand of freedom. He felt whole, and I felt whole. He gave me what money could not buy, the most beautiful seashells from a collection he started as a boy, a sketch he made of a sparrowhawk that perched in a tree on our second day, and a lacy leaf skeleton he found on his first visit and pressed into a book for me.

We returned to Seoul on my last full day in Korea. He had planned to order a meal from his favourite Italian restaurant, however, his mother called.

"My family's getting together for dinner," he said afterwards. "I told my mom I had plans already." He winked.

I did not want him to leave, but I said, "You should go. I'll stay and pack."

He shook his head. "Unacceptable."

"We'll have more time in the morning."

"She wants to meet my—"

Surprise, disbelief. "Didn't we agree—"

"... my English teacher from Cornell, who happens to be visiting Seoul."

He saw this dinner as a chance for me to meet his family and for them to meet me under neutral circumstances.

The house hid behind a tall cedar hedge. It came into view only after Adam drove through a wrought iron gate: pale stucco walls pierced by wide windows, glowing on the ground floor and dark upstairs. It had not snowed in Seoul. Autumn flowers bloomed, purple and white chrysanthemums, a few roses, and many others I couldn't name. Closer to the house, earthenware pots held ornamental kale ranging from deep purple to soft pink, jade green to frothy cream.

The front door opened before Adam had a chance to ring. A slim woman in a red sweater hugged him, patted him on the back, and beamed me a smile over his shoulder.

Introductions by Adam: his sister, Dae-moon—she bowed.

Teacher Rollins from Cornell—I bowed likewise. She shook my hand. "Please come in."

As we slipped our shoes off in the sunken vestibule, a child peeked from a doorway and retreated just as fast. In the living room, Adam's father sat in an armchair facing the door. He looked as severe as Adam had described him, with a lean face, black-rimmed glasses and a still posture. Adam made the introductions again, Principal Ahn to Teacher Rollins. "Welcome," he said.

Two sofas stretched, to his right and left, as if he presided over a meeting. For now, only another man and the boy kept him company. Dae-moon's husband held their son and bowed his head. "Pleased to meet you."

Jae-ro wriggled out of his arms and bulldozed into Adam, who turned him around to face me. "Hello." The boy repeated the words Adam whispered in his ear. "My name is Jae-ro." His eyes darted around to gauge reactions, and Principal Ahn's face relaxed into a smile.

In the kitchen, I met Adam's mother, tall and elegant in a flowered dress under her apron, and his paternal grandmother, petite and kind-looking. He translated back and forth, though most of the exchange took place through hand gestures, smiles, and bows. Dae-moon ferried dishes to the dining room and invited us to follow.

The table held plates and bowls containing a bewildering variety of food, green, pale yellow, brown, and red. Everyone kept their hands on their laps until Principal Ahn brought a piece of food into his mouth, tasted it, and nodded. Adam's mother, next to me, selected a wedge of pancake and placed it on my plate. I thanked her and felt seven pairs of eyes watching me struggle to grasp the slippery food with the metal chopsticks.

At the *hanok*, I should have insisted on practicing rather than letting Adam help me. He took such pleasure from it; now I felt embarrassed as the piece of food dropped to my plate.

Dae-moon offered me a knife and fork. "More easy."

"Thank you." I dipped my head as she had done. *"Kamsa hamnida."*

"They are called *pajeon*," Adam said, "made with potatoes and green onions."

No sooner had I lifted one morsel to my mouth than Mrs. Ahn added more must-tries on my plate, red-skinned peanuts mixed with tiny dry fish; cucumber slices—or were they zucchini?—speckled with red pepper; bean sprouts; and glass noodles mixed with slivers of red and green pepper. "Delicious," *"mashiseoyo,"* and *"kamsa hamnida,"* I kept saying.

Everyone had a covered stainless-steel bowl to their left holding short-grained rice similar to the sushi type, but gleaming like translucent beads.

Across the table, Adam helped his grandmother, doing for her what his mother did for me. I sensed a closeness between them, a bond deeper than respect for an elder. His mother said Adam had shown her a picture of the tree growing in front of my house. In full bloom, it looked like a *chima*, she said, a long skirt women wear on formal occasions. Adam had mentioned she wanted to plant a similar tree in her garden. I passed her a slip of paper with the common name, Eastern Redbud, and the Latin one, *Cercis Canadensis*.

"My mother wonders how old the tree is," Adam relayed, "how long it takes to grow to this size. If you don't know, it's okay."

"I'm not sure. All I know is that it was planted as a sapling the day Sean was born."

"Wah." Adam translated my words, and the family looked as impressed as he was, except for Principal Ahn, who maintained his stern countenance. He raised neither Adam's newly released film, *Swingtime*, nor his current work on *An Affair of the Heart*. That aspect of his son's life did not exist, according to Adam. Other family members tried to engage him in other topics with limited success. Yes, the fish tasted fresh, and the water kimchi was particularly nice.

I felt a frigid current directed at me, as if he suspected I was more to Adam than an English teacher: an American divorcée with a child to raise, a gold digger.

Adam hid his feelings for as long as the visit lasted, though he had more to say in the car. "My father should know better than to treat guests this way. My mother was mortified, I could tell. My sister came close to calling him out on his prejudices. I stopped her. It would have made things even worse for you."

They must have exchanged signals I did not see.

"I'm really sorry, Joanne-*ah*." He squeezed my hand three times, and I did the same.

Twenty-Three: December 25th, 2017 — Seoul, South Korea

On Christmas Day, Adam's mother opened the door, smiling until she saw the tiredness in his face. "You're pushing yourself too hard."

"And you look radiant, *Eomma*. Merry Christmas." Adam hugged her and handed her a cake box.

At the dinner table, his father kept the family from touching their chopsticks with a sermon about falsehoods circulating on social media. "It's a thousand times worse than the propaganda North Korea dropped on us during the war. We had the sense not to believe them. We listened to our elders. Now teenagers think they know everything." He shook his head. "But, as this is a day of celebration, let us hope for respect to prevail, and be grateful for—"

Adam's phone buzzed and he excused himself to take the call in his old room.

It was Joanne who had found a few moments to talk before Sean burst out of bed to find his presents under the tree. Adam cherished the times when she was the one to call. "Missing me?" They connected daily, pockets of time that brought respite from the myriad details swirling in his head.

She spoke about the garage set he had sent for Sean and promised to send him a video. "I love you," she said.

"I love you more." He hurried back to the table only to find everyone frozen in their chairs.

"If answering the phone takes precedence over your family, you might as well go home," his father said.

Adam apologized, saying it was a call from another time zone. He was about to sit when his father held up a hand. "No, you don't. People who think we are less important than strangers on the phone are not welcome here."

His mother and sister traded looks.

"*Aboji*, let it pass," Dae-moon said.

"This is exactly the attitude young people have these days. Checking their social media feeds at the table, answering calls. It is impolite and I will not tolerate it in my home."

Adam's mother shot Adam a look. *Apologize again.*

"*Aboji*, I'm truly sorry. I won't do it again."

"Let him sit," his mom said. "We see him so seldom."

His father held off speaking until Adam was seated. "We rate rather low on our famous son's priority list."

Adam gritted his teeth, and a hush descended over the family until his father picked up his spoon and reached for a slice of rice cake in the *tteokguk* soup. Conversation restarted, praise for the food, concerns for Jae-ro's sore throat, congratulations to Dae-moon and her husband for the sizable increase in sales at their tea shop; more congratulations to their father for success with a fundraising campaign for his school's sporting facilities. The meal was nearly over when Dae-moon asked, "It was that teacher from America, wasn't it?"

Adam warned her with his eyes, but his mother chimed in, "You spoke English."

"You like her." Dae-moon exchanged a look with their mother, who asked if she was one of his fans.

"Definitely not."

Grandmother's head turned from side to side as his mom and sister lobbed questions at him. Between his silences and half-answers, they pieced together something approaching the truth. "Maybe," he admitted. "It's too soon to tell."

Dae-moon and her family left as soon as dinner was over. Adam tried to help clear the table but his mother and grandmother chased him from the kitchen. His father continued to read a book while Adam sat to his left, at a loss for words. "Car running fine?" he asked, quickly exhausting that topic and moving on to the weather, followed by news of distant relatives. Thankfully, the women soon joined them with the strawberry cream cake he had brought and a fruit platter.

"I found a plant nursery that sells the tree your teacher friend has," his mother said as she served slices of cake.

"I like her," Grandmother said to no one in particular. She held a half-moon of pear aloft on her fork.

"She seemed quite nice," his father conceded. "Although, divorced and with a child, you have to wonder what she is after."

"You think she's after——?" His mother trailed off.

"She is not after anything," said Adam.

His father dabbed his mouth with a napkin. "How would you know?"

"I just know." Adam resisted the urge to elaborate. The more he said, the more openings he gave his father.

"Think it through: one day you will be seen with that woman, photographed with her. You will not be able to control what people say about you. Or about her."

Adam saw the truth in his father's words, though he had come to realize that unless he ignored such worries, he would never have anything resembling a normal love relationship. "It's my life. I can deal with it."

His father took a sip of tea and cleared his throat. "I don't think you are seeing the whole picture. It is not only *your* life. And it is not that we, in this family, have prejudices about Americans. Or single mothers. *Or* divorced women. We are modern." He looked around the room as if a flat-screen television equated to having modern values. "But many people in this country have not adjusted their views yet."

"That's *their* problem." The moment the words left his mouth, Adam knew he had walked right into a trap.

"On the contrary, Dae-hyun-*ah*, it has far-reaching consequences. Think of your sister and her tea business. How many customers does she stand to lose if you are indifferent to what people say about you? Your mother's gardening club friends belong to an older generation. They will not understand. And not to be selfish, but I plan to retire after the sports wing opens. I would like that time to pass without people gossiping about my famous son."

Ah yes, Father, your famous son who will always be an embarrassment to you. Adam had another forkful of cake. What had been so creamy and delicious before now tasted bland.

Two weeks later, he was charged with murdering Baek Young-hee.

Twenty-Four: April 24ᵗʰ, 2018—Danyang, South Korea

It has turned mild enough to keep the Great Room doors open. Adam prepares tea and brings a cup to Grandmother, who sits at the low table, embroidering flowers and butterflies on a white cloth. She looks frail, no larger than a child. She seemed so strong when Adam was growing up. She could move gigantic clay jars, whereas it took all his strength just to lift a cover. "When you marry," she said, "I'll make you beautiful curtains."

He will never marry now, not with Joanne and not with any other woman. He doesn't know why Grandmother is making the curtains. So much remains unsaid between them. Did his father ask her to be his guarantor, or has she come against his will? Sometimes he thinks she is at the *hanok* to take care of him—the inept male living alone, away from the city's conveniences. Other times, he thinks she is here so he has someone to be responsible for, someone he is bound to by that most inescapable of ties, filial piety.

"Have you seen the lettuce, *Halmeoni*?"

She shakes her head. He offers his arm and they make their way to the side of the house. Before the deep freeze of winter hardened the ground in January, a rectangle of land was leveled by the workers. They would return in the spring and install a swing set, a slide and a trampoline in time for Joanne's visit with her son in the summer. Adam would clear his calendar and they would spend three weeks together, go for hikes in the mountains and picnics on the shores of the river. He would don a straw hat and a pair of glasses, and they would risk the company of tourists at the Gosu Cave.

But a week after their disastrous phone conversation, he found a pickaxe in the tool shed. The hardness of the ground didn't matter. He hacked at it until the playground turned into a pockmarked field. March flurries blanketed the scars, but as soon as the snow melted, the land turned to mud. One morning, while finishing breakfast with Grandmother, he heard a ring at the gate. A truck driver.

"I'm sorry," he said to the man, "I should have called,"—meaning, In-sung should have called. "We don't need that sand anymore."

"Sand?" The man scratched his head. "Topsoil. See?" He waved a slip of paper under Adam's nose, "Ordered last week."

Grandmother had made her way from the house. "Over there," she told the man, pointing to the playground-that-would-never-be.

Adam could have left the mound there, a mountain to his indifference. He could have said, "I'm not doing that," when Grandmother told him she had seen a wheelbarrow in the tool shed. But she had already received the seed packets she'd ordered from a catalogue.

And now here they are, looking at the first frills of lettuce poking from the ground, green and perfect. He walks with Grandmother on the brick path between the rows—the bricks, another delivery—and stops in front of the biggest lettuce. The sun's heat burrows into the black earth, feeding life into anything that cares to grow, weeds and lettuce, squash and radishes alike.

Grandmother turns to him, and Adam knows she has caught him doing something he hasn't done in months. Smile. It brings a vision of the man he might become if he survives this ordeal: a hobby farmer, gangly and grizzled, scarier than a scarecrow to the children who catch sight of him on market days when he ventures into town to sell his purple carrots and blue potatoes.

In-sung returns from his vacation looking younger than his thirty-six years of age. He has slept ten hours a night and eaten his fill, he says. His cheeks have lost their hollowness, and his skin looks tanned from spending time outdoors rather than chained to a desk. One thing remains the same. He wears the kind of suits he favoured at the Star Shop Agency, informal yet refined, with impeccably shined shoes that turn muddy in minutes.

He carries a slim briefcase, the quintessential Manager Kim, as Adam still calls him sometimes. In his early twenties, whenever Manager Kim said, "Dae-hyun-*ah*, go to this audition," he hastened to follow his elder's orders. Sometimes he landed a part; most times he did not. If the script called for jumping in the Han River in the middle of February, he did exactly that, Yes, Sir!

In-sung's visits seldom vary. He arrives in mid-afternoon, eager to stretch his legs after the two-hour drive. They take a turn around the property. "Your woodpile keeps growing," In-sung might say. "You'd better start storing it under the house." Today, he points at a half-dozen jars drying upside-down over wooden slats. "Spring cleaning?"

"Grandmother wants to make fermented soybean paste, red pepper paste, and salted shrimps," he says. "And kimchi, with the jars buried underground to keep it cool." He will no doubt do all the digging and heavy lifting, and his share of the making too.

In-sung retrieves a few beers from the car, and they sit on boulders near the house. "Any more squawking from that vulture?" Adam enquires.

"Funny you should ask." In-sung relates how the owner of *The Orbiter* was accosted by television reporters to give his views on abolishing the death penalty. He gestures like Han Dok-ku. "We've become soft, and look at what's happening to our nation. The moral fibre is gone.'"

Adam chugs half his beer, churning inside over all the amoral things Han Dok-ku has done in his life.

In-sung selects a piece of paper from his briefcase and starts asking questions.

"Yes, I spent half an hour in her room, but it was the evening before the wrap party." Adam repeats what he has already said a hundred times, or sifts through his memory for a detail nobody asked before. Whether his answers are the absolute truth or versions of the truth he has come to believe, he can no longer tell.

Grandmother always invites In-sung for dinner. Tonight he talks about his holidays when he caught trout and kept them alive by tying them to a dock post in the lake. The next morning, they had all disappeared, having undone their knots.

"Do you know what happened, *Halmeonim?*" He adds a rib to the brazier. "They were all eaten. By a snapping turtle." His arms scissor the air like a mouth closing on prey. "The turtle was still in the shallows, digesting its feast. *My* feast."

Grandmother laughs and wipes tears from her eyes.

The nights that follow In-sung's visits are the worst. No matter how hard Adam tries to empty his mind, he ends up kicking off the quilt and sitting outside on the *hanok*'s ledge, his toes grazing the ground as panic battles with anger at the way fame made him a sitting duck for character assassination.

The first one who gets angry loses, his father used to say. Adam pictures him sitting in the living room, refilling his cup from the celadon teapot by his side and telling sixteen-year-old Adam that he could not go camping with his friends, or he had to paint the wrought iron fence if he wanted money to see a movie. Adam itched to storm out of the house and never return. Throw his father's precious teapot against the wall and make him jump. Most of all, he wanted him to raise his voice like other fathers, threaten to hurt Adam even, so he could yell back at him. His father invariably buried his nose again into the student assignments he marked every night. After a while, he lifted his head and caught the rage etched on Adam's face. "The first one who gets angry—"

His father was born in 1953, the last year of the Korean War. Adam's grandfather died on the battlefield and never held his son in his arms. Adam's father grew up amid such hardship that Adam cannot picture him laughing or doing anything other than studying and being the man of the house, fixing broken things, and carrying bags of rice on his shoulder.

Through hard work and perseverance, virtues he still values above all others, he became a history teacher at a prestigious high school in Seoul and, in time, rose to the rank of principal.

When Adam was in elementary school, most boys got into fights. "Stay away from troublemakers," his father said as he left the house in the morning. Adam did. The other boys called him a coward, and one day, they needled him so much that he punched one of them in the face. One blow and the boy's front tooth cracked. He spat blood and, for one glorious moment, there was silence in the schoolyard. Respect.

His father had to pay the dentist's fee and never let Adam forget it. "This is not how an eldest son behaves," he said, shaking his head. Firmly entrenched in his mind was that eldest sons should be role models. He never approved of Adam becoming an actor, not even when people began calling him Korea's Perfect Gentleman.

Interviewers used to say, "Your parents must be extremely proud." Adam nodded and looked bashful, knowing that nothing he did would ever make his father proud. His mother would have liked to attend the Baeksang Awards ceremony when he was nominated for best actor five years ago, but his father vetoed her attendance and, even after Adam won, never acknowledged the award.

Now that Adam is in trouble, his father will have nothing to do with him. How cowardly is that? How un-paternal? He has never been *Appa*, Dad, always *Aboji*, Father.

An owl perches on the persimmon tree that grows near Adam's room. The bird stands, surrounded by an aura of dignity.

"*Aboji?*" Adam asks, and the bird tilts its head, blinks, and flies away.

Twenty-Five: May 1ˢᵗ, 2018 — Danyang, South Korea

A week later In-sung is back, and Adam sits with him on the *hanok*'s ledge after their walk around the garden.

"No questions from the team," In-sung says. "I came anyway. See how you're doing, whether there's anything I can bring you, clothes, books, puzzles?"

Adam waves a hand, and they gaze at the SL55. In-sung picks a pebble and throws it over the car. "Han Dok-ku," he says, "assuming he's behind all this. Why go through such an elaborate setup to frame you for killing Baek Young-hee? Did he have any reason to fear you? Or, did he fear Baek Young-hee, and you were a convenient scapegoat?"

"I have no idea." Adam picks a pebble. "But who else could it be?"

In-sung doesn't reply, and Adam snaps. "You think *I* did it?"

"Whoa, Dae-hyun-*ah*, whatever gave you that crazy idea? No, I don't think you did it. What I think is that it helps to start from the beginning, when he first appeared in your life. Han Dok-ku fears me, or hates me, because... Start here."

"Because ... when I was a bit-part actor, I had the gall to date his daughter." Adam throws his pebble over the car.

"His one and only daughter. Keep going. You met her how? Where?"

"*High Rollers*, 2009. I had a speaking part. That meant hanging around the soundstage in case someone needed me in the next scene. One day I saw this girl—"

"How old were you? How old was she?"

"Mmm, I would have been twenty-two and Yu-mi, nineteen."

He first saw her through a maze of cables and lighting rigs. The girl smiled, and tiny dimples bloomed on her cheeks. She was visiting the set with the assistant director's sister.

Minor actors and crew members often went to a karaoke club nearby, and the girls tagged along. Yu-mi and her friend sang and clowned around. Adam banged on the tambourine, mesmerized by how she moved, how her hair swayed, fluid and shiny as satin.

Later, everyone squeezed into the assistant director's car, heading for the closest subway stop. Half in jest, Adam asked Yu-mi for her number. The next thing he knew, she was writing it on his wrist.

In-sung sends another pebble over the car. "You started dating."

"If you call waiting for her outside her school 'dating.'"

Once or twice a week, he ran the three miles from the soundstage to Yu-mi's high school. He should have been rehearsing his lines. Instead, he rehearsed the jokes he would tell her to make her laugh.

In-sung digs an elbow into Adam's side. "Didn't her parents send a car to collect her?"

Adam rolls his eyes. "She, quote-unquote, studied at her friend's house."

"Are you saying you went to a love motel?"

"A minor? Whose dad ran a gossip rag? I may have done stupid things, but not that stupid. I introduced her to the delights of cheap eateries."

The *ajumma*, the hard-working women who served the food, teased Adam whenever he came alone. His girlfriend was so pretty, was he not worried someone would steal her? Her favourite dish was a beef and mushroom soup for two that cost only ten thousand won. It came in a casserole piled high with vegetables—enoki, shitake, oyster and button mushrooms, squash, Napa cabbage and other greens—hiding thin slices of beef and glass noodles, topped with a rich broth. The server turned the burner on, and he and Yu-mi stirred the pot until the soup was ready, ten to fifteen minutes of cozy anticipation.

In-sung looks dubious. "Eating and holding hands?"

"I landed that other supporting role in 2010 and bought the Elantra. Metallic sky blue, remember? I drove her home." Adam paints the picture for In-sung. Yu-mi liked to play jokes. She found the hairbrush he kept in his glove compartment and ran it through his hair while he drove. He looked at himself in the rear-view mirror. "You call yourself a stylist, Han Yu-mi? If that's the best you can do, don't expect me to pay."

There was a secluded corner a block away from her parents' house, and they necked in the front seat.

In-sung juggles with two pebbles. "How long before her father caught on?"

Adam casts his mind back. "Six months, seven? And the last month she was away. Winter vacations."

Twenty-Six: May 1ˢᵗ, 2018 — Danyang, South Korea

Adam carries dirty dishes to the kitchen and finds Grandmother massaging her back. She stops as soon as she sees him, and when he asks if she is tired, she insists that she is fine.

"I drank too much coffee," he says. "Let me take care of those. It will reduce the buzz."

Grandmother never uses the dishwasher even though he has tried many times to convert her. He scrapes bits of food into the waste bin and loads the machine, his mind wandering back to Yu-mi all those years ago. Her family owned a house in Pyeongchang, and she spent her winter break skiing with other daughters and sons of *chaebols*, the family conglomerates that control the country's wealth. She texted Adam and told him how sick she was of hearing kids her age behave like nine-year-olds, bragging about how much their new snowboard cost and how much faster and higher it went. She begged him to come over, even if he could only manage a day.

Adam needed to report to the shooting site seven days a week. He had to be ready to jump into a scene at short notice and give a performance so remarkable that he would be offered a leading role in his next drama.

Walking out of the soundstage behind the lead actors, he passed lines of fans clamouring for their autograph. Before he met Yu-mi, he used to troll these lines and pick up the crumbs. No more. He had a real girlfriend who would soon turn twenty, and he had saved enough money for a night at a five-star hotel. He might come from a different class, but he would soon rise like the stars who flashed their smiles for the groupies and went on to party with the rich and famous.

On a frigid night at the end of February, in the line of screaming fans, Adam spotted a woman winking at him. Lacy tank top under an open jacket, miniskirt and high heels, she extended her hand for a shake and slipped him a note. In his car, strapping his seatbelt on, he smelled the woman's scent on his fingers. Visions of breasts stretching fabric, long, shapely legs, and plump, red lips played before his eyes. He read the name on the slip of paper: Candy.

Quick, before he changed his mind, he punched her number on his phone. She answered right away. Sexy, raspy voice. He suggested a love motel, but Candy had her own place. He found it in a back alley near Yeongdeungpo Market, a converted utility shed on top of a three-story building. The rooftop apartment had only two rooms, a kitchen where take-out containers overflowed from a waste basket, and a bedroom beyond. Adam glimpsed all this over her shoulder as she stood in the doorway, hair pulled into a messy ponytail, eyelashes thick with mascara. She beckoned him inside with a finger, and he slipped off his shoes, a rule she ignored, swinging her hips atop her high heels. He followed, undoing his shirt as he went, ripping the last button off, laughing when it hit the floor—one of those details that stuck in his mind for no apparent reason.

They fell on the bed and he pulled off her top—no bra, her skirt—no panties. She straddled him, bending over and tracing patterns on his chest with her nipples, wrapping her tongue around his, tasting, probing. She backed away, licking as she went until she was kneeling on the floor.

He closed his eyes and reached for her, "Come back." Through his eyelids, he saw a flash. Another. He rolled off the bed and gripped her wrists. She clutched her phone, and he fought to wrest it from her hand; he shook her arm as if shaking a branch to make a fruit fall. He shouted, "Let go," hoping an angry tone would do what strength alone could not.

She held his eyes for a split second, then lowered her gaze to his erection, smirking as if to say, *You're getting a rise out of this.*

He shook her arm all the harder until her grip slackened and the phone fell. He ducked to seize it, but her knee rose and met his chin. He bit his tongue. He heard the phone skitter away under a dresser as long as the bed. He would need light and time to find it.

How sharp could the picture be anyway? And what would it prove?

He grabbed his clothes and hurried out.

Adam jumps at a voice reaching out of the dark. Grandmother has come to put the dishes away.

"I've done this before," he says.

She gives him a tired smile. "Sleep well, then." She hugs him as if they will not see each other for a long time, a habit that formed in the early days of her residence at the *hanok* and would be hard to break now.

Twenty-Seven: May 8ᵗʰ, 2018 — Danyang, South Korea

Birdsong drifts through the morning calm as Adam dreams of a turquoise sea under an azure sky, puffy clouds hugging the horizon. Waves rock him to and fro. He feels safe, unafraid, while a familiar voice hums "Arirang."

Mother, he thinks. As soon as I rise, I will run to the beach and find her. I will fill my pail with sand and build a castle while the adults laugh and watch over me. He smiles as he opens the door to the courtyard. Grandmother is sweeping the stone path and humming. She pauses to rub an ache in her back. *"Aïgoo!"*

Adam sits cross-legged on the floor and rubs sleep from his eyes, his grown-up eyes with his grown-up hands. Dread returns.

He now starts his mornings with taekwondo, first the basic stances, hand strikes, and kicks he learned during his military service, then the complex moves he practiced for *Swingtime*'s action scenes. *Take that.* He visualizes another inmate raising a hand. *And that and that and that.* Fools who believe in his perfect gentleman image will see he can fight as dirty as anyone.

In-sung marvels at how the lettuce has tripled in size, blooms sprung from tufts of chives, and rosettes of cabbage filled the rows. Grandmother counts on it to yield enough kimchi to last through winter. He is in the middle of saying how much he looks forward to tasting it when his phone vibrates.

Adam gestures for him to answer; he will finish watering the other end of the garden. Fragments of conversation reach his ears. It sounds like In-sung is talking to his mother, *Eomma.* An English teacher once told Adam's class that the Korean word for Mom sounded like 'Oh, Ma!' to his ears. He thought students were constantly chiding their mothers for making them do something embarrassing, like wearing a scarf over their noses on cold days or holding their baby sister's hand while they walked home. 'Oh, Ma!'

Many American children called their mothers "Ma," the teacher said. Adam watched for "Ma" when he met Joanne's son. He only ever heard him call her "Mom."

For the umpteenth time, he wonders if she has tried to contact In-sung or if his final words drove her away forever. Would In-sung tell him if Joanne called? Adam is afraid to ask, afraid the answer is "no." Besides, In-sung has changed numbers twice since this all began. The odds of Joanne connecting with him are next to zero. If he borrowed In-sung's phone, or Grandmother's for that matter, and rang Joanne, would she agree to talk to him? Would she believe him?

But no pity. The last thing he wants is pity.

In-sung takes his time inspecting the new growth. "My mother's babysitting," he says. "The baby asked for a second helping of rice porridge. First time." He smiles. "But back to business." They sit on the *hanok*'s ledge with cool beers in their hands. "The Han Dok-ku story. What's next?"

Adam pulls the tab off his can and takes a sip. "Spring, eight years ago. Yu-mi's first day back at school. Afterwards, I took her to view the cherry blossoms near the National Assembly."

Adam sees the scene again, the trees making a long, white canopy, and the crowd walking underneath, food vendors, spiral-cut fries on a stick, and *soondae* that Yu-mi refused to try because the sausages were made with pig's blood. Clowns handing balloons with the names of department stores printed on them; B-boy crews performing their moves to music blaring from boom boxes; babies in strollers; couples holding hands.

"Yu-mi's mother texted to ask why she wasn't home yet. Usual routine. I drove to our special corner and we kissed goodbye." Her mouth tasted of cotton candy, he remembers. He slipped a hand under her blouse and cupped a breast through her bra.

"Next thing I knew, she wasn't in the car anymore. A man glared at me through the door. 'Out, you dirty bastard.'" Adam makes a passable imitation of Han Dok-ku's voice, and In-sung shoots him a smile.

"We stared at each other across the car's roof. You should have seen him. His chin barely cleared the top. He looked like a bulldog, sounded like one too. He called me a two-bit actor.

"He'd had me followed for quite a while, he said. If I didn't stay away from his daughter he'd slap a 'very unflattering photo' of me on the front page of his rag, as *Rapist Ahn Dae-hyun*."

In-sung holds a hand up to speak, but starts to cough. And cough. "I swallowed"—more coughing—"wrong."

Adam runs inside for a glass of water and, after a few sips, In-sung recovers. "Unflattering in what way?"

"Not sure. All I know is that he paid a woman to lure me into her apartment. She took a picture while … during … while I had my shirt off."

In-sung nods as if this confirms what he already knows. "How old was she? Did you ask?"

Alarm bells ring in Adam's brain. "What's going on? Are you saying…?"

In-sung clears his throat. "First of all, Attorney Choi is treating this as a smear campaign."

"Christ almighty."

"Unfortunately, it's par for the course in cases like yours."

"You should tell that to my parents."

"Already did. I sat in their living room and … well … now they know these attacks may feel horrible, but they're just as false as they are inevitable. I mean, the woman posted her story on KakaoTalk, for Heaven's sake: a grainy black-and-white of a man naked from the waist up. It may or may not be you. She claims you followed her to her rooftop apartment, busted the door, jumped on her and raped her. She was only seventeen."

"Oh my God. What a bunch of lies." Adam would also like In-sung to tell Joanne what he told his parents. "Do you think you could—"

"Could I what, Dae-hyun-*ah*?"

"Sorry. Too much to ask. Anyway, that woman, Candy … gave me her address. She opened the door for me. I swear she didn't look a day under twenty-two. *She* jumped on me. I'm not saying she raped me. I wanted her, and she wanted me. When she snapped her pictures though"—he shakes his head—"I felt … dirty. Violated."

"Angry, surely?"

"I'm still angry. I should have tried harder to delete the photos." He tells In-sung what made it so difficult.

"Looks like she never gave them to Han Deok-ku," In-sung says.

"He knew he could ask her anytime."

"The photo surfaced on social media, not his gossip rag. Why?"

"Maybe he didn't want to draw attention to himself?"

"Humph." In-sung scratches his head. "Now, where were we?"

"Han Deok-ku threatening me. His daughter watching from the sidelines. I said what all desperate men say under the circumstances. As soon as I earned enough money, I would ask his permission to marry her."

Adam omits details as they cannot possibly matter. He kneeled in front of the media mogul, confessed his love for Yu-mi, and vowed that he would work hard to become worthy of marrying her, peppering his plea with words parents like to hear, "humbly" and "sincerely."

"Han Dok-ku sneered. 'My daughter will never marry an actor. Get back in that wreck of a car, boy, and drive away while you can.' From that point onward, he had me followed," Adam concludes.

With a man tailing him wherever he went, Adam worried he would be fired by the Agency. In-sung—Manager Kim at the time— invited the actor to join him for dinner in a soju tent, one among thousands of *pojangmacha* that materialize as night falls. They sat on plastic stools, and In-sung ordered a heaping plate of chicken skewers, along with four bottles of soju.

This is it, Adam thought, the end of my sorry career as an actor.

But Manager Kim only plied him with more soju, until Adam's speech slurred and his reserve evaporated. "This girl," he said, "her parents have locked her in her room. I have to help her, Manager Kim. I've tried calling, texting, sending letters through the post, and waiting for her outside her school. Nothing works."

Manager Kim refilled Adam's shot glass and waited until he had swallowed it all. "First love?" he asked. "Let me guess. The girl is pretty. She's smart and she's…"

"Top of her class. She wants to be a doctor."

"Rich family?"

Adam nodded but withheld saying that her father owned The Orbiter Media Group.

Manager Kim convinced him to stop trying to contact her; it would only make matters worse. He spent time with the actor, going for dinner, to the gym, and watching films at a theatre near the Agency. He sent him to auditions, and when Adam complained that the roles were wrong, Manager Kim said, "Trust your Older Brother."

Adam had never known anyone he could call *Hyeong*, Older Brother, before, someone who could take a burden off his shoulders and make it his.

In-sung ranked in the top one percent country-wide when he passed the bar exam. He could have joined the most prestigious law firm in Seoul and put his skills to defending one well-heeled client after another. He chose to work as a public defender instead, or so the story went at the Star Shop Agency when Adam joined.

After practicing for five years, In-sung had to defend a man accused of killing a woman by pushing her off a bridge. While the prosecution built its case, In-sung took every opportunity to show that the actions of the accused could be interpreted as attempting to save the woman he loved from jumping to her death. On the witness stand, the defendant's answers to In-sung's questions supported that scenario. Under the public prosecutor's cross-examination, however, the poor man became angrier and angrier. Without realizing it, he contradicted his earlier testimony.

The judge took the inconsistencies as proof that the accused was lying. He returned a guilty verdict. In-sung wanted to appeal, but the man lost hope. He hung himself in his cell, and In-sung resigned from the public defender's office, eventually joining the talent agency.

On the ledge at the *hanok*, In-sung offers Adam another beer. "I seem to recall you were at an audition when Yu-mi finally called."

"She sounded like her dad had just told her about the other woman. How could I have done that to her? She had only been away for a few weeks. Then silence. She'd hung up on me. I typed like mad, trying to explain. A text from her popped up first. She was flying to Australia, but before that—"

"She was deleting your contact?"

Adam clinks his beer can against In-sung's.

Twenty-Eight: April 1st to May 26th, 2018 — Niagara-on-the-Lake, Canada

With Memorial Day fast approaching, my sister called to finalize the details of our visit. Before we hung up, she asked how Adam was doing. I have decided not to tell her anything about his troubles. "We broke up," I said. "Too complicated." All true.

"I'm so sorry, baby," Colleen replied.

I doubted it. Not long ago, she said, "He'll use you then leave you, my naïve little sister."

My friend Emma from the Center is the only one who knows what transpired. On Easter weekend, in the middle of a chickenpox wave sweeping through Sean's school, Adam's fan sites erupted with screen captures of a post on Korea's KaKaoTalk. A kindergarten teacher claimed Adam had raped her in 2010. She'd managed to take a grainy cell-phone picture of her assailant. Thinking about this image wounds me every time. He looked so violent, so terrifying.

Emma now combs Korea's English news sites and fan sites while I force myself to stay away.

The drive to Canada takes four hours, and I pack sing-along CDs, sliced fruit, colouring books, and DVDs, Sean's current favourite being *The Knights of the Round Table.* By mid-afternoon, we reach the outskirts of Niagara Falls and stop at a café.

"I saw two white horses," Sean says while we wait for our beverages.

"I thought only King Arthur had a white horse."

"No, outside."

"Ah, the horse farm we passed."

"Do they have white horses in Korea?"

Where did *that* come from? "I'm sure they do, sweetie."

We arrive in Niagara-on-the-Lake with the late afternoon sun still high in the sky. Colleen and Jeremy live in a Victorian-era farmhouse made of warm red bricks adorned with white gingerbread along the roofline and second-story gables. A sketch of the house forms the logo for their wines.

Colleen wears a purple dress that belongs more at an art gallery opening than at a family dinner. Dad looks well, a relief after last fall's pneumonia scare. Sean tugs at his sleeve, and my father takes him to the back of the house.

Colleen has invited a neighbour, Ted Burns, to join us. He shakes my hand with a firm grip and a warm smile.

Jeremy announces that dinner is ready and Colleen shepherds us to the dining room where scents of herbs, caramelized onions and roasted meat herald a feast. Bold floral prints complement the honey tones of the wood floor, table and chairs. I help Sean put his napkin on his knees, and catch Colleen directing Ted to the seat on my right.

Jeremy serves everyone a bowl of mushroom soup, not the pureed kind that Sean would eat without realizing what the vegetables were, but a creamy version with slices of various fungi he names, though they go in one ear and out the other.

"You can leave it there, buddy," I whisper in Sean's ear. "Have a piece of bread."

My father knows how difficult it is to keep a child sitting still through a family dinner. He pulls something from his pocket—a figurine of a knight mounted on a horse—and slides it over to Sean, who abandons his bread in favour of his fantasy world.

"What do we say, Sean?" Colleen asks. He doesn't even hear her.

Up to me to intervene. "Honey, your grandfather gave you a gift. Isn't there something you want to tell him?"

Sean looks up at five keen faces. "Umm."

My father beams him encouragement.

"I'll call him Arthur," Sean declares. "Even if his horse is black."

Colleen leans toward him. "How about, 'Thank you, Grandpa?'"

"Oh, I forgot," and he repeats her words.

Jeremy replaces the soup bowls with salad plates and Colleen casts her eyes across the table. "Ted, tell us about Mount Everest."

"I only went to base camp." He describes spectacular icefalls, monasteries, and bazaars. He keeps his story short and lifts his glass to

Colleen and Jeremy, complimenting them for pairing their Riesling with this dish.

"Such a gentleman," my sister says. "Ted's wines have won international awards."

"We've had a few good years."

"So modest." Colleen takes a sip. "Ted, you must tell Joanne about your 2014 Icewine."

Whenever he stops talking, she launches him in a fresh direction while she helps Jeremy serve the roast lamb.

My father has lived here for the past ten years. He hasn't touched a drop of alcohol in nearly three decades. Colleen took a picture before my parents left for the New Year's Eve party that would be their last together. Dad looks dapper in his rented tuxedo, and Mom smiles confidently in a moss-green taffeta gown. Champagne was drunk. Dad has never been able to talk about the accident on the way home, but his abstinence speaks volumes.

People say that the pain of loss dulls with time; that our lives fill again with the business of living; that even if we don't forget, we try not to show it. My father keeps a quiet conversation going with Sean as if nothing devastating ever happened in his life. For my part, I remember him singing happy songs while he pushed me to and fro on a swing, yet I doubt that meant he had forgotten my mother. At night, alone with his thoughts in his empty bed, I am sure she visits him.

Profiteroles, puff pastries filled with ice cream and drizzled with chocolate sauce, have been served and picked at, if not actually eaten.

"Come and help Grandpa with a puzzle," my father tells Sean.

Colleen sits back, one leg crossed over the other, and dabs the corners of her mouth with her napkin. "Joanne, Ted, you'll get a laugh out of this one." She tells a bawdy joke—poorly—and Ted chuckles out of politeness. I sense he is mildly embarrassed by her innuendos.

"If you'll excuse me," I say, "I'll check on Sean. And Dad."

They are in the solarium, standing around a square table, fitting puzzle pieces together. "Mom, look, I did this whole corner."

Dad stoops a tad more than he used to, not only because he is bending over a table. "Have a seat, Dad. You'll tire yourself out."

He sinks into a chair and I lay a hand on his shoulder. He pats it with his. "And you, Joanie, how are you managing?"

"Splendidly, Dad. Don't worry." Tears pool in my eyes, and the puzzle piece I hold melts out of focus. I fight for composure, staring at the picture on the box cover, a parking lot filled with cars of all colours, models and sizes. "Here, Sean." I hand him my piece and point at random on the box, "I think it goes there."

I take refuge in the bathroom.

Colleen talks about the busloads of Chinese tourists visiting the area. "Great for business," she says, "no question about it, but do they ever inflate the prices we locals have to pay."

Jeremy gestures to a chair. "Joanne, I'm glad chickenpox didn't leave scars on Sean's face."

Colleen carries on. "Worse than the Japanese years ago."

She sips her wine, and Ted pushes his chair back. "I'm sorry, but I have an early start tomorrow."

He's a nice man, though I feel no attraction whatsoever.

"The weather's amazing," says Colleen. "Why don't we all walk Ted home? You must see his place, Joanne. An Art Deco dream."

I suspect Ted is no keener on showing me his house than I am to see it. "It's past Sean's bedtime." A ready excuse, although the odds are he is too keyed up to sleep.

I read him three bedtime stories and answer a dozen questions about tomorrow's egg hunt—postponed from Easter—before I can leave the room and take a shower.

"Damn you, Colleen," I mutter the moment the water runs. "Ambushing me with Mr. Next-Door Neighbour." I lather my hair and massage my scalp with more vigour than necessary. "Ambushing us both."

Last Christmas, after returning from Seoul, I finally told Colleen that Adam was a film star.

"Is that so? Well, well. I wouldn't be surprised if he sees you as his ticket to a green card."

Twenty-Nine: May 26th to 30th, 2018 — Danyang, South Korea

For their shopping trips, Adam drives a leased sedan while Grandmother sits in the passenger seat, planning meals for the next few weeks.

"Shall we have *soondae* tonight?" She names the shop that makes the best sausages in the district. "Must remember to buy rice. Oh, and we need poles for the beans to climb." Trivial talk. Never, "Your father called this morning," although Adam heard her talk to him before breakfast. Never, "He believes you're innocent."

Mountains ripple across the horizon in shades of indigo, violet and mauve, fusing clouds and sky. Rather than losing himself in the beauty, he looks forward to finishing the shopping and returning home.

He drops Grandmother outside the butcher shop and drives on to fill the tank. The attendant is the same as last time. "Look who's here," he cackles. "What d'you do with all that gas?"

Adam tolerates his tired joke because the attendant at the other station refuses to serve him. "We don't take murderers' money," he said the first time Adam tried.

At the supermarket, he pushes the cart. He keeps his head down, reading the backs of packages: flour, yeast, milk. Such a contrast with Wegman's in Ithaca. The smell of fresh bread used to trick him into buying more than he could eat in one day, defeating the purpose of buying fresh bread. He could keep his head level without worrying about being mobbed by people who begged him for a selfie or wanted him dead.

Grandmother asks how much they paid for ten kilos of rice at another store. "Wasn't it 21,000 won? The cheapest here is 25,000. Let's stop by the other store."

"It was on special, *Halmeoni*."

"It's always cheaper there."

"It's only a few thousand won."

They debate in low voices.

"You've no idea what it's like to watch every won. Young people." She clicks her tongue.

"It's not important." He lifts a bag at random and dumps it in the cart.

At the checkout Grandmother gives him the silent treatment. *Fine.* Outside, he loads their purchases in the trunk, making as much noise as he can until he realizes he is behaving like a spoiled child. She is only trying to help.

Grandmother sits and fans herself with a flyer. Adam lowers his head by her window. "I'll run over to the hardware store." He points across the street. "How many bean poles?"

On the road home, they pass over a stream all but drained of water. "So dry," Grandmother comments.

"The rains are late." If he is pronounced guilty, these bland exchanges will be all he has to look forward to, talking to his family through a perforated window.

He should not be thinking about prison. He inhales—Joanne— exhales; inhales deeper—Joanne. She was upset with him on the drive to the *hanok* six months ago. Living in a private oasis might have seemed ideal for him; for her, it might have felt more like a prison.

Our Fifth Season is carved into the crossbeam over the entrance, a place where people can live outside the natural cycle of the seasons. He opens the gate with his remote. He has become his own warden. The sound of gravel popping under his tires feels oddly reassuring after the perils in the outside world.

Adam works by the lamp glow spilling from his room, brushing sealer on the beanpoles bought earlier in the week. In-sung has left, and Adam ponders a remark his friend made. "You haven't been lucky with women."

Or rather, Adam thinks, women have not been lucky with me: Baek Young-hee, who accepted the leading role in his directorial debut and died on the night of the wrap party; Yu-mi, sent away to Australia by her father because of him; Joanne, for the horrible way he pushed her out of his life; and Lee JinAh—JinA by her stage name—who committed suicide within months of knowing him.

He met JinA at a gala reception for Screenwriter Kang Min-chae's sixtieth birthday. The guest of honour, trained in America and a pioneer among Korean women in her field, looked like a fuchsia bloom in the billowing skirt of her *hanbok*. Everyone who had worked with her was there, including A-list actress JinA, dressed in an electric blue gown with a plunging neckline, moulding her every curve and setting off her copper hair. Kang Min-chae put a hand on JinA's arm. "This is Ahn Dae-hyun-*ssi*. Something tells me he will go far."

Adam was twenty-four and had yet to land a leading role. He blushed. JinA, already in her thirties, looked amused. "I wouldn't mind a scotch."

Later in the evening, Adam mustered enough courage to approach her again and invite her for a nightcap. She surprised him by accepting.

Going to a bar was out of the question, dressed in full gala regalia. Paparazzi and social media followers would not fail to recognize her. Luckily, he had moved out of his parents' house. "Your place or mine?" He drew another amused smile from JinA.

She complimented him on his apartment, the neighbourhood, the size of the rooms. "I hope this place isn't run by the mob," she said. Over glasses of beer in his living room, she asked about security in the lobby and other practical matters, to which he could only give partial answers.

Within a month she had moved into a suite on the top floor, with a sweeping view of the Han River. View or no view, they could see each other without KakaoTalk exploding with gossip.

Adam often mentioned his family, but JinA hardly ever did. Her parents lived in the country and did not fit in with her Glamour Queen image. Her closet overflowed with designer clothes she called "gifts."

It had been a year since Yu-mi left, a year of coming to terms with reality. They would always belong to separate classes, no matter how famous he became. JinA, on the other hand, knew how hard it was to climb the show business ladder; how fickle fame could be. "Enjoy being an unknown while you can," she said. "Every day, I have to kick my feet like crazy only to keep my shoulders above water. Not easy, huh? Try making it look effortless."

Where Yu-mi was prone to playing practical jokes, JinA was practical, period. During the summer of 2011, there was an eclipse of the moon. They stood on her balcony, fingers entwined, and watched the shadow of the earth turn the moon reddish brown. "It's hot," JinA said before the orb had made it halfway. "Let's go inside. We can catch it online tomorrow. The whole show in one minute."

Outside the *hanok*, Adam cleans his brush. Without JinA's suicide, he might never have enrolled in university, never finished his studies in America, and never met Joanne. Does she still think of me, he wonders. Better if she doesn't, although he still hopes the impossible hopes he cannot voice for fear of jinxing them.

Thirty: May 27ᵗʰ, 2018 — Niagara-on-the-Lake, Canada

After breakfast the following morning, we all walk to the winery for our much-delayed Easter egg hunt. Sean skips ahead and runs back to pull on his grandfather's hand. Colleen is giving me the cold shoulder.

As soon as Jeremy unlocks the glass doors of the barn-like building, Sean scoots under the tasting table, remembering a few years ago when he found his first foil-wrapped egg hidden behind one of the barrels that serve as legs. No luck today. My father, our official Easter Bunny, seldom reuses his hiding places.

Jeremy investigates behind the sales counter, save for the shelves where bottles of wine lie on their sides. Out of bounds by the family's unwritten rules. Too easy to break. He opens drawers, and his eyebrows lift. Maybe he spotted a plastic egg with someone's name marked on it, or possibly the chocolate treat destined for Sean.

I follow Colleen through the arch beyond the shop and into the hallway leading to the wine-making rooms. She enters the cellar on the left while I explore the fermentation room on the right, looking around and under each of the steel tanks lining the walls. I find a handful of mini eggs and pocket two. I also spot a purple plastic egg marked for my sister.

In the hallway, we come face-to-face. "We need to talk," Colleen says. She opens the office door and locks it behind us. Two identical desks face each other and hold two identical computers. Piles of paper on each. On the wall, a corkboard overflowing with postcards and, beside it, framed in silver, the picture Colleen took on the eve of New Year 1990, when my mother's concern over wrinkling her taffeta dress took precedence over wearing her seatbelt.

"Do you realize how rude you were?" Colleen leans back against the door. "You left the table just as we were starting to have a real conversation. You were gone for half an hour, Joanne. Half an hour."

"I wanted to see how Dad was doing."

"Dad's fine. Although he wasn't that well when you went gallivanting to Korea last December." She makes it sound so crude.

"Listen," I say, "what possessed you to invite Ted? Playing matchmaker."

"Ted's the nicest man ever. He lives all by himself on that property. Wouldn't you like to come back, live close to Dad?"

"Whoa, that's a major leap; as if living close to my family means I'd be willing to settle for any lonely guy."

"You prefer 'settling' for a two-timing Korean star who kills women and rapes girls?"

What the –

"You thought I didn't know? Wake up, Joanne. Everything's online. The minute you told me you were dating Mr. Movie Star, I checked him out. He's easy on the eyes, I'll grant you that. I had my suspicions. Once I heard you'd broken up, it wasn't hard to discover why."

I should have known she'd ferret it out. "He had nothing to do with that woman dying. He is—" I want to say, "kind and sweet and wonderful." It is how I felt once upon a time, except that the rape, if true, sickens me.

"Putting your head in the sand won't make things disappear, Joanne. Be thankful it didn't go any further. Forget him. Date a normal guy."

"Are you saying he's not normal because he's Korean or because he's an actor?"

She holds my eyes: *both.*

"Charlie was 'normal' and look what happened."

"No surprise to me that a postdoc would hit on a grad student. All that time together in a lab."

Major things, minor things, there's nothing Colleen likes better than showing people she knows best. "Don't fold that sweater, Joanne," she said while I was packing on a past visit. "Roll it. Fewer wrinkles."

As much as I'd like to threaten never to return, she holds the key to seeing Dad, to Sean spending time with his grandfather.

His sweet voice pipes up from the hallway. "Mom, Mom, I found your egg."

"I'll be right there, buddy."

"We'd better go." Colleen points to a low shelf behind me where the side of a chocolate bunny box mixes with the spines of manuals on *terroir* and varietals.

"In a minute." I keep my voice low. "Listen, Colleen, stop meddling. Stop thinking you have to mother me, tell me what kind of man I should date, how to raise my son, how to fold my clothes."

"I'm only trying to help."

"Wrinkles happen, Colleen. You and I both know what a few extra wrinkles can do." The snapshot of my parents winks in the sun streaming through the window. "They can save your life. Even if I have wrinkles, even if I make mistakes, they'll be my mistakes." I brush past her and hurry out.

Thirty-One: June 12ᵗʰ, 2018 — Danyang, South Korea

"Let's trek uphill," In-sung says on his next visit. He has secured the necessary permission.

They follow the *hanok*'s perimeter wall under the beating sun and enter the aspen grove where green light shivers and sighs. Adam's breathing eases. I should come here on my own, he thinks.

In-sung lags and calls for a halt. He pants, hands on knees, "You're in better shape than me."

Adam leans against a silver trunk and closes his eyes. He empties his mind of the ceaseless chatter: fears, hopes, despair.

In-sung clears his throat. He holds a sheet of paper in one hand. "Could you cast your mind back to 2011? You spent a week in Busan for a location shoot."

"What does this have to do with the mess I'm in?" He has enough worries as it is.

"A misunderstanding, I'm sure," says In-sung. "No need to panic. We simply need to know where we stand. Start with how you went there—plane, train, or car?"

"The SL55," says Adam. He had landed another supporting role with twice as many scenes as the one before; he appeared in commercials for a line of casual clothing featured in the drama. The windfall was enough to buy the silver Mercedes SL55 AMG roadster 2008, second-hand, though in great condition. "It must have been November," he says. "Lots of ripe persimmons on the trees along the way. Did I ever tell you I made it there in three hours?"

In-sung whistles, impressed.

Adam can still hear the engine growling and roaring, the tires rasping on the road and squealing in the switchbacks up and down the mountains.

"And JinA," In-sung says, "I assume she was busy in Seoul?"

"Acting-wise?" Adam shakes his head. "Nothing. A complete drought. She claimed it was the natural ebb and flow of fame. I think she felt her career was over. She phoned a lot for no apparent reason: she was boutique hopping; she was meeting a friend for dinner."

"It's a while back," In-sung says, "but I seem to recall she drove over one day."

"Yeah, well, more night than day, really. She rang me at three in the morning. She was downstairs in the lobby. I let her in and she disappeared inside the washroom. She took a shower that went on forever. I had time to drink a beer and could have finished two more. She finally emerged—hotel bathrobe, hair dripping wet. 'I shouldn't be here,' she said. She rushed out and slammed the door."

"Strange."

"She used the elevator. I took the stairs."

In-sung makes a T with his hands, time-out. "Alright. Tough question—were you angry?"

"Whoa, why do you ask?" Dread seizes Adam as he gestures for them to resume walking "More of those nasty rumours?"

"Relax, Dae-hyun-*ah*. I'm on your side. Think motivation. What did you hope to accomplish by going after her?"

"She'd already driven four hours from Seoul. I worried she'd fall asleep at the wheel if she drove back right away. Or worse, that she'd… "

"… drive in the wrong lane?"

The words feel like a kick in the belly, and Adam struggles to move past. "She wasn't a runner, that much I can say. I reached her just as she tried to open her car door. You should have seen her eyes, *Hyeong*. Wild with fear."

In-sung blinks in sympathy. "And you argued."

They must have yelled at each other, breaths puffing in the night air. He remembers urgency but not anger. Both shivered, JinA with her feet bare, and he without a shirt. "She gripped the door handle real tight. I might have fought with her; I don't remember. All I know is I convinced her to come inside and sleep for a bit."

In-sung nods. "Tallies." The two men forge a path through the meadow of tall grasses. "Yes, another smear attack. A crew member on your drama sold his story to *The Orbiter*. Shouting in the parking lot kept him from sleeping. He recognized you. You were fighting with a woman who had red hair, JinA. He claims you knocked her to the ground and carried her inside the hotel against her will."

"Damn it, *Hyeong*. She crumpled to the ground on her own. She was crying. I carried her inside and tucked her into bed; end of story." Except it is not strictly the end; the rest is private. Lying beside her, he'd felt her shoulders heaving. 'What's wrong?' He touched her cheek, but she did not reply. Poor JinA. In time, her sobbing eased, and Adam was on the verge of sleep when she rolled over him and lowered his shorts.

In-sung and Adam have reached the top of the hill. Danyang appears below, ringed by a deep blue river, as if inside a bowl of mountains.

Adam is in no mood to admire the view. First a murderer, then a rapist, and now a woman-beater. He shakes his head, unable to contemplate the consequences. "What do I...?"

"You do nothing. You don't worry. You let us deal with it."

"You'll issue a denial. Give my side of the story."

"It would only give these allegations more oxygen."

"But people will think... They'll be prejudiced against me: 'a pattern of behaviour.'" His reputation had been in shambles. Now it was completely ruined.

In-sung taps him on the shoulder, there, there. "The truth will triumph, Dae-hyun-*ah*."

Easy for you to say.

Thirty-Two: June 12ᵗʰ, 2018 — Danyang, South Korea

After their walk, Adam and In-sung stand in the kitchen doorway while Grandmother ladles pork bone soup into three stone bowls, each set on a gas element. Blue flames lick the sides, and the spicy broth bubbles. Grandmother adds bean sprouts and perilla leaves to top the meaty bones and potatoes.

In-sung carries the heavy tray to the Great Room, places the bowls on the table and, as they wait for the soup to cool, shows Grandmother a video of his daughter calling him *appa*, the tiny voice precious and perfect. Adam is happy for his friend; he truly is. Yet envy rises like a bear waking from slumber. He should slap him on the back, *Well done, Hyeong*, but all he can manage is a choked-up "sorry" as he hurries out.

He walks around the *hanok* and beats his arms against his sides. *Jerk, bastard, asshole.*

It takes two circuits for his head to begin clearing. He passes the kitchen's open door. The appliances he chose to make country life more comfortable for Joanne—the Italian espresso machine, the programmable rice cooker and the French skillets—have been replaced by cast iron woks and stock pots.

Grandmother's room is next to the kitchen. Through the paper door, he glimpses the glow of the nightlight she leaves on day and night, worried she will stumble in the dark and break a limb. Condemned to fears in the night. Condemned to endure Adam's doom and gloom.

The next room, originally two, now combined into one, is a washroom, including—folly of follies—a sunken Jacuzzi Adam has never cleaned. Over the months, it has accumulated a layer of grime that would take considerable effort to clean. Grandmother tried. He was chopping wood and saw her shadow filling a bucket from the shower tap and adding a squirt of cleanser. He rushed in. "Don't!" And appalled by his rude tone, "I mean, you'll hurt yourself, *Halmeoni.*" Bending over to reach the bottom struck him as taxing even for a younger person. "I'll take care of it. Today. Later today." He never did, sentencing them to stare at the caked-in dirt every time nature calls.

The evening air can still be cool, especially along the wing that faces the hill. This side was supposed to house the master bedroom. He has not been inside since he inspected the renovations and brought in the bedding purchased in anticipation of Joanne's visit in the summer. The quilt and mattress pads are probably still wrapped in plastic. The paper on the doors has lotus watermarks, invisible without light on either side.

The corner room was destined for Sean. It had spacious cupboards to store his toys and spare bedding for a friend, the boy from across the street in Ithaca, or Adam's nephew, Jae-ro. Now the room holds the treadmill he uses when neither wood chopping nor garden chores fill his days.

The side facing the garden was meant for guests or any other use Joanne might dream of—for those children they will never have, a girl, perhaps, who would snuggle in his arms and call him *appa*.

Sandwiched between two empty rooms, is his, like a cabin on an ancient ship where the captain spends a few hours in restless sleep, worrying about what the next day, the next hour, the next minute will bring.

Adam has come full circle again. Grandmother is saying something that ends with a plea *jehbal*. They must be discussing the pre-trial hearing.

"There is no need for *Halmeonim* to worry." In-sung talks about "circumstantial evidence," "procedural errors," and uses other impressive-sounding terms. "We have a really strong case. The legal team has been working late into the night every day for weeks." People of her generation have an unshakable belief in the power of hard work.

In-sung keeps mum about the fifty-fifty chances their lead attorney gives them of convincing the judge to drop the charge. He remains doggedly hopeful, yet Adam cannot share his optimism. He takes a step toward the light when Grandmother's voice stops him. "He hardly eats," she tells In-sung.

"He has put back weight. He loves *Halmeonim*'s cooking."

"He uses a rope to keep his pants from falling."

"He's not in his right mind. You shouldn't worry, *Halmeonim*. It must be the first thing he found."

After the episode in Busan, JinA was offered the lead role in an arthouse film shot on Wando Island. She played a woman frightened into submission by an abusive husband. The film would likely be distributed worldwide.

Between shooting his drama and making the requisite appearances on talk shows and promotional events, Adam was hardly ever home except to sleep. On her island, JinA rose before dawn and fell into bed exhausted every night. This must be normal for acting couples, he thought. They teased each other on the phone, saying how boring they'd become. "It's so nice to laugh," JinA said.

"Are you not laughing where you are?" he joked before remembering she was playing the role of a battered woman, and the importance of staying in character, even when not on set. "Sorry, I wasn't thinking."

Time moved on: Christmas, New Year. Adam came home from a shoot after midnight and found an origami heart, JinA's trademark, on his coffee table. She must have let herself in, waited, and returned to her apartment. He showered before unfolding the note. The words remain seared in his brain:

My dear Dae-hyun, please don't cry. None of this is your fault.
I had an ultrasound and I am ten weeks pregnant.
I can't bring myself to have an abortion, and I can't face all the gossip that is bound to come.
I truly loved you.
JinA

What did she mean by "None of this is your fault?" That she was pregnant? That if he married her, a woman seven years older, there would be too much gossip? He called her cell phone and landline with no success. He ran the five flights to her floor and tried her entry code—punched it in, over and over. It didn't work. He hammered on her door until a man peered from another apartment and threatened to call the police. Adam slumped to the floor beside her door and prayed to God to let him hear a sound on the other side. He did not.

There was no avoiding work the next morning. He kept bungling his lines, dragging everyone into re-takes. By mid-afternoon, the director had had enough. "Don't you ever come on set when you're not fit to work."

Adam reached the side street where he'd left the SL55 and found Manager Kim parked behind it. The older man rolled down his window and asked the actor to sit beside him.

JinA had been found by her housekeeper hanging from the ceiling fan in her room.

Recalling that horrific death while Grandmother and In-sung fret over him gives Adam the same choking feeling he felt at the time. If there is a death he must be punished for, it should be JinA's. He should have seen her distress and made time to help her.

On the heels of these thoughts: Would he have been any better with Joanne? Does he—*did* he—have what it takes to make a relationship work? For the long run?

Grandmother's voice filters to him. "But a rope—"

After he was charged with murder and disgraced his whole family, the lure of suicide took hold in his mind. Ropes, neckties and kitchen knives, which were readily available. Poisons, drugs and pills, which were not. For three days, he ate nothing and drank hardly any liquids. He had one or two spoonfuls of soup, but only to put Grandmother off the scent. He rose from the table, and black spots danced before his eyes. His wood-chopping sessions dwindled to a few logs a day. He sat on the floor in his room, mentally composing his farewell note. He envied JinA for her determination.

His death-by-dehydration bid ended only because In-sung came with his questions and his beers. The cool liquid had never tasted so good, so life-giving.

In-sung tells Grandmother that ropes were in fashion a few years ago. "For all of three weeks." He laughs, and Adam uses that moment to rejoin them.

Thirty-Three: June 13ᵗʰ, 2018 — Danyang, South Korea

Adam is hammering beanpoles into the ground on a day with a postcard sky. The trick with the poles is to wet the soil, climb on a stool and hit them square on the head, otherwise, they go in crooked and break.

JinA's suicide still torments him. Had he paid closer attention, he might have prevented it. He could have married her; they could have gone to America for a year or two. After her funeral, he stopped going to the auditions In-sung registered him for; he did not shave, did not bother with haircuts, did not leave his apartment.

Two months turned into six, and his contract with the Star Shop Agency lapsed. In-sung tried to lure him away for dinner, but Adam declined. He had other plans: he drank shot glass after shot glass of soju and played *StarCraft* online. Every night he passed out on his couch and dragged himself to bed a few hours later, only to dream of being pursued, tumbling off cliffs or facing off with monsters. He woke past noon and sat in his armchair, listless, waiting for his vision to clear before ordering a bowl of hangover soup.

One night, he dreamt that his soul, wispy and thin, lifted from his body and passed through the window. He heard In-sung calling him, but his soul kept going, like a helium balloon escaping a child's grip. It drifted over the Han River, and, halfway across the river, his legs disappeared into mist that thickened into fog threatening to engulf him. If this was death, it wasn't too bad. He felt no pain, no regrets.

A boat glided by with a copper-haired figure on the prow.

"I'm ready to follow you," Adam said.

"You're still upset with me," JinA replied.

"Not anymore. I haven't felt this great in years. This is where I belong. You were right to come here."

"This is where *I* belong. You still have a purpose to fill."

He sighed. He wanted to lay in the water and let it carry him where it chose. He still heard In-sung's voice calling him. An entreaty. A plea.

JinA said, "Listen to In-sung and you'll find your way."

Who was she to tell him about finding his way?

"Fulfill your duty as the eldest son."

"How?"

"Your ancestors will be proud of you."

Maddeningly oblique. And what about my descendants, he wondered.

He had blamed the unborn child for JinA's death—if only she'd had a miscarriage. With time, however, he came to mourn the baby as well. "Was it a boy or a girl?"

JinA's boat drifted away. Fog was on the verge of reclaiming her when he heard: "There will be another boy."

A gust of wind lifted Adam's spirit and blew it home, through the open window and into his body. In-sung was slapping him on the back. Hard.

Adam's pillow felt wet and sticky; his mouth tasted foul. He would have choked on his own vomit had his friend not dropped by.

In-sung changed Adam's sheets while he took a shower. His friend sat in an armchair by his bed until he fell asleep.

At the *hanok*, under the azure sky, Adam stops hammering to feel the sun on his back and listen to bumblebees buzzing. The beanpoles are in, with only two lying on the ground, broken. He kneels on the brick path and guides the tendrils around the poles so the plants can soar and bear fruit. Full of life yet so easily trampled. Life hanging by a thread.

Hawks circle the hill behind the *hanok*, wing feathers splayed as they ride the thermal drafts. One of them plunges, intent on something near the house. Grandmother is on the ledge, shaking a rug.

Adam runs, waving a near-empty watering can at the bird. "*Yah!*"

The bird changes course and Adam throws water upward. The bird is too high. Adam holds the can over his head like a shield. He can't see anything. If the hawk hits his container, it could knock him to the ground. He braces for a fall that doesn't come. A dark shape swoops over his head, talons outstretched and pushes air on him as it pumps its wings.

Grandmother hobbles down the steps with the rug clutched to her body. "Did you see the rat?" She points to the space under the *hanok* where a rat scurried. "I'm going to make tea. Come in."

Adam's eyes need a moment to adjust to the semi-darkness in the Great Room. He sits on a cushion at the square table and rolls his shoulders to ease the tension in his muscles. Grandmother returns with the teapot, and he asks about her morning. There is not much else to fill the silence. She tries to avoid anything that will rub him the wrong way. Even a simple, "Did you sleep well?" can trigger an "I don't sleep at all," and a look that says, "Never ask me that again." Adam knows he owes her countless apologies. Whenever he says, "I'm really sorry," it never seems enough to express his shame for having exploded at her.

There was a time when she told Adam stories she would not share with anyone else: how she raised a child—his father—as a widow, trying to fulfill her in-laws' expectations, to find a way to laugh through the hard times, be comforted by everyday events. Now, silence and words unsaid bind them together.

Adam finishes his tea and returns to the pump, the endless trips with the watering can and his ruminations about the night six years ago when he nearly died choking on his own vomit.

He woke to the sound of In-sung cleaning the dishes that he had been too lazy to wash. His friend sat him on a kitchen chair and poured two cups of coffee. It tasted like a miracle: rich, chocolatey and smooth. In-sung must have gone out to buy fresh beans. He let Adam finish the demi-tasse, made him another and, with shining eyes, told Adam the news: he had found a role for him, a leading role, at long last.

Poor In-sung. Adam had made a decision. He was done with acting. He told his manager the first excuse that came into his head: he wanted to study film directing at the Korea National University of Arts.

In-sung's face fell, but he recovered quickly. "You'll need reference letters from people who are pretty pissed at you right now."

They made a deal: if In-sung could obtain the letters for him, Adam would take on the role as his farewell to acting.

A month later, with his application to K-ARTS submitted online, the cast of *Reunification*, the television series that would change his life, met for a table reading. Adam had shed the pounds gained while doing nothing in his apartment. He had used the advance to reclaim his SL55 from repossession. He practiced his lines in front of the mirror until they came naturally, and his expression matched what he wanted to convey. He made a favourable impression—the photos in the papers and the captions attested to it—but the press was there for the real star, Baek Young-hee.

Adam was a bundle of nerves through filming the early scenes, whereas Baek Young-hee was in her element. "You must believe," she said when he commented on how easy she made it look. Her advice seemed self-evident, yet watching her embrace the fears of a refugee from North Korea and inhabit her screen persona, the actor began to enter his.

The script was penned by the celebrated Kang Min-chae. Adam learned later that she had recommended him for the role. The combination of her script and Baek Young-hee's star power gave *Reunification* an early lead in the ratings. Over thirty percent of Korean households tuned in for the first episode, growing to forty, then fifty percent over the ten-week run.

Throughout the punishing schedule that yielded over a hundred and twenty minutes of prime-time serial each week, Baek Young-hee remained focused, energized and humble. Adam became nervous when they rehearsed the love scenes. "Don't hold back," she said.

Other dramas used camera angles, mouths aligned, though not actually touching, but they kissed fully on the lips. Adam gave it all the passion his character felt for the fearless activist she played. He was her anchor, the man who renounced his love for her in favour of the greater good.

Viewers flooded the network with passionate messages for him. Some asked if the actors were in love in real life.

Their respective agencies instructed them to leave the public guessing, yet not to socialize. It would destroy the mystery. In any event, nothing happened between them. He had gone through enough heartache with Yu-mi's disappearance and JinA's death. His first term was about to start at K-ARTS. He wanted to leave the acting world and live like an ordinary student.

That his intended farewell to the screen turned him into a megastar, not only at home but in other Asian countries, is one of those twists of fate that even JinA's words— "Your ancestors will be proud of you"—did not prepare him for. *Reunification* helped raise South Korea's cultural profile from below the line to well above it. If his ancestors watched from their perch high in the sky, surely they turned to each other and nodded sagely while stroking their white beards. Whereas with this latest turn of events, they must be shaking their heads in disappointment.

The sky behind the *hanok* is darkening. Fast.

When he doesn't water the garden, the rain holds off. When he does, the heavens open wide. As he races up the stairs, he spots a rat darting from underneath the house and scurrying under the *pyeongsang*, the wooden platform that keeps people above the dust in the yard. He throws a shoe at the rodent. Misses. Now his shoe is filling with water.

Thirty-Four: July 3rd to 4th, 2018 — Ithaca, New York

Children run up and down Library Slope on Cornell's campus, waiting for the Independence Day fireworks to begin. Among them, Sean and Byron, whose capes ripple as if they were knights riding horses. Emma sits on the grass beside me.

"You checked online recently?" I whisper close to her ear.

"You managed to stay away?"

"I've stopped caring what happens to him. Or what he's done before." My heart says otherwise and I stamp on it. "I'm glad I'm out of it."

She pats my leg.

Sean returns, out of breath. "Mommy, how much longer?"

"Ten minutes? Hey, how about you two rest your horses?"

Byron flops down beside Emma. "My horse would like more strawberries, please."

She brought a whole basket, sweet and juicy, and we enjoy a second round—simple, local pleasures. No drama.

I pick up on our earlier conversation. "Anything new?"

She waits for the boys to gallop down the hill. "Better you hear it from me."

"Awful?"

"Not awful, Joanne. Preposterous. Rumours pass for facts and speculations for indictments."

The first firework cracks in the sky to the crowd's hoo's and ha's. A girl on her father's shoulders calls out the name. "A peony, Daddy."

Two capes slalom uphill as palm fireworks cascade down the darkened sky. The boys stand in front of us while rings, haloes, and smiley faces blossom then dissolve into smoke. A baby cries.

A volley of Roman candles fires up and fizzles down. "That gossip rag claims that Adam hit a woman—" The rest is drowned by rapid-fire shots.

"Chrysanthemums," says the girl.

Emma wraps an arm around me. "'Fake news to sell copies, Joanne." She gives me a one-sided hug. "Wow," she exclaims at the diadems expanding across the blackness.

"The Cake, Daddy," says the girl as a cluster of fireworks zooms up and showers down. "It's going to be over soon."

I take Sean's hand. "The Granny Finally," I say, our inside joke for "The Grand Finale."

Fireworks bloom, each bigger and more spectacular than the one before. I block everything except Sean and the wonder we share right now. I lift him in my arms—how much he has grown—and we wait for one last firework, hear the high-pitched sound, and watch it blossom, red, blue and green, enormous, with fiery drops that stream down, twinkle and sparkle, then dissolve into puffs of smoke that coalesce and drift away.

It is late, but tomorrow's a holiday. Over wine and snacks at my house, Emma reads excerpts from *The Orbiter*'s article. An eyewitness claims that Adam yanked a woman named JinA away from her car and knocked her to the ground.

"'Yanked,' they used that word?" Eerily similar to what he did to me on his terrace.

"The article is translated. Who knows what the original said? 'Pulled away from a car; pushed her to the ground?'"

Did he have it in him to push *me* to the ground?

"Joanne, listen. This paper is Korea's equivalent of *The National Enquirer*. You're so emotionally invested that every little rumour out there wounds you."

I would like nothing better than to believe Emma and absolve him of all wrongdoing. This ceaseless tug-of-war between "innocent" and "guilty," "unjustly accused" and "monster," and, concerning me, "aching in sympathy" and "ashamed I ever believed him," is exhausting. I have stopped listening to any music that reminds me of him. I no longer dance. In May, the Eastern Redbud bloomed in its most spectacular display ever. *Why now?* I was angry for as long as the blossoms remained on the tree.

Emma opens a second bottle of wine and refills my glass. "Cheers."

Thirty-Five: July 10th, 2018 — Cheongju, South Korea

Glassy sheets, like puddles after a rainfall, reflect off the highway. No matter how fast In-sung drives, the mirages race faster. They morph from horse to elephant to dinosaur, and Adam wishes he could continue chasing them all day long. In-sung takes the exit for Cheongju, and reality returns. The town is quiet, with nearly everyone in school or at work. In-sung stops for a mother and child to cross. The boy stares, his feet moving only because his mother pulls him by the hand. He cannot see Adam behind the tinted glass. It is the sports car that draws his attention. Adam's throat tightens thinking about the people bent on convicting him. They will scrutinize his body language and note any weakness they can exploit .

"Excellent," In-sung says. No paparazzi, no crowd to cheer or jeer, only four uniformed officers waiting to escort them. The multistoried courthouse looks more like a company headquarters than a civic institution, painted in mauve and green waves, with round windows adding to the ship-out-of-water impression.

The sun beats on Adam's scalp as he crosses the open space. He holds his head level, neither like a film star nor a guilty man, only an ordinary citizen who did nothing to deserve being dragged into court. He is here of his own free will, confident he will emerge with his name cleared. Acting. Covering his fears: that Attorney Choi will miss the mark; that the judge is in Han Dok-ku's pockets. That there will be a trial, where he will be found guilty and sentenced to death; that the steps he takes today, following In-sung past the trees growing among the pavers, lead him closer to the noose.

His hands shake, and he presses them against the metallic cool of the elevator's wall. They exit, and a short man with a boxer's build nods their way: Attorney Choi. He grips Adam's hand with such confidence that he finds himself believing. Praying. God, please, help us win.

"Ready?" Attorney Choi leads the way into a conference room where two people rise amid a shuffle of chairs. It is all happening so fast.

Public Prosecutor Park, an elegant man wearing glasses, and Assistant Public Prosecutor Ryu, a cream-suited woman, introduce themselves; Adam's counsel reciprocate. The two teams sit on opposite sides of a table. Assistant Prosecutor Ryu turns the pages of a binder with her delicate fingers. Mother-of-pearl nail polish. No ring. She shows a line to her superior. He flips to another page, and she nods.

Adam jumps at a rap on the door. Judge Yeom enters, accompanied by a secretary, and everyone rises. Bows. He has a cocker spaniel face with drooping jowls and bags under his eyes. According to In-sung, he has been a judge for over three decades—the most senior in the North Chungcheong Province, with a reputation for being scrupulously fair.

He asks Attorney Choi if his client still intends to plead "not guilty" to the charge of first-degree murder on the person of Baek Young-hee.

"That is correct, Your Honour, not guilty."

Adam's heart hammers in his chest. *Breathe! In. Out. Small breaths are better than no breath at all.* He focuses inward until the pounding subsides.

Public Prosecutor Park's chair angles toward the head of the table. "We have a healthy woman who died from drowning under highly suspicious circumstances; we have clear evidence, (a) that the accused was with her at the time she died, (b) that he pushed her into a bathtub full of water, (c) that she suffered blunt force trauma to the back of the head, and (d) that the accused forced her nose and mouth underwater until she drowned."

Adam and his attorneys shake their heads. *What horrible acts.*

The prosecutor outlines the evidence: the Danyang guesthouse owner's sworn statement that Ahn Dae-hyun followed Baek Young-hee upstairs that night; the owner's unanswered knocks on Baek Young-hee's door the next morning; finding her submerged in the bathtub, dead.

In the deceased's room, the Cheongju police found Adam's sweater and a mug bearing his fingerprints. Scattered on the bathroom floor, they photographed a toothbrush, a toothpaste tube and a plastic cup, their evidence for a struggle where a presumed perpetrator overcame Baek Young-hee.

The prosecutor shows the judge photos that he examines through a magnifying glass, occasionally nodding or frowning. Adam's legal team has pored over this evidence in the weeks leading to the hearing.

The assistant prosecutor lifts the iced water carafe provided for their use and pours a glass for the judge and a second one for Attorney Choi, who declines, as do In-sung and Adam. They must demonstrate they can withstand hardships without flinching, according to the senior counsel's instructions. Adam's mouth is parched. He avoids looking at the beads of condensation trickling along the jug's sides.

Judge Yeom invites Attorney Choi to respond.

"Your Honour," he bows, "my client admits that he accompanied Baek Young-hee-*ssi* to her room the evening *before* the wrap party at the Danyang guesthouse. They both drank tea in the mugs pictured in the police evidence, hence the fingerprints. However, on the night of the party, Ahn Dae-hyun-*ssi* remained on the ground floor throughout his visit to the guesthouse. He and Baek Young-hee-*ssi* both wore black zippered cardigans and draped them over the backs of their chairs. They switched seats a few times to lead each table in cheers, and it is entirely possible that Baek Young-hee-*ssi* brought my client's cardigan to her room by mistake." Attorney Choi gives the judge a set of photographs to illustrate his points.

Prosecutor Park moves on to the drug found in Baek Young-hee's bloodstream matching a sleeping pill prescription the accused admits he gave her; and to Adam's lack of a verifiable alibi for the time of death, pinned between 23:30 that night and 1:00 the next morning. "And, most—"

Attorney Choi interrupts. "Your Honour, if I may respond before my esteemed colleague continues? In his police deposition, Ahn Dae-hyun-*ssi* said he left the guesthouse by car no later than 11 o'clock. Since no one can vouch that they saw his car at, or near, the guesthouse at the time of death, we submit that any further inference is circumstantial."

The prosecutor looks unperturbed. "Your Honour, we can show, beyond a reasonable doubt, that Baek Young-hee-*ssi* tried, albeit unsuccessfully, to fight off her assailant. Our evidence is five strands of hair"—he places a photograph in front of the judge—"she managed to pull from the accused in her final desperate moments alive. The National Forensic Service compared DNA extracted from the hair with two samples obtained from the accused." He hands the judge a printout. "Both attest to a perfect match with the hair clutched in the unfortunate woman's hand."

Attorney Choi proffers a different printout to Judge Yeom, who declines to take it. "I will hear defence counsel after we take a one-hour break." He gathers his papers and leaves while everyone bows.

Attorney Choi, In-sung and Adam are escorted to a conference room with three bento boxes on the table. Between bites, Attorney Choi and In-sung compare notes: what went as expected and what was a surprise—the prosecutor's insistence that the objects scattered on the bathroom floor were proof of a struggle, for instance. In-sung likens this case to one involving a man convicted of pushing his girlfriend off a bridge when he was fighting desperately to keep her from jumping.

Once finished eating, In-sung takes his jacket off and loosens his tie. He stands and stretches. "You should move too, Dae-hyun-*ah*. Long afternoon ahead."

Adam stays in his chair, and Attorney Choi asks how he is managing.

"Fine."

"I am glad to hear that."

Saving face.

Thirty-Six: July 10th, 2018 — Cheongju, South Korea

In the afternoon, Attorney Choi begins by summarizing the events. "The film's cast and crew stayed at the Danyang Guesthouse from January 7th to the 11th of this year. This included everyone except my client, Director Ahn, who slept at a house he owns twenty minutes away by car. On January 9th, a day before the wrap party, Baek Young-hee-*ssi* requested a few minutes of Director Ahn's time."

Adam sees the scene again: the trestle table by the window in Baek Young-hee's room, the plastic chairs where they sat, coats still on against the ambient chill, the actor making them mugs of tea and apologizing for bungling her lines earlier. "I haven't been sleeping well," she said. "It's cold even with the mattress heater set at the highest level."

"Let's move you to a proper hotel."

It would mean bringing a bodyguard with her, and they were already short-staffed. "It's only one more night," she said.

Adam had sleeping pills in his car, a prescription he meant to take home. He ran over to get it, but Baek Young-hee declined. Sleeping pills made her feel "dead to the world," she said, words that have haunted Adam ever since because he put a capsule in her hand. "Take one. Just in case."

Attorney Choi is saying, "... neither forced nor tricked her into ingesting it, Your Honour. On January 10th, to celebrate the end of 'principal shooting,' as it is called, the cast and crew held a party in the guesthouse's common room. It was informal and hot; many shed bulky layers and moved from seat to seat. At the start of the evening, Baek Young-hee-*ssi* and Ahn Dae-hyun-*ssi* both wore black zip-up cardigans. Baek Young-hee-*ssi* retired to her room earlier than most. It is entirely possible that she took my client's cardigan with her, mistaking it for her own, and hung it in her room."

Attorney Choi hands a sheet of paper to the judge. "Your Honour, I found this online." He names an American actor—blond hair, blue eyes—and says that his fans collect mementos: towels from hotel gyms, hair from his regular salon. "Unlike my hair"—he pulls at his wiry locks, which get swept in the trash, "Ahn Dae-hyun-*ssi*'s hair is prized. We have to think more broadly in this case. Could someone with an axe to grind against my client have used this 'commodity,' his hair, not only to deflect suspicion away from themselves but to frame a celebrity? As Your Honour knows, everyone in the public eye has enemies, people envious of their position, who want to topple them."

Public Prosecutor Park rolls his eyes, and Adam's hopes dim. Insung scribbles on his legal pad, "Theatrics."

Attorney Choi continues. "Your Honour, we put it to your sound judgment that the police enquiry was conducted along simplistic lines: my client's fingerprints and sweater—both in the deceased's room for perfectly benign reasons, resulted in the police believing that an upstanding citizen was the only possible perpetrator. They overlooked the likelihood that their single solid piece of evidence, his hair found in the deceased's hand, could have been planted there by the real murderer."

The judge's hangdog face remains impassive.

"The prosecution has brought forth zero evidence to take this charge against a law-abiding citizen, Ahn Dae-hyun-*ssi*, to trial. There is a conspiracy here, and the authorities have failed to investigate it. They have rushed to the conclusions that the real killer wanted them to draw, and they have charged the wrong person. We ask you to release my client from this unfounded charge. He is as bereft as everyone by Baek Young-hee-*ssi*'s untimely death. He is eager to assist any further investigation into who murdered an innocent woman that night in Danyang." He bows low over the table.

Hope swells anew in Adam's chest. How can the judge possibly rule that the prosecution has sufficient evidence to warrant a trial?

Assistant Public Prosecutor Ryu lifts a finger. "May I remind Your Honour that to extract DNA from hair samples, one must have the follicles, the roots planted in the head, intact. No cuttings from a salon will do. The strands of hair in Baek Young-hee-*ssi*'s hand were undisputedly pulled from the perpetrator's head. No matter how many 'innocent' reasons may account for other pieces of evidence, no one can dispute the match with the hair. It points to this man and this man only."

Her superior picks up the baton. "Fighting for her life, Baek Young-hee-*ssi* hung on to the only anchor within her reach, the man trying to kill her. She managed to take with her, beyond death, one vital clue. It is all that concerns us here, Your Honour."

Another break follows. Attorney Choi excuses himself, citing his need to return calls, while Adam and In-sung retreat to the conference room where they ate lunch earlier. The panelled walls are lined with black and white photographs of former judges. In-sung hands Adam a water bottle and finishes his in a few gulps. "Ha, that Public Prosecutor Park. Your trial's his number one chance to get his face on the nine o'clock news. He's running for a seat in the National Assembly. He'll twist all the facts he can to achieve his goal. The judge is key. I can't see him rule that he's satisfied with that evidence. Too many holes. He'll ask for the investigation to start again." In-sung paces in front of the portraits until Attorney Choi enters the room.

He gives them a tired smile, approaches In-sung, and tells him something Adam cannot catch. "What is it?" he asks.

"Nothing." In-sung replies.

Attorney Choi examines the portraits, his back to Adam.

"It's not nothing," Adam says. "It can't be nothing if the two of you need to talk about it."

"Nothing that should worry you."

"Who are you to decide what should or should not worry me?" This is one too many things In-sung has not told him. "Stop treating me like a child."

"Alright, but please don't let this bother you. The media's outside, waiting for the—"

There is a knock on the door: time to return to the conference room.

Adam wishes he had brought a water bottle with him despite his attorney's interdiction. His throat feels like tree bark.

Judge Yeom adjusts a pair of half-moon glasses over his nose. "I am well aware that, taken in isolation, many pieces of evidence in this case are circumstantial." He reviews each one and concludes with questions. "Should we believe that the defendant went home at the time he claims, or did he stay at the Danyang Guesthouse for another hour or two? Can no one vouch for seeing him leave? Should we believe that the defendant's sweater was carried by the deceased to her room, thinking it was hers, or that the defendant left it there himself that night? Where is the deceased's sweater? Why hasn't it been found?"

The two public prosecutors nod. The judge highlights the DNA match between the hair found in Baek Young-hee's hand and Adam's, and the two prosecutors sit taller in their chairs.

"Taken together, this evidence amounts to a case with sufficient merit to stand trial. This is the decision that I have taken this afternoon. Both sides will be contacted shortly with a court date. Until then, I advise you all to dig deeper into the unanswered questions raised today."

Thirty-Seven: July 10th to 13th, 2018 — Danyang, South Korea

The SL55 passes through the gate, and a small woman taking small steps shields her eyes from the headlights. "You look exhausted," Grandmother says. "Come and eat. It will do you good."

Both decline. In-sung swings the car around for home, and Adam goes to his room. He lies on the mattress and wishes he had a sleeping pill hidden somewhere. He wants to forget what happened, the public prosecutor with his political ambitions, upright-citizen looks, and disregard for whomever he has to crush to reach them; the judge with his faithful dog face that drives defendants to expect sympathy and receive none; even In-sung with his prompts—Sit. Nod. Bow. He wants to wipe off the mayhem on the plaza when they tried to reach the car, the reporters closing ranks around them, sticking their microphones in his face through the arms of the officers escorting them, yelling questions, one on top of the other. Greedy voices, harried voices coming from mouths hungry and never satisfied. Burly men with cameras hitched on shoulders, pointing lenses at him, trying to capture disappointment and tiredness in his face, in the slope of his shoulders and the heaviness of his steps. He felt like a beast in chains paraded through town before the inevitable stoning on the public square: dirty, stinking and mad. Instead of lashing out, he had to focus inward and follow In-sung's cues: Walk. Now left. Faster. Bend your head. Easy does it. Sit.

It took In-sung forever to inch the SL55 away from the mob. He honked the horn and mouthed, *Please*, while grumbling through his teeth, *get the hell out of my way.*

The reporters had time to push their cameras against the side windows and take pictures at random, hoping to catch Adam scowling or even crying. He had to appear unbowed, serious and confident, although he felt the exact opposite. He wanted to pound on the dashboard and curse everyone in sight; storm out of the car, and push away the woman who had the nerve to paste a page from her notebook on the windshield: *Will you take the stand in your defence? Nod once for Yes and twice for No.*

After they pulled away from prying eyes, Adam began to shake. His head felt squeezed in a vice, blocking all thoughts except "no" echoing in his skull.

"Can we—" Adam fought to tame his voice. "Can we appeal?"

"Not after a hearing." In-sung shifted gear on the ramp to the highway. "Only after the trial. If they find you guilty, we can appeal at that point."

Adam's stomach lurched. He hoped willpower would overcome his nausea but the waves kept building. "Stop. Stop the car."

He held the vomit in while In-sung checked his rear-view mirror, eased on the gas and stopped on the shoulder. Adam opened the door and fell on his knees, retching and coughing, tears gushing from his eyes.

In-sung stood beside him and waited. He slapped Adam on the back whenever he choked and passed him tissues that Adam threw to the wind after wiping his mouth, his nose, his eyes, his hands, his jacket and his pants. He felt ashamed. Better if he had been with someone he barely knew rather than the man always by his side in his moments of weakness.

It is morning now, and Adam weeds the garden. His mind can't stop replaying the scenes in the pre-trial conference room. How will he cope with days of sitting still and keeping his emotions in check when his life hangs on so many constructions of truths and untruths, so many combinations of words, tones, looks and gestures?

Grandmother acts as if the hearing never took place, although it looks like she had prepared a feast. They eat leftovers for days, including when In-sung returns later in the week.

The legal team embarked on a full re-examination of the evidence, he says. They are appealing on social media to anyone able to vouch for seeing Adam leave the guesthouse.

"And?"

"Nothing yet. Still, whether or not someone saw you leave remains circumstantial evidence. Innocent until proven guilty, not the other way around." In-sung drapes his jacket over his arm while they walk in the garden. He scrapes the soles of his shoes on a brick at the exit.

"Are they trying the Japanese fans?" Adam asks.

"The nice ones and the stalkers. I called Nijima-*san* at Rising Sun Tours yesterday."

"That smarmy excuse for a man?"

"He begged me to get you off. Implied that money can do things in Korean courts that it can't do in Japan."

"Despising us. I wouldn't put it past him to have had a hand in this."

"What would he gain?"

"I don't know. He's always two steps ahead. Perhaps he wants to write a book, *The Fall of Mighty Ahn Dae-hyun*. Lord knows he has followed me around enough."

"Didn't sound like it. Without you, he has lost a lot of business."

"To hell with his business. There are plenty of Korean idols left to stalk; bring his contingent of fans to Seoul and make them stand in front of their apartment buildings." Adam has no problems with fans attending his public appearances. Stalkers, especially when they cannot be stopped because of diplomatic repercussions, are another matter altogether.

In-sung wanders off to the car, and Adam takes a turn around the *hanok* to clear his mind.

"You texted Joanne that night." In-sung hands Adam a beer. "We discussed this. Are you absolutely sure you wrote that you were at the *hanok*?"

Adam needs a moment to connect what In-sung is asking with their earlier conversation. The night of the wrap party. His alibi. "I'm one hundred percent sure. Still, didn't the prosecutor say I could have sent that text from Baek Young-hee-*ssi*'s room? Something about the signal tower on the hill behind the *hanok* also serving parts of Danyang?"

"We'll find a way," In-sung says.

For now, they have to endure—the neo-Confucian equivalent of a stiff upper lip with the added flourish of beating one's chest with one's fist. Humble suffering.

Thirty-Eight: July 17th, 2018 — Danyang, South Korea

"We found the missing sweater," In-sung announces as soon as he arrives. Raindrops dot his blue shirt as he tells Adam the tale. The law firm's private detective re-interviewed everyone who attended the wrap party. In-sung runs through photos on his handphone and shows Adam a face he recognizes as belonging to a grip handler.

"Get this: he wanted to return it to her personally in the morning. After what happened, he kept it as a souvenir. He didn't realize it had anything to do with the investigation."

"Does it help?"

The rain starts pelting down, and they run for cover under the roof's overhang.

"Not much, unfortunately."

"I know. The hair. We shouldn't have given them the DNA sample. I'm the one who pushed."

"It showed that you had nothing to hide."

"Yeah, well." They have rehashed this story many times: the wrap party at the guesthouse at the end of the third day of filming in the Gosu Cave, the call Adam received at the *hanok* the next morning: Baek Young-hee, dead in her room.

Everyone connected with the film was questioned by the Danyang police and allowed to go, subject to being contacted by the authorities as the investigation progressed. The next afternoon, Adam received a call from the Cheongju District police asking him to answer a few more questions at the station, an invitation he accepted readily, arriving within the shortest possible delay.

At first the detective in charge, a chubby man who wore rumpled jeans and chewed gum, seemed to suspect Baek-Young-hee's husband. Was Adam aware of any marital issues? Or did the deceased have personal problems or maybe a health condition?

Adam mentioned her insomnia and was about to relate how he had given her one of his sleeping pills when the detective was called away. "Hold that thought," he said as he left the interview room. Adam waited more than half an hour to tell his tale, and no sooner had he done so than the detective left again.

Matters escalated. Adam became a "person of interest." The detective directed him to make a written statement covering everything he had done or observed in the twenty-four hours before he learned that Baek Young-hee had died. "You're entitled to consult a lawyer before you sign," he said.

It was past two in the morning when In-sung arrived, bags under his eyes and deep lines creasing his forehead. Between the birth of his daughter and the death of Baek Young-hee, he had hardly slept. Behind him was a short man with broad shoulders, Attorney Choi, who shook Adam's hand with an iron grip.

The rest of the night passed with Adam retelling his story to the newcomers, answering their questions, and writing his statement as dictated by his lawyer.

In the morning, the chief of police entered the room. Tall and ramrod straight, he wore a black uniform with gold trim and a crisp white shirt. He was with the detective and a few underlings. "I have troubling news," he said. "We have evidence that shows Ahn Dae-hyun-*ssi* was in the deceased's room. What would help is a DNA sample."

"What kind of evidence?" Attorney Choi asked.

"We're not at liberty to tell."

Adam's team assumed, as most people would, that they had recovered semen. A DNA test would definitely clear him.

"I'll do it," Adam said.

But Attorney Choi asked for a few moments alone with his client. "Are you absolutely sure you want to give a DNA sample?" he asked.

"I've never been surer of anything in my life."

After the mouth swab, they were asked to wait. Attorney Choi questioned the need, arguing the DNA results would take a minimum of forty-eight hours. The detective said he might have further questions.

The three men dozed on and off on their chairs. When the chief detective officer returned to the interview room, it was late in the afternoon. A full day had passed since Adam's arrival. The detective had changed clothes but not shaved. Men in uniform crowded behind him.

"Ahn Dae-hyun-*ssi*," he read from a document, "the Cheongju authorities are arresting you on suspicion of murder."

"I'll need to see that warrant," Attorney Choi said. The piece of paper had barely changed hands when handcuffs closed around Adam's wrists. He was pulled along a corridor lined with police officers and pushed inside a detention cell, the door clanging behind him. In-sung was a step away, looking horrified through the bars.

This can't be happening, thought Adam. In-sung said, "Don't worry, Dae-hyun-*ah*. Give us twenty-four hours and we'll get you out."

There were already three men in the cell—cut lips, blooming black eyes, reeking of sweat and soju. Adam sat on the floor in the corner farthest away. *He* wasn't like them. Not at all. It was a horrible mistake. The DNA would clear him

He did not sleep, not even doze off. The weak light of dawn and the cold that keeps it company began seeping through the high window. He shivered. The other men lay sprawled on the floor, snoring, jerking awake, and uttering an angry "*aïsh*" before falling into oblivion again.

A guard came for him.

But the man took Adam to an interview room where In-sung waited.

"We'll get you out of this," he said again. "It's all circumstantial. The sleeping pill, the sweater, the fingerprints."

The next day Adam learned that his DNA matched DNA extracted from hair found in Baek Young-hee's hand. He was formally charged with first-degree murder.

In-sung has left the *hanok*, and so have the clouds. Adam sits outside his room while the stars pierce the darkness, and crickets shriek, *mori, mori, mori*, hair, hair, hair. Who could have put strands of his hair in Baek Young-hee's hand? Any notion that she committed suicide or that her drowning was accidental flew out the window. Somebody killed her and planted evidence in a deliberate bid to frame him. It is the only possible explanation.

Thirty-Nine: July 18th to 24th, 2018 — Ithaca

Emma waves me into her office and closes the door "New development," she says. "His law firm's looking for information from anyone who saw him on the night Baek Young-hee died."

"So?"

She snaps her fingers before my eyes as if I'm sleepwalking. "It means they're looking for someone who can give him an alibi for the night of January 10th."

"Are you saying his lawyer doesn't believe him?"

She shakes her head. "You're still too close to him. Where was he when that woman died?"

"It depends on when she died."

Emma is already ten steps ahead. She called her brother, a criminal lawyer, who told her that a victim's time of death is never revealed publicly until the trial. "Standard police procedure here and likely in South Korea."

"That means…" I am tempted to rush home for my "Adam phone," but our staff meeting begins in five minutes.

Emma and I regroup during the afternoon break. "Show me that video again, when he arrived at that old house," she says.

Six months ago, I muted the sound to show her Adam's tour of the renovated *hanok*. This time, I let his commentary play: "I'll sleep in this room," he says, scanning a guest bedroom from side to side. "The master bedroom is reserved … for when you come." How can his voice not stir me?

"It's even better with the sound." Emma winks. "Okay, now for the night when that woman died."

Adam sent me another video, much shorter, of him collapsing on the bed and saying, "We're there, Joanne-*ah*. All principal photography is done," followed by love talk that hurts more every time I hear it.

"Whoa." Emma fans herself with her hand. "It's undeniably … the same room as in the other video." She touches my arm and asks if I'm okay. "Let's check the metadata, the 'details' on your phone for the date and time recorded. Ah, here it is: *Wednesday, January 10, 2018 – 11:23 p.m.* That would have been local time for Adam."

"What if it sinks him instead of helping him?"

"Look at his face, Joanne. Listen not only to what he says but also how he says it. Could he have killed a woman in cold blood that same night? He must have left the guesthouse close to eleven, given the distance he had to drive. That's pretty early to quit a party. Contact the lawyers. They need to see this."

Over the next few days, I send messages through the online form, ranging from, *Kim In-sung can confirm that I was Ahn Dae-hyun's girlfriend at the time,* to, *Ahn Dae-hyun sent me a video that categorically shows he was at his house at 11:23 p.m. on the night of January 10ᵗʰ.* I lay everything out clearly, but the emailed replies never vary: *We are sorry, but you must prove that you were in Danyang, North Chungcheong Province, between 22:00 on January 10ᵗʰ and 7:00 on January 11ᵗʰ. Signed: Ko, Shim and Choi, Attorneys at Law.*

As I did all those months ago, late at night here, so it's morning there, I try to connect with the people I met in Korea, starting with the number In-sung gave me last December. It rings three times, and a woman's voice delivers a message in Korean. Is it busy? If so, why is there no *beep* to leave a message at the end? Is it no longer in service?

I tap on the Star Shop Agency's number. Same message; statements ending in "mnida." Verbs, but which? I try the number for Kora Zone, the teashop Adam's sister owns. Come on, Dae-moon, answer the phone, I plead. It rings and rings and then cuts off.

What was I expecting? For months now, every sign points to numbers no longer in service. My fingers hover over Adam's number. What will I say if he answers? "Were you acting the whole time with me? Why did you try so hard, buying the house, reading stories to Sean?"

No reply there as well.

Library Slope spreads before my eyes, a placid lake of green radiance. I sit on a bench in the dappled shade of honey locusts' feathery leaves. The peace of the morning contrasts with the feelings warring inside.

Should I take the next step to help Adam, even though I know so little?

Emma arrives, two lemonades in hand: freshly squeezed lemons, iced water, and a dash of honey. So generous of her to soothe a confused soul like mine.

Deep breath. "I'm thinking of going to Seoul. Once Sean has left for his dad's. It's risky since we don't know the time of death, but…"

She shakes her head. "They wrote twenty-two hundred. That's ten p.m., likely the last time anyone saw the poor woman alive."

"That still gives him a good hour."

"To do the deed?" she asks, raising an eyebrow.

The pendulum refuses to stay still: not guilty, guilty, incapable of, capable of, trust, distrust.

Emma drinks her lemonade. "It's likely they set the period much wider than the evidence tells them."

"There's hope? I'm not crazy?"

"Think of it this way: could you live with yourself if you didn't try?"

Forty: July 20th, 2018 — Seoul, South Korea

It is broad daylight, and the Gentlemen's Club is closed. The pink neon silhouette of a woman flashes above Adam's head, blending with the barrage of bright signs enticing people to part with their money in Seoul's Myeongdong district. He lowers the visor on his cap and steps out of the SL55 while his friend presses the club's call button.

In-sung was dead set against Adam coming with him on this fact-finding mission, but he was so sick of playing gardener at the *hanok* that his friend gave in. On the drive from Danyang, In-sung received a call from Attorney Choi. The trial, originally scheduled for December, had been moved to September.

On the hot sidewalk in Myeongdong, In-sung shakes his head again. "Only six weeks left to prepare."

A woman in a slim grey dress opens the door. Smooth white skin, high cheekbones, dark eyeliner and cherry-red lips. "Follow me, please." Husky voice.

She ascends a flight of stairs lit by a low-wattage bulb, her steps constrained by the narrowness of her dress.

In her office, she introduces herself as Misty, and they reciprocate. Business cards and bows. She invites them to sit in twin mahogany chairs and settles behind a matching desk. The blinds are drawn. Only a desk lamp illuminates the room.

In-sung speaks. "You told our detective you still had footage from last January."

"Before we go any further, I must ensure you will abide by the assurances he gave me. Han Dok-ku-*ssi* owns this club. I cannot endanger my staff's livelihoods over this … fishing expedition."

In-sung lists their commitments on his fingers. "One, no one will receive a subpoena as a result of this visit. Two, the police will have no legal ground to requisition any of the videos you show us. Three, no copies will leave these premises today or any other day."

"No matter what the videos show," Misty adds.

"Agreed," replies In-sung. "The Gentlemen's Club owner isn't on trial. We're looking for lines of enquiry. Not evidence."

"How can you be sure? What if the owner gets in trouble later? Aren't you here because you suspect he paid someone to kill that unfortunate woman?" She steals a glance at Adam.

"Is that in the videos?" In-sung asks.

She looks at each in turn. "We have standing orders to turn the CCTVs off whenever the owner uses the party rooms."

"But you don't. Not always."

"The cameras that feed into the control room are switched off without fail." She presses her lips together. "I must think of my staff. I—" Her gaze falls to the desk, and she rearranges a misplaced pen. "I have my own camera in the party room he typically uses—picture and sound. No one knows, and I'm taking a huge risk by telling you. I have to trust that you'll keep it a secret."

In-sung reiterates his earlier assurances.

"The camera links only to my computer. I normally delete the videos the same night unless something unusual happened."

"Unusual in what ways?"

"Oh." She shrugs. "Nothing like that has happened in a long time. You know, actions that make our hostesses uncomfortable."

"As in 'rape?'"

"That's a strong word, Kim In-sung-*ssi*. Let us say 'intimidations.'"

"What do you do when that happens?"

"I'm sorry. We're drifting away from why you came. No such action took place between the owner and anyone on the premises last January."

"But you said you still have the footage."

"An oversight on my part. I was away. I didn't even know I had the videos until your detective called."

In-sung has impressed upon Adam that he would do all the talking, though Adam can't help asking, "Han Dok-ku-*ssi* came more than once?"

"As I said, I can't let you see the videos until I'm absolutely sure that their existence and content will remain strictly between us."

Discovering this footage took delicate sleuthing by the law firm's detective, who traced Han Dok-ku to this club and convinced Misty to meet with In-sung.

"How much?" In-sung asks.

She says fifty million won. In-sung shakes his head. "Out of the question." He signals for Adam to rise. "We're sorry to have troubled you, Misty-*ssi*."

"How much are you willing to pay?"

"No more than five."

She gives them a scornful look. "They're worth at least forty."

"Not when all we can do is watch. How many are there?"

"Four."

"I doubt they'll tell us anything we don't already know."

"Hard for me to judge."

"Could you give us the dates?"

She purses her lips. "Let me see." She scrolls through her laptop files. "There's January fourth, ninth, twelfth, and sixteenth."

In-sung makes a note. "How many guests?"

"I only viewed them once. I don't remember exactly."

"Big parties? Small parties? If you could check your records to see how many hostesses were present?"

"I suppose." More scrolling on her laptop. "Would you care for something to drink?" She calls from her desk phone and asks for refreshments.

"Ah, here. We have a party of three, then two, another two, then six."

There is a knock on the door, and a short woman wearing baggy clothes enters with a tray she deposits on the manager's desk: a flower-patterned teapot, three matching cups with saucers, and a plate of cookies arranged in a pyramid.

In-sung scribbles Misty's numbers and Adam lowers his head, again using his visor as a shield, while the *ajumma* leaves.

"Five million won," In-sung says.

Misty pours the pale green tea and hands them each a cup. "They're worth a lot more. Twenty-five for all four."

"Twenty for all four. Five each, with the option to choose the order and decline continuing as we see fit."

"Cash," Misty says.

The negotiations continue, Misty insisting that payment precede any viewing and In-sung arguing that Adam has to be in Danyang before nightfall. "I'll bring the money myself tomorrow. On my honour," he says, rising and extending his hand.

Misty rises and shakes on the deal.

In-sung and Adam have been to these perks of the business world. The party rooms' layout rarely varies: leather benches fixed to the walls on three sides forming an elongated U around a low table.

In-sung elects to start with January 9th, the eve of Baek Young-hee's death. In the video, Han Dok-ku enters with another man and sits at the top of the room while his guest settles on his left, leaning back against a cushion.

"Who is he?" In-sung asks Misty, who has come to stand behind their chairs while they watch her laptop's screen. "I'm not at liberty to say."

The men wear suits, jackets open, ties loosened. They are soon joined by two women in sequinned bustiers and barely-there skirts, who bring a bottle of what looks like scotch, an ice bucket, four glasses and a plate of fruits and nuts. The hostess who sidles up to Han Dok-ku pours his drink neat, without asking for his preference, whereas the one who sits beside the other man enquires first and leans across his lap as she makes a production of filling his highball with ice cubes and pouring the tawny liquid over them.

The talk turns to a rising golf star who had a bitter argument with his wife in the lobby of a chic hotel, leading to revelations that he had been serially cheating on her, a story that dominated the news cycle until Adam was charged with murder. *The Orbiter*'s coverage of the golfer's fall from grace had been particularly biting, and the men laugh at the finer points, clinking glasses and congratulating each other. Han Dok-ku never calls the other man by name, and both men use semi-formal speech. The hostesses fawn over them and giggle behind their hands whenever the guests say anything remotely witty. The men treat them more or less like pets.

The hostess next to Han Dok-ku suggests they dance, and presses a button on the table to start the karaoke player. The women rise and make willowy moves with their arms above their heads as they sashay out of camera range. They reappear with microphones and tambourines. One sings and the other keeps the beat.

Into the second song they close in on the men and mock-pull them by their ties until everyone is on the dance floor. Han Dok-ku seems to enjoy himself as he lumbers around. Adam thinks he looks ridiculous.

His guest shimmies in time with the music as the women take turns brushing against him. The music drowns the conversation. A few high-pitched words surface, the kind said by women whose job entails showing men a good time. Nothing important happens, although Adam and In-sung suffer through the whole playback just in case.

Forty-One: July 20th, 2018 — Seoul, South Korea

"Could we watch the footage from the twelfth?" In-sung asks. The date coincides with when the Cheongju District police drove Adam to the station for further questioning.

This time Han Dok-ku's guest is a younger man who tends to lean forward. He turns away from "President Han" whenever he drinks, addresses him in formal speech and bows subserviently. The conversation turns to Baek Young-hee's death, so sudden and so sad. "Although it won't hurt our circulation numbers," they agree with wry smiles. The same two hostesses pour drinks and act cozy with the men. When the talk subsides and one woman suggests turning the music on, Han Dok-ku declines. "You two may go." The women strut out of the room, stiletto heels clacking on the cement floor.

"I want you to lead the coverage," Han Dok-ku says. "Go to Cheongju and camp at the police station."

"Do they have a suspect?"

Han Dok-ku raises his glass and gives the man a look. "Big fish." He leans over and whispers something in his ear.

The other man's eyes widen. "Crime of passion?"

"Who knows? She had a sizeable bruise at the back of her head. He must have attacked her."

"*Aïsh*! I'll drive over first thing in the morning."

"He's already in for questioning. Go now."

The man chugs his drink and leaves. Han Dok-ku sits alone and pops a few nuts in his mouth while he finishes his scotch.

Adam mentally compares the timing of the events in the video with the timing of his own experience with the Cheongju District police. Something doesn't compute. He proposes a break.

He and In-sung find the washroom and, as soon as the door closes, In-sung points to the camera mounted in a corner of the wall, tiled in shades of coffee, chocolate and caramel.

Adam shields his mouth as he speaks into In-sung's ear. "He knew I'd get arrested." It emerges as a loud whisper, and In-sung makes a 'down' gesture as they stand at the urinals.

In-sung speaks, barely moving his lips, "A day before they clamped the handcuffs on you. He even mentioned the head injury. How did he know? The autopsy was done that same afternoon. I checked."

Adam's heart thumps as he zips his pants. They wash their hands and dry them with cloth towels piled on a shelf below the mirrors. In-sung pats the pocket where he keeps his phone. "All recorded here. The conversations."

Adam matches his friend's way of speaking. "Is that going to be admissible?"

"*Pssst.*" They stiffen and hold their breaths while opening the four cubicle doors. Nobody inside.

The *pssst* comes again, and a cinnamon scent on the edge of Adam's consciousness intensifies. His eyes dart around until he spots a dispenser above the urinals, sending periodic spritzes of freshener.

In-sung resumes their conversation. "Knowing a detail earlier than anyone doesn't amount to catching Han Dok-ku red-handed."

Adam argues for pushing ahead with the remaining videos. In-sung counters that it is already late relative to the time on Adam's pass. "I'll come back tomorrow with the cash."

Adam swallows his disappointment as they return to the manager's office. The taste of freedom and the surge of hope he experienced today make the prospect of returning to the *hanok* all the worse.

Misty sits at her desk, reading glasses on, signing documents. Her laptop is still facing the door and has switched to screensaver mode. A snapshot of a younger Misty appears; she and another woman eat ice cream cones in front of a brightly painted carousel. They mug for the camera in a happy, carefree way, and it takes Adam a moment to recognize the other woman.

"You were friends with Lee JinA-*ssi?*" he asks.

Misty lifts her eyes. "I'm sorry?"

Adam repeats his question.

"Mmm . . . why do you ask?"

He explains what he saw on her screensaver, and she comes around the desk. "She worked here, yes." Her eyes hold Adam's as if trying to communicate a message, but he has no clue what it could be. "Now, let's see," she says, pivoting on her heels and waking the computer. "Which video would you like to see next?"

"When was that?" Adam asks. "JinA-*ssi* working here."

"Oh, a long time ago. Over ten years."

Before she became an actress, thinks Adam. "Did Han Dok-ku-*ssi*—" he wants to say "take her under his wings," but amends it to "help her along? In her career, I mean."

She considers the question. "I couldn't say. I'm sorry." Again, she holds his eyes and silence hangs over them until In-sung relates their decision regarding the remaining two videos.

Forty-Two: August 6ᵗʰ to 9ᵗʰ, 2018 — Seoul, South Korea

I booked seven days in Seoul, anticipating delays between meeting Adam's lawyers and going through the necessary procedures to prove my video evidence was genuine and been taken come at a time that proved helpful to him. I would use any spare time to learn about South Korea, visit museums and perhaps a palace.

Yet here I am at the end of day four with zero progress. I tried to gain admittance to the offices of Ko, Shim and Choi. I insisted I was bringing an alibi for Ahn Dae-hyun, only to be escorted to the street by security. I travelled an hour to a Rubik-cube-like building that housed Adam's sister's teashop, only to discover that it closed after his fall from grace. I found the Star Shop Agency and pleaded with an employee to ask In-sung to contact me, only to learn he had "gone," and was "not here." I followed the handful of clues I had—near the Canadian embassy; house number 19-90, matching the year my mother died—to screenwriter Kang Min-chae's house. She was not home.

I have stewed in traffic at the back of a cab with a driver who could not find my hotel, yet charged me 185 dollars; followed a helpful local to a cheaper hotel where he offered to hop in bed with me—no thanks; misread subway directions multiple times; walked through drizzle and waited in bus shelters for downpours to end; experienced the varied faces of Seoul: gritty, hurried, harried, hard-working, and helpful.

I have cried in frustration; ranted against Adam for causing me so much grief; threatened to quit trying; imagined myself telling him he was not worth all the trouble he put me through, not to mention my growing credit card debt; that if he indeed raped the kindergarten teacher or assaulted JinA, he deserved to go to jail even if he did not kill Baek Young-hee.

I have cried from lovesickness, certain that the Adam I knew could never commit any of these acts, praying, hoping that what I tried so hard to deliver into the right hands would tip the balance toward his acquittal.

Morning of day five: I have returned to Kang Min-chae's gate and rung the bell. Will she be home today and if so, will she agree to talk to me? Agree to help me?

A voice comes through the intercom, words in Korean. I say my name, and the gate swings open, leaving me to follow a path lined with big-leaved hostas. Kindly Kang Min-chae stands outside her front door, a blend of surprise and concern on her face. She opens her arms and pulls me into an embrace. "You poor dear." She pats me on the back.

Too choked up to speak, I follow her inside, sit on a stool at her kitchen island, and debate how to explain what I am doing here while she pours me a glass of water.

"You want news?" she asks, and after I shake my head, "You *have* news?"

I place the phone Adam gave me, the one reserved for his calls, on the countertop and play his last two videos with the sound on— this is no time to be shy. Kang Min-chae leans against the island from the other side and gives them her undivided attention.

Next to the sink, pale green vegetables soak in a blue plastic vat. "I interrupted your cooking."

"My cabbages can wait." She points at my phone. "If the last one was taken after Ahn Dae-hyun-*ssi* left the wrap party, Kim In-sung needs to see these right away."

"You have his current number?"

"*Aïgoo*," she says. "But here." She shows me her screen. "Dae-hyun-*ssi*'s law firm."

Everything is in Korean.

She presses the call icon and stands, poised to speak. "On hold," she whispers. She presses one more key, and music—piano, classical—plays.

A male voice comes on. The conversation sounds polite and business-like. Brief.

"In-sung is out of town." She nods at her phone. "The man promised to text him. Right away." Her voice bubbles and rolls like a river over stones.

She reaches across the island and clasps both my hands. "Everything will be alright."

I want to believe her so much, tears swim in my eyes.

It is darker now, and rain beats on a window, hard, soft, and hard again. I am lying on a sofa with a blanket over me. I want to rise but my legs feel heavy; my arms feel heavy. Moments later, someone touches my shoulder. "Come and have something to eat." It is Kang Min-chae.

I obey like a sick child, following her to a dining room with a low table cut from live-edge wood. The surface holds half a dozen bowls brimming with vegetables, including two kinds of cabbage kimchi, the one she was making when I arrived and the well-fermented kind Adam loves. Kang Min-chae's phone lies within reach.

I try a few bites but I am not hungry. I keep eating, not wanting to offend; I bow my head at my host when she deposits a piece of stewed meat on top of my rice, assure her that everything is delicious, that I'm not a big eater.

The television murmurs at my back while Kang Min-chae tells me about her five grandchildren. I struggle to keep their names straight. I must be hallucinating; Adam is standing in the garden beyond the glass doors. Kang Min-chae's chopsticks freeze in mid-air. She stands, hunts for the remote and shuts off the TV. Adam disappears.

"What were they saying?"

"Nothing much." She spoons rice into her mouth and chews while I hold her gaze. "The trial," she says. "Whether he will testify in his own defence?" She selects a slice of cucumber from a side dish. "People think he should tell his side of the story. It would go a long way to proving his innocence. Legal experts all say that it's risky because the prosecutor would cross-examine him."

"Why is that risky?"

"The prosecutor might try to revive old scandals."

My throat constricts. "Such as?"

"Anything. Allegations in gossip papers. Rumours on social media."

The disturbing picture pops into my head.

"According to legal experts," Kang Min-chae goes on, "if no one comes forward to give him an alibi, he'll have no choice. He'll have to testify. That's why your videos are so—"

Her phone is ringing. From her tone and body language, it can only be In-sung. She scribbles a few words, nodding, and concludes with her thanks.

She beams me a broad smile and shows me her note: "Est. TO death bet. 23:30 on 10th and 1:00 on 11th."

Forty-Three: August 7ᵗʰ, 2018 — Danyang, South Korea

In-sung found nothing more in the Gentlemen's Club videos. The lawyers' appeal to delay the trial has failed, and the public prosecutor is pushing for television cameras in the courtroom.

"'Justice must be seen to be done,'" In-sung quotes him as saying. "'There are too many people in this land who can buy their way out of trouble.'"

Adam bristles. "There are too many people in this land who can buy their way into making trouble for others?" He shakes his head. "You know what that means? The whole time, I'll have to worry about what they're beaming to the masses. I've been through enough already with this fame thing, *Hyeong*. Remember *Reunification*? Everyone and their dog had a camera phone ready to flash in my face. I couldn't even go to the convenience store for a pack of gum. Now this? Damn them all to hell."

"Listen," In-sung says. "No television camera has ever been allowed in a South Korean courtroom. Dangerous precedent. A parallel trial in the court of public opinion. Due process denied. We won't let it happen. I swear to you."

Cicadas screech as if the sun would fall to Earth without their deafening support. Adam feels the same about In-sung's promises. Strong words, though woefully inadequate against a man like Han Dok-ku.

He lets it pass, and they go on to Attorney Choi's questions: At what time did he leave the *hanok* on the last morning of shooting his film? How can he be sure it was that particular morning, not the one before or the one after? Did he go directly to the Gosu Cave, or did he swing by the guesthouse in Danyang? Details but possibly important details.

Grandmother misses the variety shows she used to watch on television. She never says so, though Adam remembers how much she enjoyed them, how they induced a happy frame of mind before she went to bed.

After dinner, she takes her time tidying the dishes. She showers and hand-washes their clothes in the bathroom. She emerges smelling of soap and likes to take a turn around the garden, a tiny elderly woman in her pyjamas surveying the work of nature. Twilight gives way to darkness, and when Adam goes with her, she mutters, "This is nice." Trying to convince herself that they are not living in a nightmare.

The trial starts in four weeks. Merely thinking about it can trigger a panic attack. It is like stage fright, except a thousand times worse. He will have to give the performance of his life to tell the truth in a way that topples whatever case they manufacture against him. If he fails, they will lock him in a tiny room with three convicts who will make it their mission to punish him for everything they hate about rich people, the life of ease, the countless women they think he laid, the crime they think he committed. Who is he trying to fool with his taekwondo practices? When it is three against one, with only a strip of floor between two sets of bunk beds, he would no sooner kick one man than the other two would jump on him. According to Attorney Choi, his best strategy is to focus on turning any lingering doubt in his mind—about what he did, saw, or heard in the days leading to Baek Young-hee's death—into certainties.

It sounds easy, though his mind keeps drifting: to Joanne (Is she well? Has she moved on? How much does she know about what's happening here?); to his parents, his sister and her family; to In-sung; to that despicable Han Dok-ku; to JinA, who worked as a hostess in his club.

He uses Misty's business card as a bookmark. The temptation to call her comes and goes.

Grandmother's hair is wet, and she has draped a towel around her neck to prevent soaking her pink pyjamas. Adam stays with her while she hangs the clothes she washed. They say nothing. It is enough to be together. *I'm here for you.* Her phone, a clamshell hand-me-down from Adam's sister, rests on a stone. Grandmother laughs about it sometimes, "An old woman like me, carrying a talking egg."

She closes the lid on the clothespin box and walks toward the garden. Adam doesn't move.

"Coming?"

"I'll read in my room." Once her back is turned, he pockets the phone, feeling like a thief. He could have asked to borrow it, but there would be questions afterwards and he would prefer not to invent lies.

Misty answers on the second ring. Adam doesn't waste time on trivial talk. "I have a few questions."

"Yes?"

"When did you last see JinA-*ssi*?"

"Seven years ago. In November." She answers without hesitation, as if she has been waiting for Adam's call and questions.

"You went for dinner together," he says.

"You were in Busan for a shoot."

Adam gulps. "What happened?"

"After the meal, she came to the club with me. She wanted to talk to another hostess." Misty pauses. "To warn her about that man—"

Han Dok-ku.

"It was just our rotten luck. He arrived at the club at the same time."

The pieces of the puzzle are beginning to fall into place. JinA decided to move to Adam's building seven years ago because it wasn't run by the mob. "And?"

"He acted all nice. Asked her to have a drink with him for old times' sake."

"In that party room. The one with the cameras turned off."

"That's right."

"And you took your secret footage."

"No, I didn't have the camera at the time."

"You mean—" Adam recalls Misty's words, "actions that make our hostesses uncomfortable," and "nothing like that has happened *in a long time…*"

"How did JinA-*ssi* look when she came out?" he asks.

"I didn't see her. Maybe she left without looking for me. I'll never know. No one saw her. I called her number. She didn't reply."

"Did you hear from her after that?"

"She landed the leading role with that indie director. She was ecstatic."

"Do you think Han Dok-ku-*ssi* was blocking mainstream offers from coming her way?"

"She was sure he did."

Han Dok-ku didn't only want to keep me away from his daughter, he hated me because I stole his woman. "Did she mention taking a test. I mean a medical test? After you last met."

"I was her closest friend."

Adam is still reeling from the revelations coming on top of each other when, on the edge of consciousness, he hears Grandmother speak into the darkness, "This is nice."

He holds his breath and listens for her footsteps through the crickets' chirps. Is Misty saying that Han Dok-ku raped JinA in a party room at the Gentlemen's Club while Adam was in Busan? It might explain the long shower, the sudden urge to drive back, the sobs.

"Are you still there?" Misty asks.

"I have to keep my voice down."

Adam hears a familiar *squeak*, the hinges on Grandmother's bedroom door, and the question that leaps from the turmoil in his mind surprises even him. "Who was the baby's father?"

A pause at the other end. "JinA-*ssi* didn't know. She hoped it was you, but there was an equal chance it was him. That man might have done God knows what so the baby wouldn't surface one day and claim his share of inheritance. It has happened before. Why didn't JinA pre-empt that by having an abortion? I blame myself. I should have taken her to a clinic rather than expect her to go on her own."

"He is to blame Misty-*ssi*. Not you and not me."

Forty-Four: August 10ᵗʰ, 2018 — Seoul, South Korea

The coffee shop where In-sung will meet us is a short walk from my hotel, in Insadong, another part of Seoul with a unique personality. The pedestrianized street is lined with art galleries and boutiques selling pottery, jewelry, and hand-painted scarves. Despite the threat of showers, tourists meander along the cobblestone pavement. The coffee shop has a European flair, with bricks the colour of espresso, cappuccino and latte, and mullioned windows open to downpour and drizzle alike. I climb to the top floor, too early for our rendezvous, but In-sung is already sitting at a table, head bent over his phone.

He rises and shakes my hand, holding my gaze this time rather than looking through me. The worry lines on his forehead dig deeper than I remember. Otherwise, he is the same straight-backed man I met last December.

We sit, and he turns his phone around. "My daughter." The video shows a little girl with a ribbon in her hair holding on to a low table. She takes four wobbly steps before sinking to the ground, her blue dress ballooning around her, a one-tooth grin on her face.

I keep an eye on the stairs while we chat: his wife is taking the baby for a check-up this morning; my son is returning to Ithaca in less than two days. In time, Kang Min-chae's head comes into view, followed by her shoulders and the rest of her, one laborious step at a time. In-sung springs to his feet. He bows twice and says something in a solicitous tone.

"It's quieter," she replies.

We order beverages, and the server disappears to a lower floor. Time for my big scene. I manage to say what I have come to say without major errors and touch the phone's play button.

In-sung watches both videos straight through then asks me to replay each and pause whenever he needs Kang Min-chae to interpret. His expression remains neutral. He compares the metadata with a table of numbers on a printout.

The server brings our cups and leaves. In-sung ignores his coffee and transcribes Adam's words on a yellow pad. I should have done that myself to save him time. I could probably do it from memory. The words are innocuous, yet it feels like laying us both naked in front of In-sung and Kang Min-chae.

In-sung re-reads his notes: "'Joanne-*ah*, hello,'" he says.

More doubts assail me. Did I come here to legitimize what we had? To throw it in In-sung's face?

He stirs his coffee but doesn't drink. "Times can be—" He searches for the right word, "changed."

"Can't the videos be analyzed? I mean, isn't there a way for experts to figure out whether the timestamp has been tampered with?"

In-sung raises the cup to his mouth and drinks. I wait until he lowers it to see the expression on his face. A smile, possibly at my naiveté. "We find someone, but make alibi…" he says a word in Korean and turns to Kang Min-chae for help, "suspect." He scratches his head. "Why Dae-hyun-*ssi* not tell police right away?"

"Nerves?" offers Kang Min-chae. "Maybe they only asked if anyone saw him leave the guesthouse?"

In-sung considers the possibility while drinking a few more sips. "Well, is okay alibi." He raises his fist in the air and says something that sounds like, "fighting."

Kang Min-chae interprets. "Kim In-sung-*ssi* will not surrender without a fight."

There are details to attend to, phone calls In-sung must make at another table while Kang Min-chae and I gaze out the window. Teenagers in school uniforms spill out of an art gallery and mill around on the cobblestones, talking in excited tones.

I can't follow what In-sung is saying. Kang Min-chae translates the main points. "He needs to take you to the public prosecutor's office in Cheongju. That's where the case will be tried." She offers me a mint. "You'll have to hand over your phone and sign an affidavit."

My Adam phone. I expected as much, but losing that illusory link to him is like abandoning all hope that he will ever call. I quell the tears that threaten to spill.

"Can't you come as well?"

"His wife is using the family car," she says. "His other car only has two seats."

We are in an underground garage, and I stand by the passenger door of Adam's sports car, looking at In-sung over the roof. How wounded Adam must have felt to give it away.

"He loved this car," In-sung says.

As we reach the highway, scenes from last December's drive play in my private cinema: Adam pointing at an owl perched on a tree with branches interlaced against the winter sky, reeds with crinkled hair blowing in the wind, horses galloping up a slope and veering in unison as if to a signal only they could hear; me, sulking, refusing to accept the fleeting moments of beauty he wanted to share; allowing movie-star stereotypes to mask that Adam, despite his foreign-ness, remained a kindred spirit.

In-sung weaves through traffic, shifts gear up and down hills and along sharp curves, letting the tires screech at his rough handling. He is oblivious to brooks rushing past and willows drooping their branches along the road.

I ask him for a map that I unfold slowly to prevent obstructing his view; it is all in Korean. I try to match the scenery to the topography. Hopeless. The windshield wipers sweep fields, crops and cows to the same manic beat.

In-sung stretches a finger to a point on the map. "He's there," he says. "I saw him three days ago." We pass a school bus, yellow like ours. "He like to chop wood."

In short sentences punctuated by long pauses, he paints a picture of Adam living with his grandmother, tending a garden and running errands once a week. He says nothing about his mood. I don't expect him to spend each day with a smile on his lips, happy for the forced vacation. I wish we could stop and watch from a distance. See how he's doing but not test how he feels. Avoid an in-person rejection.

In the distance, Cheongju looks like a miniature Seoul: white apartment towers, although not as high, and mountains close by, although fewer.

"They never handle a case like this before," In-sung says at a traffic light. He explains that the prosecutor plans to run for a seat on the National Assembly next spring and expects the visibility of the trial to propel him to victory. "Always big delays when ask for evidence—" He shakes his head. "Police worse. They not search his *hendepone* when in jail and give to him when leave. Police should keep *hendepone* and make him unlock."

Only after the second time do I realize that he is saying "handphone," cell phone.

"Prosecutor, very angry. Police must go and ask. But Dae-hyun say he lose." At a stop sign, In-sung presses a button and the roof lifts away. Banners hang over the streets announcing what looks like a fair. Now that the rain has stopped, families walk in the direction opposite ours, children skipping ahead of their parents.

"We look for *hendepone* together." In-sung downshifts while climbing a hill. "He say drop it under wood. Took long time to move wood and store under house. *Hendepone* flat ... like beer can.

"I say no one believe is accident and he angry. Say 'quashed'—Is that right word? 'Squashed,' yes, thank you—squashed between logs. He ... hmm ... strong head but I ask and ask. Change story: fell out of pocket to chopping block. He bring axe down and try to—"

"Deflect the blow?"

"Yes. But still hit *hendepone*. He swore he talk true." In-sung checks his side mirrors. "*Hendepone* card broken. Prosecutor cross-examine hard on *hendepone* if Adam on witness stand."

This is not the In-sung I met in December. He hoarded information and doled out only what he thought I needed to know. Now he keeps going even though he trips over his limited English. Maybe he has nobody else to share these stories with.

In-sung leads the way to a building painted in swirls of mauve and green. We take an elevator and reach the public prosecutor's suite. Despite the calls In-sung made from Seoul, we have to wait before being shown into the office of the assistant public prosecutor, a tall woman in a pale grey suit.

In-sung explains why we have come, going by his hand gestures. He asks me to show my phone and refers to it many times.

The woman's black hair frames alabaster skin set off by glistening pink lipstick. She shoots dubious looks at In-sung and occasionally at me, as if she cannot fathom what Adam ever saw in the frumpy woman before her. My lip gloss has faded long ago, my curls turned frizzy, and my clothes—a wrinkled blouse and capri pants—belong at a campground rather than a government office.

It looks as if In-sung and the woman have dealt with each other before. We are seated now, and the verbal match continues. He attacks with emphatic nods and she parries with shakes of the head. His voice is forceful while hers is conciliatory, yet immovable. Somehow, he manages to convince her to view the videos.

Her demeanour says "So what?" I feel like crawling into a hole. She asks rapid-fire questions, and In-sung waits for her to finish. He replies in a few words. He turns to me and translates what he is telling her: the reasons Ahn Dae-hyun sent the videos are not important, only the timing of the last one is. Once in a while, I hear a word that could be "affidavit."

More talk, ending with a request for us to wait.

"Prosecutor is at fair," In-sung tells me. "She say come back in the morning." He shakes his head. Ludicrous. He convinced her this had to be done today.

It is not dinnertime yet, but we skipped lunch. He suggests a place nearby.

We sit under a dark green umbrella on an otherwise deserted patio. Humidity hangs in the air and makes our clothes stick to our skin. In-sung takes his jacket off and rolls his shirt sleeves, exposing an expensive-looking watch. We order from a girl in pigtails who seems too young to wait on tables. Our cold soups—In-sung's suggestion— arrive in plate-sized steel bowls with pieces of ice floating in the broth.

There are times when enjoying food is indecent, and this is one of them. I recognize slices of cucumber and a hard-boiled egg; the rest is a mystery, will forever remain a mystery. We have more pressing matters on our minds. "What about the rumours online?" I ask.

Light drains from the sky. Fast. Dime-sized drops splash on the stones, and the sky rips open. Rain pummels the umbrella. We stand behind a curtain of water, cut off from the rest of the world. "Bad,"

In-sung replies to my earlier question, pitching his voice above the deluge's din.

Lightning throws the scene into the arc light of a film set, then it's darkness. Thunder rumbles deep into the earth. "Bad people. Not true."

Forty-Five: August 10th to 11th, 2018 — Cheongju and Danyang, South Korea

The downpour forced the public prosecutor to go home and change before coming to the courthouse. He seemed approachable, charming even, not the arrogant man I imagined. He insisted that we work through an official interpreter, which added another hour to our wait. Still, I did what I had come to do: I left my phone as evidence with the Cheongju authorities and signed an affidavit attesting that the video supporting Adam's alibi was genuine and had not been tampered with. Both In-sung and the prosecutor assured me that neither side, defence or prosecution, would ask me to testify in person or remotely as a result.

In the elevator, In-sung is as close to ecstatic as I've ever seen him. "Thank you," he says repeatedly, bowing each time. "This could save him."

What balm, what vindication to banish the doubts I harboured in coming here. He opens the car's door and says, "*You* tell Dae-hyun."

It's so unexpected, I don't know what to say.

"No, I can't," finally comes out. I am not ready to face him.

Walking around to the other side, In-sung doesn't hear. He fastens his seatbelt and checks his watch. "Half-hour." On the ramp to the highway, drizzle begins to fall.

"Maybe we should call ahead?" I say.

"Ah, hmm, Dae-hyun no *hendepone*. Grandmother has." He makes no move to contact her.

I hesitate, but I will never find a better chance. "That photo. The woman who says he … raped her?"

"Bad man gave money."

What does he mean? A bad man paid her to fabricate the story and picture? Or a bad man paid her to trap Adam with the picture? Or is In-sung spinning a tale to protect his friend?

"He hurt another woman. JinA? Someone saw him," I say.

"Help look like hurt."

How?

We speed along in the dark, each wrapped in our own thoughts.

A few nights ago, in search of fruits near my hotel, I chanced on a public square where people watched a shadow theatre performance. In a bedchamber behind a paper door, a woman in a loose dress unpinned a long braid of hair coiled around her head. A man in a wide-brimmed hat sat on the ledge outside her room with his back to her, legs dangling over the ground. He took a thick rope from the depth of a sleeve and began to caress it while the woman stroked her hair against the length of her arm. She rubbed lotion on her face; he ran his rope against his cheek and brought it to his nose, drawing laughter from the crowd.

The woman behind the paper door started to pluck a daisy, and the petals appeared to fall on the man's head. He extended a hand, touched the brim of his hat and pulled out one petal after another, enough to make a whole daisy by pressing them to the side of his hat. Accompanying music alternated between hope and sorrow—he loves me, he loves me not; he loves me still, he doesn't love me anymore.

We have reached the road that zigzags up and down the mountain, scary enough in broad daylight and downright terrifying on a night of drizzle. I pray that In-sung knows what he is doing.

Soon, we roll through the gate and stop on the wet gravel. In the car's headlights, the *hanok* looks forlorn. In-sung lowers his window and listens for movement. "I'm sure someone hear."

Nothing stirs save for rain dripping from the notches in the roof. In-sung wants me to stay in the car while he retrieves umbrellas from the trunk. Since there is no escaping from meeting Adam, I am too anxious to wait. I run up the steps to the house and knock on the door.

In-sung touches my hand. "This way." He walks along the ledge and rounds the closest corner. Light shines from a room, and a voice, *his* voice, asks a question that In-sung answers in English. "Is me. With surprise."

He makes space for me to step into the light, and there is Adam, standing just steps away. He wears loose shorts and a stained T-shirt. He looks even more haggard than I expected. He smiles—tentatively—as he looks from me to In-sung and back. "You came," he says, as if asking, "Why are you here after I said I didn't want you in my life anymore?"

"Joanne-*ssi* give you great alibi," In-sung says, and Adam's expression goes from puzzled to hopeful to radiant as his friend explains.

Adam slaps his forehead with a hand. "I'd completely forgotten." He takes a step toward me, but something stops him. In-sung asks a question in Korean, and he replies in English, "Yes, this calls for a celebration. I'll tell Grandmother."

It has stopped raining. In the Great Room, with the lights burning bright, we sit on floor cushions around a low table. Adam is on my right, and his grandmother, on my left.

She ignores her glass of champagne and clasps my hand, thanking me repeatedly, bowing like In-sung, but with tears, and the exclamation Kang Min-chae uses so liberally, "*Aigoo!*"

For Grandmother's benefit, the conversation is in Korean, with a few asides to me in English. In-sung places the cake we bought in Cheongju, a white confection decorated with cascades of glazed fruit, on top of its box. No one makes a move to cut it. I yearn not for sweets but for a few moments alone with Adam. His hand trails on the floor; I long to take it, but what if he pulls away?

In-sung's phone rings. He needs to hurry home. And I must finish packing. If I miss my flight tomorrow, I'll have to impose on Emma to meet Sean at the Syracuse airport when he returns from California.

We rise, and Grandmother says something that, from the direction of her gaze, concerns me. "I'm sorry," Adam says. "I should have asked… Would you like to freshen up?"

Freshen up? Is this all he's going to say?

"Good idea." In-sung drains the last of his Dom Perignon.

"This way," Adam says. I follow him along the ledge to the back of the *hanok* where he opens a door and turns on a light.

The bathroom is twice the size of the one we used in December. Tears swim in my eyes as I sit on the toilet. I never should have come. He meant what he said on the phone all those months ago.

Struggling for composure, I stand at the sink and splash water over my face.

The next thing I know, arms encircle me from behind, blanket me in warmth. "Joanne-*ah.*"

I wriggle out, instinct slamming on the brakes, and face him.

He looks miserable, schooling his lips to stop trembling. "I did not murder Baek Young-hee, Joanne-*ah.* I swear. I did not beat JinA. She was too tired to drive. I pulled her away from her car. I may have been rougher than I intended, but I didn't push her to the ground. Her legs gave out." His tiger eyes plead with me to believe him. "I did not rape that other woman, Joanne-*ah.* She gave me her address and opened the door. Wide. Someone paid her to manufacture a scandal."

How can I be sure he's not lying?

"I'm sorry for what I said on the phone. I've regretted it ever since." He searches my eyes. "Even if you don't have those feelings anymore, may I love you, silently, in my heart?"

A lump rises in my throat. I sense what he doesn't say: loving me will help him through his ordeal. "I love you, Adam." I hug him, bringing back memories of our early days, when his respect for my wishes was unwavering, even when they went counter to his own.

We kiss, forgetting seven long months of estrangement, the media attacks that eroded my trust, and the trial in less than three weeks. We stop only long enough to fill our senses with the sight of each other, the scent of each other, and kiss again.

"Don't cry." He wipes tears from my cheeks.

"I'm not crying." I laugh, and laughter fills his beautiful eyes.

"Adam," I say, if only to hear his name fill the space between us, for the comfort of saying it aloud.

We return to In-sung and Grandmother hand in hand. We hug, tight, long, and warm, and I get in the two-seater that used to be his. He keeps pace as the car rolls along the driveway and through the gate, waves, and blows me a kiss. Hope thunders in my heart.

It is morning, and Seoul offers its first blue sky since I arrived. The train to the airport rushes over mudflats awash with birds: pelicans standing at the water's edge, ducks bent over the shallows, and sandpipers with long pointed bills, lifting in waves and landing again as if to have one more delicacy buried in the silt before they set off, this time for good.

Forty-Six: August 15th to 31st — Seoul, South Korea

Adam would be inclined to view Joanne's visit as a figment of his imagination, except that Grandmother has taken to patting his hand and saying, "Nice woman." It is as if he was crossing a desert for weeks on end and came upon an oasis, quenched his thirst for the briefest of moments then returned to sand and grit, to *mori, mori, mori*, hair, hair, hair, as the crickets like to remind him every night, all night long.

With less than three weeks to go until the trial, the question of how he should react at various points of the proceedings occupies his legal team as much as the evidence. He is to convey humility, respect, and sincerity at all times. Neo-Confucianism for the age of cameras.

Attorney Choi is not planning to call Adam to the witness stand. The accused typically makes their case worse under cross-examination. "Besides," he says, "you were never at the scene of the crime."

Nevertheless, against the eventuality that Attorney Choi changes his mind, he insists on a half-day of training. The rules are not given to Adam beforehand but explained whenever he makes a mistake. Often. His job is to provide clear yet brief answers and remain calm whenever the attorney who acts as the public prosecutor tries to provoke him into getting defensive, angry, or argumentative. "Think of it as a game of chess," his attorney says, "but without the option to attack. The calmer you remain, the more pieces you keep," another way of saying, "the first one who gets angry loses."

"You know you will be taken into custody on Sunday night?" Attorney Choi asks.

Why doesn't he just say "jail?"

Forty-Seven: September 3rd, 2018 — Cheongju, South Korea

The police van approaches the courthouse amid progressively louder shouts. The vehicle stops, and the crowd bangs on the sides. The four guards escorting Adam spring up from their seats to stand by the back exit, holding plexiglass shields. At the sound of a whistle, they open the doors. Blinding sunlight.

Outside, four more guards struggle to hold the crowd in check, leaving barely enough space for Adam to jump. *Are you crazy?* he thinks. The men in the van hold him under the armpits and lower him into the pocket of safety secured by their teammates.

While in mid-air, Adam looks for In-sung. He sees only scowling faces, hears only shouts of "MURDERER," "RAPIST," and "WOMAN BEATER." The sun blazes overhead. By the time the phalanx protecting Adam reaches the elevator, his shirt sticks to his back.

After a brief ride, the doors slide open, and In-sung greets him. "Sleep alright?"

Adam shoots him a look. *What do you think?* They march. Between the bodies shielding him, Adam glimpses wall, door, wall, door. He finds himself in the courtroom before realizing they passed through any entrance.

The room is immense, church-like, with a high ceiling and rows of wooden pews. Every seat is taken, and a hush falls over the crowd as Adam and In-sung walk to the front, their progress relayed to the masses by one of two cameras at the front, in the corner opposite the defence table.

Attorney Choi takes both of Adam's hands in his and they greet each other with formal bows, a piece of theatre he did not expect. Oddly, it settles his nerves, and he sits more or less composed as Judge Yeom makes his entrance. He is the judge who presided over the pre-trial hearing, with the same drooping jowls and bags under the eyes. Of the two assessors, one is a man, and the other, a woman. She reminds Adam of his grade five teacher, an unforgiving woman: moon-shaped face, narrow eyes and a thin line of red on lips that never curl into a smile.

The bailiff calls for order, and Judge Yeom asks the accused and his counsel to rise. "Ahn Dae-hyun-*ssi*," he says, "to the charge against you of murder in the first degree on the person of Baek Young-hee-*ssi*, between the night of Wednesday, January tenth of this year and the following morning, Thursday, the eleventh, at the Danyang Guesthouse, how do you plead?"

Bile rises to Adam's throat and he forces it down while his legal counsel speaks. "My client pleads not guilty, Your Honour." Adam's legs feel like tofu as he settles back on his chair.

Judge Yeom states that Adam's attorneys asked for, and were granted, a trial without jury on the ground that it would be next to impossible to find impartial jurors given the rumours swirling in the media.

Public Prosecutor Park rises to make his opening remarks, alternating between facing the bench and the spectators. His lengthy address concludes with, "The victim, beautiful, talented Baek Young-hee-*ssi*, realizing she was in mortal danger, took one last desperate action to point the finger at her assailant. We will show, beyond a reasonable doubt, that her assailant was none other than the man sitting there." He looks straight at the actor.

One camera remains on Adam, while the other swivels to the audience, catching people nodding in agreement. In the front row, Baek Young-hee's husband, a handsome man with strong features, her mother, wiping tears, and her father, shoulders bent under the weight of sorrow, clasp each other's hands.

Adam wishes his parents were there to show their support. In the back row, he spots his grandmother and Kang Min-chae sitting together. The screenwriter raises a hand to her ear in a discreet greeting. On his second sweep in her direction, she points to the man sitting one row ahead, Han Dok-ku.

Adam tries to hide his shock, but it is like trying to ignore an eyelash in one's eye. He takes a steadying breath, knowing that a million people will see his chest rise and subside, and draw all sorts of conclusions from an act that everyone does thousands of times a day.

Attorney Choi's opening remarks cover the same ground as in the pre-trial hearing: circumstantial evidence with perfectly benign explanations; the sleeping pill Adam admits to giving the deceased—not *administered* to her, and certainly not *tricked* her into ingesting; the ready availability of Adam's hair from salons and possibly combs and brushes at film locations.

"Public Prosecutor Park has not offered a single word on a possible motive. What would my client gain from the death of the leading actress in his upcoming film? Mischief-makers speculate that box office receipts would go through the roof. In reality, the passing of an actor always leads to significant delays in finishing a project, sometimes years, a situation no director would ever willfully cause.

"The evidence against a defendant in a first-degree murder case must be clear and unambiguous: innocent until proven guilty. Social media have sullied the names of both the deceased and my client by casting her death as a crime of passion. There is not a scrap of evidence that supports this notion. She was a fellow artist, a co-worker, and a friend. He is utterly devastated by her untimely departure from this world."

Finally, someone is telling his side of the story. Tears prickle Adam's eyes, and he lets them flow. Attorney Choi sits and clasps Adam's hand while In-sung hands him a pack of tissues.

The same counsel who assisted Public Prosecutor Park at the pre-trial hearing calls the owner of the Danyang Guesthouse to the witness stand. A middle-aged woman walks up the aisle with clickety-clack steps that echo against the walls.

Under the assistant prosecutor's questioning, the owner describes the arrival of the cast and crew on the evening of Sunday, January 7th and, with the help of floor plans projected on twin monitors, the layout of the guesthouse: the residents' lounge on the ground floor, the bunk rooms where the crew slept, and Baek Young-hee's private room on the first floor.

In-sung scribbles on his legal pad: "Are you okay?" Adam makes a checkmark on his.

The assistant prosecutor moves to the wrap party on the night of January 10th. "Where were you at the time?"

"I was at the reception counter." The witness describes the party as rowdy, with many people drunk, including Ahn Dae-hyun.

Adam struggles to look unperturbed. Faking no emotion is much harder than faking emotions. In-sung adds another question mark to his earlier one and, try as he might, Adam cannot make his check mark as light as before.

The guesthouse owner testifies that Baek Young-hee drank mostly bottled cold tea poured into a beer glass. She was the first guest to go to her room, around 22:45.

"Can you tell the court what happened next?"

"Yes, within minutes, a man who did not have a room at the guesthouse followed her."

Prompted by the assistant prosecutor, the guesthouse owner identifies Adam, and the three men at the defence table shake their heads.

"If you could now turn your attention to the following morning, starting with a wake-up call you made," the assistant prosecutor says.

"Ah, yes. Baek Young-hee-*ssi* had asked me to give her a wake-up call. At six o'clock."

In the laborious way counsel question witnesses, the guesthouse owner testifies that she tried three times by phone before going to her door and knocking repeatedly while calling the actor's name. Receiving no answer, she unlocked the door with her master key. "Baek Young-hee-*ssi* lay in the bathtub. Her face was underwater." The owner looks horrified. Baek Young-hee's parents and husband cry openly.

The assistant prosecutor gives them a moment to compose themselves. "And did you go farther into the bathroom? To help her, perhaps?"

"I did not. Her eyes were wide open." She demonstrates. Her seat faces the judge's bench, with the prosecution table on the left and the defence table on the right. People in the audience can only see her back, however, the camera catches the scene and relays it to the two monitors and anyone watching the broadcast. "Her mouth too," the woman adds. "I could tell she was dead. I called 119." She looks immensely sad.

Adam forces himself not to look at the audience. He focuses elsewhere: In-sung rolling his ankles under the table; Attorney Choi writing on his legal pad with a fountain pen. Adam practices a mantra the attorney gave him: *It's not too awful. I can take this.*

Court resumes after lunch with Attorney Choi cross-examining the guesthouse owner. He asks for the slides with the floor plans to be shown again, starting with the ground floor. He reassures the witness that he has only a few easy questions regarding the guesthouse's layout. He points to an area with four self-contained washrooms. "Are there additional washrooms on the ground floor?"

"No."

He calls for the next slide with the plan for the floor above and points to two self-contained washrooms. "Are visitors, by which I mean people who do not have a room at the guesthouse, allowed to use these facilities?"

The owner makes a sour face. "Visitors should use the ground-floor washrooms."

Attorney Choi guides her to revisit her assertion that Adam followed Baek Young-hee to her room. She reluctantly agrees that he might have had a different reason for climbing the stairs, such as wanting to use an upstairs washroom.

Relief washes over Adam, although he has no recollection of using an upstairs washroom on the day of the wrap party. "Reasonable doubt," writes In-sung on his legal pad.

At the table opposite, the prosecutor and his assistant cultivate impassive looks, repressing any show of agitation.

Attorney Choi thanks the guesthouse owner, hand on chest, "From the bottom of my heart." He bows. Adam and In-sung do likewise. Adam's eyes well up, and a few tears spot the defence table.

The coroner testifies next. His main contribution is to attest that the time of death occurred between 23:30 that night and 01:00 the next day.

The video Adam left Joanne confirms he arrived at the *hanok* at 23:23 p.m. However, the prosecutor's emphasis on pinpointing the latest possible time of death telegraphs where he is going. He can still argue that Adam had time to go home and drive back to the guesthouse.

The public prosecutor calls the detective in charge of the investigation to the witness stand, and the man marches up the centre aisle. No rumpled jeans or two days' growth of beard this morning. He wears a beige suit with a matching tie.

"Will you please describe the scene as you saw it when you arrived in the victim's room at the guesthouse in Danyang?" the prosecutor asks.

Attorney Choi rises. "Objection, Your Honour. Only if murder has been proven beyond a reasonable doubt can anyone refer to Baek Young-hee-*ssi* as 'the victim.' She should remain 'the deceased' throughout these proceedings."

"Objection sustained."

The prosecutor bows toward the bench and signals for a photograph to be projected on the twin monitors. The guesthouse room has a single bed on one side and a rectangular table with two chairs on the other. The table holds a suitcase, a kettle, and two mugs. There is no closet or wardrobe, only hooks on the walls with hangers that hold Baek Young-hee's clothes, including a black zip-up sweater.

Next come photographs of the bathroom, starting with the floor where a toothbrush, toothpaste tube and plastic cup are scattered—the "evidence of a struggle." Adam hears gasps from the audience. For him, it is not as awful as it could have been, since he already saw these pictures at the pre-trial hearing.

The prosecutor wrings one detail after another from the detective: "Was the mattress heater on?" or, "Were the curtains drawn?"

Why should any of this matter, Adam wonders. Sitting still and looking engaged, yet neutral, requires all the effort he can muster. He resorts to imagining Joanne next to him, holding her hand under the table. His breathing eases but not for long. The next photograph shows Baek Young-hee from the shoulders up, her hair floating, Medusa-like, around her head, horror on her face.

In the front row, her mother covers her face with both her hands.

The prosecutor probes the water level and the temperature, and Adam's mind wanders. *Who did this?* The male assessor watches him, and Adam shakes his head, *No, I had nothing to do with this.*

More photos: her legs, knees bent above the water; a close-up of her left hand, open wide; her right hand, clenched tightly.

"Did you look inside that hand?" the prosecutor asks.

"We tried, but *rigor mortis* had already set in."

"Meaning that she had already been dead for some time, is that correct?"

The word "dead" echoes in Adam's head, and he does not know how to react. It is like a heavy rock pressing on his chest, and yet, to the eyes watching him, any sign of distress is bound to look like guilt. Adam tries to steady his breathing while the judge and assessors file out, and In-sung and Attorney Choi whisper in each other's ears behind their hands.

Forty-Eight: September 4th, 2018 — Cheongju, South Korea

The next day begins after a night of tossing and turning on the narrow bed in Adam's cell; a night spent hearing the night guard grunt and sigh as he watched porn on his phone and fumbled with his crotch. The toilet disinfectant has invaded his nose, his lungs, and his blood. His clothes have absorbed the sickly-sweet smell, and when the police escort comes for him, it follows them into the van and through the mayhem outside the courthouse. "MURDERER," "RAPIST," "WOMAN BEATER."

In the courtroom. Attorney Choi appears calm and rested., In-sung looks like he hasn't slept a wink.

The prosecution calls the Director of Forensic Analysis at the National Forensic Service in Seoul, Doctor Cha. She wears a khaki pantsuit and matching walking shoes that make no sound as she walks to the witness stand. More pictures are enlarged on the monitors. More talk about what was where, what was in the mugs—tea bags and dregs of tea.

In-sung writes a question mark on his pad, and Adam answers with a light check mark.

Doctor Cha projects a slide of the electrophoresis she ran with amplified extracts from each of the hair strands clasped in Baek Young-hee's hand in the five central columns, flanked by the two separate mouth swabs Adam provided. The patterns leave no doubt; they match perfectly. Attorney Choi declines to cross-examine the witness, to the apparent relief of the assessors who were eyeing the clock, eager for a break.

Baek Young-hee's husband and parents stare at Adam with swollen eyes. Kang Min-chae and his grandmother show no emotions. Adam had hoped to come across them in the hallways but the path to the conference room set aside for his legal team never passes through the public corridors. Same for trips to the washroom, where four guards always accompany him, two standing inside and two outside.

This time, as they walk back to the conference room, a head peeks from the women's washroom and retreats swiftly. Did Adam dream it? Wasn't that Yu-mi, spooked when his eyes met hers?

The pathologist who conducted the autopsy, a white-haired man named Doctor Im, is sworn in. He wears granny glasses and looks like someone who would have trouble boarding a subway car in the morning rush, forever pushed aside by other commuters.

This time, the courtroom is treated to a video. The forensic pathologist wears a lab coat, giving him the air of authority he might lack in the tweed suit he has underneath. The video camera surveys the legs of Baek Young-hee, both front and back. Her face looks more placid than in yesterday's photographs, although the frozen stare is no less chilling. Adam is past caring that the camera catches him hanging his head, filled anew with sorrow for losing a woman with such talent and kindness. People may interpret his reaction as they want—shame, remorse, guilt. There is nothing he can do to change that. Once again, he imagines Joanne sitting by his side, telling him with the pressure of her hand that she believes him no matter what.

On the courtroom screens, the pathologist lifts the hair at the back of Baek Young-hee's head and shines a light on a purplish bruise. "This shows that the deceased sustained a blow to the head."

"Can you tell us what kind of object might have done this?" asks the prosecutor.

"This bruise was likely caused by her head hitting the edge of the tub."

"As might happen if she was pushed by her assailant?"

"The evidence is consistent with that scenario, yes."

"Was this blow the actual cause of death?"

"No. We will see later that water infiltrated her lungs. She drowned."

The video restarts. A broad-shouldered assistant turns the body face up on the steel table and disappears from camera range. The pathologist directs the camera toward the right hand. The clenched fingers from the crime scene pictures have loosened considerably. In close-up, strands of hair lie dark against Baek Young-hee's pale hands.

All eyes are on Adam. It's not too awful. I can take this, he tells himself, although he is shaking; tiny tremors that feel like he is outside in the cold, naked and alone. Baek Young-hee's mother struggles to control her sobs. Her husband wraps an arm around her shoulders and takes her outside.

In the video, the pathologist collects the strands of hair between tweezers and deposits each in a separate evidence bag held by someone out of camera range.

The testimony continues. Adam disconnects, the image of the five strands lying in Baek Young-hee's hand seared in his brain. What if someone at the National Forensic Service changed the hair in the sample for his hair, rather than what his legal team assumed, namely that the real murderer planted the hair? That's a possibility neither In-sung nor Attorney Choi has mentioned.

As soon as court adjourns, Adam voices his theory. His counsellors look at him with pity. Attorney Choi explains that samples go through a chain-of-evidence process so rigorous at the National Forensic Service that tampering is virtually impossible.

The crowd outside is louder than this morning and larger than yesterday. People hold signs plastered with captions like, *Ahn Da-hyun deserves DEATH*.

"Please keep your head down," the lead guard says as they march through. Once they have all climbed in, the van shakes, rocked by the crowd, while Adam's tremors continue.

How can you SLEEP at night? one sign screamed.

His cell reeks of disinfectant. A wave of nausea rises in his throat whenever he lies flat. He sits on the bunk, resigned to staying that way for the whole night if he wants to hold in whatever threatens to spew forth. His mind circles to the autopsy video, the inert body lying on the metal table, the wound at the back of the head, the straight strands of hair lying against Baek Young-hee's pale palm, the tweezers collecting each strand and transferring it to a separate evidence bag held by a hand with a slim wrist. I am dreaming, Adam tells himself. Impossible. But the more he sits in this half-dream state, the less improbable it seems.

Forty-Nine: September 5th, 2018 — Cheongju, South Korea

Hope, dangerous, beguiling hope, fills Adam's chest as he dresses in the morning. The police van arrives at the courthouse earlier than usual, and the crowd is thinner, quieter, except for a group he has not noticed before: people holding signs with messages of support for him.

"We BELIEVE in you," they shout as police guards rush him through the doors and into a waiting elevator. In-sung beams at Adam and hands him a printout. The picture is grainy, yet the bracelet, with porous black beads and gold Buddhas, is unmistakable.

By the time Attorney Choi joins them in the courtroom, the two counsel have at most ten minutes to confer before the public rushes in and the trial resumes. Adam's Attorney begins to cross-examine the pathologist by asking the clerk to project a photograph taken at the guesthouse. Baek Young-hee's clenched hand fills the twin screens. Only her husband attends the proceedings this morning.

"Dr. Im, as we see, the deceased's right hand was folded in a tight grip when the police gathered evidence at the scene."

"Indeed." Despite his meek appearance, the pathologist projects a quiet confidence bolstered by many years of experience as an expert witness.

"Can you tell us if you took note of the state of the hand when you began the autopsy? I ask because we heard nothing about it yesterday." Attorney Choi turns to the bench, implying they were denied crucial information.

The pathologist's lips purse as if he agrees that relevant information was withheld. He consults a blue binder. "I examined both hands in detail at the start of the autopsy. It's standard procedure. I certainly noted the tight clenching of the right hand."

"Can you tell us if you noticed any difference from what we are seeing on the screen?"

The pathologist reviews his notes again. "I did. In the photograph taken at the scene, four of the fingers are folded so tightly that we can only see the deceased's thumbnail. In fact, the thumb is folded right over the other fingers. I understand that the police photographed the scene around mid-morning of the day in question, and death occurred no less than eight hours earlier. That's long enough for *rigor mortis* to have set in completely.

"I conducted the autopsy two days later and saw evidence that *rigor mortis* was releasing its hold. The thumb was not clenched as tightly. I noted seeing three nails out of the four folded fingers." He demonstrates with his hand, leaving only the nail of the finger closest to the thumb hidden.

"Now, concerning the strands of hair you recovered later, did you notice any tips protruding outside the clenched hand when you began the autopsy?"

The pathologist takes the time to consider the question and consult his notes. "I saw nothing protruding outside the clenched fingers. I would have noted it."

Attorney Choi repeats the expert witness's words as he jots them down. "In light of what you found later, would you have expected to see at least a portion of what was clenched in the deceased's hand before the hand fully relaxed?"

"Objection, Your Honour." The public prosecutor rises. "Speculative. The defence counsel must limit his questions to the facts of the case."

"Your Honour, we have the benefit of a seasoned expert," Attorney Choi says. "The case against my client rests on this crucial piece of evidence: hair with DNA matching his, assumed to have been pulled by the deceased seconds before she died; or, possibly, hair placed in her hand by a third party at an opportunistic moment."

The judge whispers to each assessor in turn.

"You are aware that the defence is at liberty to call its own expert witness to render such an opinion," he says, implying that Adam's counsel runs a serious risk in soliciting an untested opinion from a prosecution witness.

Attorney Choi turns to Adam for permission and, once granted, addresses the judge again. "Your Honour, in the interest of saving everyone's valuable time, the defence wishes to hear Dr. Im's view."

The prosecutor, seated by now, waves away with his hand. *Fine. Hang yourselves.*

Attorney Choi repeats his question, and the pathologist blinks several times. "I must say, this puzzled me at the time. In my experience, when someone grasps somebody's hair"—he demonstrates by clawing at an imaginary head—"the strands tend to catch *between* their fingers rather than inside the hand. It seemed strange, though I have seen too many strange occurrences in my professional life to dismiss it as impossible."

"You must admit that it seemed too neat."

"One might say that."

Attorney Choi remains the consummate professional. No smile. No gloating. "Now, we come to the autopsy itself. We saw a video yesterday, an *edited* video. You were in it, and a camera operator was present, naturally. This court saw someone turn the deceased's body and possibly someone else holding evidence bags for you to deposit"—he clears his throat—"the strands of hair. Counting your good self, that makes four people in the room by my reckoning. Is this correct?"

"Yes."

"Can you give this court the names of these people?"

"Of course. They are all members of our staff. There was—"

"Objection, Your Honour." The public prosecutor rises again. "Useless line of enquiry. This court should not waste 'valuable time' reviewing the National Forensic Service's operations."

Attorney Choi bows to the judge. "Your Honour, if you would allow the question. The identity of anyone who assisted in an autopsy is a matter of public record. The court will soon see where this is leading."

The prosecutor grumbles about fishing expeditions, however, the judge rules that the question should be answered.

The pathologist names those present, and Adam holds his breath. One name, two names then it comes, "Han Yu-mi."

He locates Grandmother in the back row and gives her a hopeful look. His eyes travel to the centre of the court, and he notices a floppy mint-coloured hat on a woman sitting beside Han Dok-ku. The wearer keeps her head down.

"Yu-mi is here," he writes on his legal pad. In-sung replies with a check mark that fills half the page.

Adam's mind swirls with theories on the role she most certainly played in this drama. Why? What was she doing at the National Forensic Service? Wasn't she supposed to be studying medicine in America? What crazy coincidence put her in the room where Baek Young-hee's autopsy took place?

"May counsel approach the bench?" Attorney Choi asks.

The group holds a whispered conversation, with much shaking of heads, yet no sign of a resolution. The judge announces a break, and all four lawyers follow him out. Inside the courtroom, the forensic pathologist reviews his notes, the public fills the space with a low hum, and both Yu-mi and Han Dok-ku have disappeared.

In-sung re-enters from a side door and sits beside Adam. "We asked to subpoena Han Yu-mi-*ssi*, but the prosecutor objected. Most vehemently." He smiles. "Doesn't matter. You'll see."

By now, the judge and the two assessors have regained their seats behind the bench. Attorney Choi addresses the pathologist. "You agreed earlier that it seemed too neat for five strands of hair to rest in the deceased's hand when none showed between her fingers while her hand was clasped." He turns partly toward the bench, as stage actors do with an audience. "You have told us who was present during the autopsy." Attorney Choi pauses. "Now, remember you are still under oath. Did you, Dr. Im, deposit those hair strands in the deceased's hand?"

"I most certainly did not."

Attorney Choi nods. "And the camera operator? Could he have approached the body without you seeing him?"

"No, he could not. He did not."

"Which leaves us with two assistants. Let's start with the person who turned the body. Can you remind the court of his name?" Attorney Choi nods to the judge, who presumably approved this line of questioning. Public Prosecutor Park sits with his body angled away from the bench. He takes his glasses off and polishes them with a dark fabric square.

"Lee Soo-bong-*ssi*," answers the pathologist.

The next few questions establish that this employee has assisted Dr. Im many times, over many years, in conducting autopsies.

"Now let's focus on the other assistant, Han Yu-mi-*ssi*, as you said earlier. Same questions: how long has this employee worked at the NFS, approximately, and how many times has she assisted you in conducting autopsies?"

The pathologist blinks again. "I am not certain how long Han Yu-mi-*ssi* has been with the NFS. She normally works in Dr. Cha's laboratory."

"Dr. Cha, who testified on the DNA evidence?"

"That is correct. I only met Han Yu-mi a few hours before we began the autopsy."

Attorney Choi shows surprise. "Really? What led to that situation?"

"It came as a special request."

"By whom?"

Dr. Im clears his throat. "By the Director of the National Forensic Service."

Attorney Choi lets the implications sink in. Han Dok-ku, who returned to the courtroom without his daughter, is bending over whatever he keeps on his lap. His eyes travel up and meet Adam's while the judge says. "Attorney Choi, if you would please bring this cross-examination to a close. I have already allowed you a fair amount of leeway."

"Your Honour." He bows before returning to the pathologist. "Final question: could either of the two assistants have inserted something—for example, five strands of hair—into the hand of the deceased as it relaxed from *rigor mortis*, and while your attention was diverted to other aspects of your post-mortem examination?"

The pathologist gives the question due consideration. "It is not impossible," he finally says.

Attorney Choi repeats the words as he jots them down.

No sooner has he thanked the witness and turned on his heels than the prosecutor rises, a puzzled look on his face. "Dr. Im, I suspect that everyone is as perplexed as I am. 'Not impossible,' you said. But still rather improbable, wouldn't you agree?"

"Yes, although—"

"Thank you. That will be all," the prosecutor hastens to say. Baek Young-hee's parents have returned to the front row; they look mystified.

The judge asks the witness whether he wishes to elaborate.

"Your Honour, I meant to say that, from an autopsy point of view, all aspects of this death were consistent with an accident, a dreadful accident, until we found the hair."

Public Prosecutor Park thanks the pathologist again and announces that the prosecution rests.

Adam follows his legal team—three associate counsels in addition to Attorney Choi and In-sung—to the conference room with the photographs of former judges. In-sung looks as if he could lift a car with one hand. "Let's call the pathologist as a witness for the defence," he says as soon as the door closes.

"There is another way," Attorney Choi says.

"Re-apply to subpoena Han Yu-mi? Our chances have sky-rocketed after that cross-examination. Whatever she says, she'll look like a liar."

With all the wild thoughts zooming around Adam's head, he is still puzzled over why Yu-mi took the risk of planting evidence during a videotaped autopsy. "Couldn't she have done as much damage by doctoring the DNA tests? She worked in that lab."

"There would have been no DNA test without what was found in Baek Young-hee-*ssi*'s hand," Attorney Choi replies.

"How did she scheme to assist with that particular autopsy? That's what I'd like to know," In-sung says.

"Or how did she know Baek Young-hee-*ssi*'s hand was clenched in the first place? Only a few people knew that," Attorney Choi adds while flipping through his legal pad until he finds what he is looking for. "Change of strategy," he announces. "Except for the metadata expert to validate Ahn Dae-hyun-*ssi*'s alibi, we no longer need to call on additional witnesses. Contact the others. Divide the task amongst yourselves."

The associates who have spent months combing through the evidence and trying to poke holes trade deflated looks.

"Now," Attorney Choi commands, and the room morphs into a hive of activity.

Attorney Choi addresses In-sung and Adam. "I'm tempted to say that the defence rests. I am ready to give my closing arguments: A few pieces of circumstantial evidence. Nothing solid. No motive. And the clincher, 'It is not impossible.' More than enough to argue reasonable doubt."

A fresh wave of hope washes over Adam.

"It would take the prosecutor by surprise," In-sung says. "He must be waiting to hear what our expert witnesses say before he prepares his closing arguments."

Attorney Choi dismisses the notion with a hand. "That's his problem. However, it might help to have one more testimony. I mean, it may help *you*, Ahn Dae-hyun-*ssi*, prove that you truly are not guilty; that you won this trial on substance, not technicalities." His eyes search Adam's. "Are you willing to testify?"

Fifty: September 7th, 2018 — Ithaca, New York

What was the point of going all the way to Korea if Adam is where his lawyers did not want him to be, testifying in his own defence? For three days, I have been streaming condensed versions of his trial, subtitled in English overnight by his fans.

Here he is, raising his hand. "I solemnly swear that I will tell the truth, the whole truth, and nothing but the truth, and agree to receive punishment for perjury should there be any falsehood." He looks less bowed by the events than when I visited him, although his face is still gaunt, his cheeks hollow. "I love you, Adam," I beam through the ether. Just those words, over and over again, hoping he will feel less lonely, less scared, less vulnerable; remembering his kiss at the *hanok*, the strength he drew from knowing I believed him.

His lawyer asks, "At any point during the night of January tenth to the eleventh of this year, did you go into Baek Young-hee-*ssi*'s room at the Danyang guesthouse?"

"I did not." His tone is just right: not too forceful, not challenging, and not offended either, as if it were the simplest question in the world.

"Did you go into Baek Young-hee-*ssi*'s room at any other point during her stay at the Danyang guesthouse in January?"

"Yes, I did."

Jealousy flares inside me. I can't help it.

He explains: "She wanted to discuss an upcoming scene with me. The common room was noisy. We sat at the table in her room. She made us mugs of tea."

"When did this meeting take place?"

"The scene in question was the final one we shot, so it had to be January ninth, the day before the wrap party."

Adam and his lawyer establish that he was at the *hanok* from 23:20 onward on the night in question, that he knows Han Yu-mi "fairly well" (*What does that mean?*), and once gave her a bracelet with beads made of black lava stones and three gold heads of the Buddha.

The monitor shows a photograph of Adam taken at the prayer ceremony for *Swingtime,* and zooms in on a bracelet he wore around his left wrist. The screen splits into two, with the right side running a video clip from the autopsy, where a similar bracelet comes into view, worn on the wrist of the person assisting the pathologist in collecting evidence.

"What was your relationship with Han Yu-mi-*ssi* when you gave her that bracelet?" Attorney Choi asks.

"We were seeing each other," Adam says. Neutral expression.

Does he really feel so matter-of-fact telling the world he was "seeing" someone? He certainly kept me well hidden. "And by that do you mean 'romantically?'" (*Euphemism for sex?*)

"Yes." (*No qualms admitting it.*)

"When did you last speak with Han Yu-mi-*ssi?*"

"In June of last year." (*Ah, around the time he called me.*)

"That makes it approximately seven months before Baek Young-hee died," Adam's lawyer says. "Did anything out of the ordinary happen between you and Han Yu-mi-ssi in June of last year?"

"I told her I wanted to end the relationship." He looks shaken. The hum of whispered conversation fills the courtroom, and an annoying comment bubble added by a fan pops up, "Hell hath no fury…?"

Attorney Choi bows to the judge. No further questions.

The video shifts to the public prosecutor standing in front of Adam. "Yes or no, did you have a prescription for sleeping pills called Chalja?"

Whatever question Adam expected, it was not that one. He looks surprised. "Yes."

"Meaning a medical doctor determined that you needed this drug?"

"Occasionally. I needed it occasionally."

"Oh? What kind of occasions would those be?"

Adam's lawyer rises. "Objection, Your Honour. Not relevant to the charge my client is facing."

"I would like to hear the answer," the judge says. "Objection overruled."

"When we did night shoots. I used the pills when I needed to sleep during the day."

"And that same medical doctor presumably determined the dosage right for you?"

"Ah … yes."

"Which may not be right for someone else. Yes, or no?" The prosecutor moves closer.

"I'm afraid I don't know."

"You don't know, and yet, in your statement to the police, you admitted to giving Baek Young-hee one of your sleeping pills. Why?"

"Because I hoped it would help her get the sleep she needed."

"Because you hoped it would help her get the sleep she needed. I see." He keeps his eyes on Adam as he addresses the judge. "No further questions, Your Honour."

Adam walks to the defence table as if on autopilot. He looks stricken, and an event I had pushed to the back of my mind surfaces. Before he was arrested, while he was still reeling from Baek Young-hee's death, he called me.

"It may have been my fault," he said.

"You don't even know if she took the pill."

"But if she did, then fell asleep in her bath—I pushed the pill on her, Joanne-*ah*."

"Even so, she would have woken from coughing as soon as water entered her windpipe."

"You think?"

"I'm sure. Involuntary reflex." I wasn't sure, but it made sense.

"What if—"

"Stop torturing yourself."

I wish I could tell him again, "You did not willfully kill anyone. She could have slipped and hit her head. Who knows for sure? She was unconscious, and she drowned. It's horrible, but your pill had nothing to do with it."

Fifty-One: September 7th, 2018 — Cheongju, South Korea

In the conference room lined with judges' portraits, In-sung paces the floor while Attorney Choi writes on his legal pad, taking an occasional sip of coffee and a bite of cinnamon bun. Adam sits, his chair turned sideways from the table, as his mind replays the scene. "Take one," he said, putting a capsule of Chalja in Young-hee's hand, "Just in case."

He is barely aware of a knock on the door; of Attorney Choi and In-sung leaving. A new recollection pops into his head, "Stop torturing yourself." Joanne's face floats in his mind's eye, and he remembers what she said a month ago to comfort him, to bring him peace.

She travelled all the way to the hanok. It truly happened. I did not dream it.

"Dae-hyun-*ah*, listen, this is important." In-sung and Attorney Choi have returned.

The senior attorney sits to his right and clears his throat. "The prosecutor is offering to reduce the charge from first-degree murder to involuntary manslaughter. If you plead guilty."

"Don't do it, Dae-hyun-*ah*."

"Let him think about it," Attorney Choi tells In-sung. Addressing Adam, "You need to understand what your choices are."

He explains three possibilities from worst to best: firstly, twenty years in jail if the judge rules that he is guilty of first-degree murder, the original charge; secondly, only two years if he pleads guilty to involuntary manslaughter; thirdly, no jail time if the judge rules to acquit him.

"If he finds you guilty, we'll file an appeal. Right away," adds In-sung. "And we'll win, I guarantee you. Nobody in that courtroom testified that the *dosage* of the drug made any difference whatsoever. She slipped, knocked a few items to the floor as she tried to grab hold of the sink, hit her head on the edge of the tub hard enough to knock herself unconscious and the rest happened. Nothing you should be held responsible for."

The mid-morning break stretched into the lunch hour. They have now returned to court, taking their chances with the judge, hoping they made the right decision. The prosecutor stands at the centre of the floor, facing the judge, and delivers his closing arguments. He presents a scenario where Baek Young-hee swallowed Adam's sleeping pill, ran herself a bath, slipped on the bathroom floor before entering the tub, then fell into a sleep so deep she could not rouse herself when water started entering her lungs.

In the front row, Baek Young-hee's family draws close together. The camera, normally fixed on the accused, swivels to her husband, whose tormented expression stabs Adam like a knife.

Attorney Choi argues that every piece of evidence is circumstantial and has since been refuted in open court; that the scenario put forth by the public prosecutor in closing is only a hypothesis, a *farfetched* hypothesis, that utterly fails the test of "beyond a reasonable doubt."

Attorney Choi returns to the defence table, and In-sung whispers, "Brilliant!" Adam has not heard a word his lawyer said. His mind is stuck in a loop. "Couldn't rouse herself, couldn't rouse herself." He has already admitted to giving Baek Young-hee one of his pills. How can he expect the judge to dismiss the part it played in her death?

In their usual conference room, In-sung tosses his jacket on an empty chair. "I bet the judge and the assessors will come out with their verdict before dinnertime. They won't want to drag this through the weekend. It's too simple for words: a woman our client broke up with a year ago doctored the evidence. Dragged him through a highly public character assassination."

Adam would like to believe his friend, but he is convinced Baek Young-hee would be alive today had she not been groggy from the pill.

Cream-filled pastries have been brought in for refreshments. The smell of the toilet disinfectant rises to Adam's nose. "I'm not feeling too well," he says.

He expends his last drop of energy walking through the crowd and ignoring reporters who keep asking how confident he feels about winning.

In his cell, he collapses on the cot and stares at the ceiling. He cannot think. Too many contrary winds buffet him, keeping him beached on a desert island with no rescue in sight.

The day guard comes with food on a tray and leaves it on the floor. Adam ignores it. I'm catatonic, he thinks. That's how a doctor would describe my condition. He doesn't care. He played doctor on one occasion, and it was one occasion too many. A stupid, preventable, *fatal*, accident.

He hears movements: a door opening, footsteps approaching, voices, and he thinks, that's it. They'll ask me to rise, and I won't be able to. What can they do? Was there ever a case when the accused couldn't appear in court to hear the verdict? Too sick, which would be understandable. But petrified? A man who can't confront his actions is a coward. The shame.

He wants to shut his brain off, keep his thoughts from swirling around his head. Where's the switch to oblivion?

"Dae-hyun-*ah*," a voice in his brain says. "Sit."

So much for switching off. I'm not moving. I refuse to move.

"Dae-hyun-*ah*, what's the matter?"

He ignores the voice. *Go away.* He keeps his eyes shut, but the bed shakes. A hand touches his arm.

"Dae-hyun-*ah*."

Hyeong. He cannot say the word, however, he manages to open his eyes. In-sung's worried face bends over him. "It's a good thing you came to rest. I'd forgotten how exhausting it is to wait for a verdict. They need more time. In a way, this bodes well. The prosecutor has thrown them a curveball." He prattles on, something about "expert witness" and "no direct testimony." Adam knows what In-sung is doing. Trying to give him hope, to give himself hope, otherwise how could he justify putting his career on hold for Adam when he should have been securing the future of his wife and child?

"Get some rest," In-sung says. "I'll be back as soon as they come to a decision. Don't worry. There's no way he'll convict you." He squeezes Adam's arm. "Do you hear? Have you heard a single word I said?"

Adam assents with his eyes. *Yes. You're feeding me lies, but I'll play along.*

Adam can hardly feel his body. Even if the guard were to forget to lock up the cell, if everyone were to leave the station, he wouldn't move, couldn't move. He would still be there when they returned. He would have a pulse, and they would think he was fine. Just tired.

His mouth feels dry but drinking means sitting and that is beyond him. A mosquito has found a way in. It buzzes in Adam's ears, one side, the other. He feels wings brushing his cheek, a stinger piercing his skin. *It's not too awful. I can take this.* It gorges itself on his blood. The blood of a murderer. An involuntary murderer, but a murderer just the same.

When he was a child, he sometimes let a mosquito bite him only to watch the red liquid fill the insect's belly. When it tried to pull away, Adam would slap it. Kill it. *You want my blood? It's going to cost you your life.* What an arrogant bastard he was.

Sirens rush past. An emergency. A man is having a heart attack. A fire. A woman is drowning in a bathtub, too drugged to rouse herself, her lungs filling with water, her hair floating around her head like a Medusa. He should have warned her not to take a bath.

Fifty-Two: September 8ᵗʰ to 9ᵗʰ, 2018 — Cheongju, South Korea

Night moves on, slow but inexorable. Through closed eyelids, Adam sees the darkness lifting on Saturday morning.

Bustling sounds outside: footsteps, voices, and a key turning in a lock. A voice, but not In-sung's. "Dae-hyun-*ah*, wake up. You need to eat to stay strong." He has known this voice all his life. "Sit, child."

To his surprise, his limbs obey.

Grandmother sits on the only chair in the cell, eyes filled with concern, and opens a thermos container. She pours rice porridge into the lid that serves as a bowl and hands it to him with a spoon. "Eat, it will do you good."

"I'm not hungry," he croaks.

She busies herself with another thermos and pours a brown liquid. For a fleeting moment, the aroma masks that of the disinfectant. "I used your Italian machine," she says. Adam shakes his head, no.

"You have to drink something." She walks to the door and asks for a glass of water.

"*Halmeoni,* I'm not thirsty."

She holds his hand as if he is in a hospital bed, and when the guard brings the water, she holds the paper cup to his lips and tips it until the liquid wets them. "Only one sip."

He wants to let the water pour off the sides of his mouth, but the reflex is too strong. The water flows in. He takes the cup from her hands and drinks. The water is lukewarm; the tap has not been run long enough, yet he drains it. He takes the coffee mug that Grandmother offered him earlier. She didn't use enough grounds, though it's better than any coffee he has had all week. She coaxes him to eat the porridge again, and he tries one spoonful. Abalone, typically made at great cost to help very sick people recover. Tears fill his eyes.

In-sung must have told her he looked ill, Adam reasons, otherwise why would she be here? How did she get permission to minister to him like this?

"Five minutes," the guard says, and she rises. She hangs the jacket Adam flung on the floor before he collapsed on the cot. She places his shoes side by side under the bed. She straightens his blanket and packs away her coffee thermos.

He hands her his bowl, ignoring the tears wetting his face. He tells her he is full but she pours him another bowl. "Promise me you'll finish it."

He doesn't want to. "I can't."

She sits again and brings a spoonful of porridge to Adam's lips. He cannot refuse her the way he refuses In-sung. He takes the spoon and continues to eat.

The guard unlocks the door, and she touches Adam's arm. "I'll come again with lunch."

He scrapes his bowl clean before lying on his side and pulling the blanket to his neck. He sleeps. Fitfully but it's sleep, sleep filled with Joseon-era jailers in checkered robes and pointy hats. They brand him on the forehead with a red-hot iron. They bind him face-down on a cross-shaped bed and beat him with a bat until his back, legs, and buttocks throb with pain. They tie him to a crude armchair and force his knees apart with strong posts until his joints crack and, in a paroxysm of agony, he admits his guilt. Adam wakes drenched in sweat, not knowing where he is until the toilet disinfectant reasserts itself and he knows only too well. The day passes in this half-asleep state, interrupted by Grandmother sitting by his bedside while he eats the food she made.

She prepares to leave. "No court on Sunday. We have to wait until Monday."

That's a relief. Adam had not realized how much of his energy went to dreading the call to return to court. He swivels on his cot, and his feet touch the ground. *"Terra firma"* pops into his head, solid ground. Cold. He feels a measure of comfort.

He walks. Around the cell in one direction, then the other. *Don't think about anything, just walk and do thirty push-ups, walk and do sit-ups. Count the repetitions and beat that clock.* He sets a goal: six hours of exercise, an hour reading, then sleep. It is four in the morning when he lays his head on the pillow and tries to silence the voices that say sleep doesn't obey orders like walking and reading do. He has to be strong. He has to show himself to be strong. He feels hungry, but he will have to learn to sleep on an empty stomach. Breakfast at seven. He holds on to that thought. Weak coffee and a ham sandwich. And a banana. He will ask for a banana. He needs potassium.

Joanne always ate a banana with breakfast. He wonders if she still does or if it is one of those habits that has already come and gone.

By the time Grandmother arrives, he has already eaten his prison breakfast and is reading, seated on the floor. Relief washes over her features as she unpacks her thermos flasks.

"I'll have them for lunch," he says. "I'm fine." He is dismissing her.

"Stand, child."

He wanted to circumvent what's coming by staying seated, however, there is no avoiding it. She still has strength in her slight frame, and she hugs him as if they will never see each other again. She releases him, and he cannot disguise the lump in his throat.

"*Halmeoni*—" He wants to ask her to buy a banana—the guard refused earlier—but that will lead to more awkwardness when she returns. "Thank you."

She gestures that it is nothing, repressing tears.

Fifty-Three: September 10ᵗʰ, 2018 — Cheongju, South Korea

It is Monday afternoon, and the crowd outside the courthouse has split into two camps. People on one side of the roped area stare, faces stern and unyielding; people on the other side cheer and meet Adam's eyes with hope. He has found his courage. No matter what happens in the courtroom, he will maintain his dignity. He will not crumble in front of strangers. He held on to that simple resolution as he paced his cell yesterday, as he wrestled with sleep. He will try to atone for his mistake by enduring whatever comes his way. He will stay strong.

In-sung greets him by the elevators.

"You went to Seoul?" Adam asks. He can already see the pattern of his friend's visits to jail. Every week in the beginning, but stretching to every month, then longer spans as new talents claim more of his time at the agency.

Attorney Choi gives Adam a handshake that is neither warm nor cold, already disassociating himself from his client. He will no doubt say—again—that they will appeal if the verdict is "guilty," but who will he be trying to fool, himself or Adam?

He takes his seat. Baek Young-hee's family is in the same pew as always, her mother angled away, dabbing at tears with a checkered handkerchief, and her father leaning forward, shoulders sagging. Her husband acknowledges Adam with a glare and resumes patting his mother-in-law's hand.

"Over there." In-sung directs Adam's eyes to the left.

His father, with his school principal aura, sits in the front row, face devoid of expression, although Adam knows why he is there. To witness his downfall.

It doesn't matter. He will show him what dignity looks like. His mother holds his gaze while Dae-moon gives him a smile that blends encouragement with apologies. Apologies for what, he is not sure. He wishes none of them had come.

The hum of conversation subsides as the judge and two assessors enter and take their seats. The cameras start rolling. Judge Yeom tests his microphone with a finger and surveys the room. "Will the defendant please rise?"

Adam stands. *I am not afraid.*

In-sung and Attorney Choi stand beside him, yet he might as well be alone with the judge. *I am not afraid.* Adam hangs on to his mantra.

The judge holds an envelope but waits for absolute silence before opening it and extracting a sheet of paper that he unfolds.

I am definitely not afraid.

"On the charge of first-degree murder, this court finds the defendant, Ahn Dae-hyun-*ssi*—"

"I AM NOT AFRAID," rings so loudly in Adam's ears that it covers the judge's words.

What did he say? Adam's heart races as he looks to In-sung for clues.

His friend pulls him in a hug. He is crying.

"What did the judge say?" Adam asks in his ear.

"Good God in Heaven, it came so close to going the other way."

Over his friend's shoulders, Adam spots his mother. She hits her fist repeatedly on her heart. She nods at him. His father nods as well.

Adam nods back, with dignity. He pulls away from In-sung and holds him at arm's length. "Guilty or not?"

"Not guilty."

Adam breathes in the words, the hoped-for words, and they slide into his chest, easily at first, wonderfully, until they hit resistance. He coughs a few times but cannot dislodge the dregs of guilt still lingering over the part he played—no, not "part," and not "played"—the responsibility, rather, that he failed to meet.

Judge Yeom and the two assessors exit. Everybody else stays where they are until Baek Young-hee's family, the two men supporting the mother, walk along the aisle, and the courtroom's double doors close behind them. Attorney Choi pumps Adam's hand and wipes away tears.

Adam thanks him for all his hard work. He glimpses Grandmother at the far end of the room, but the press is closing in, and his family cannot reach him. Reporters' questions crisscross each other. "How do you feel?" "What will you do next?"

In-sung pushes forward. "Let us through, please. Let us out." In the elevator, with no guard escorting them, he slaps Adam on the back. "It's over, Dae-hyun-*ah*. You're free."

"It will take time to sink in," Attorney Choi says.

On the plaza outside, the sun lends the scene a festive air, and the crowd's cheers clash with the remorse Adam feels for the role he played in Baek Young-hee's death. He walks between In-sung and Attorney Choi and tries to summon the man these hungry eyes want to see. In-sung feeds him lines that he repeats into the microphones thrust in his face: "I feel vindicated. I'm glad that justice has been served this afternoon."

Only when In-sung opens the car door do his own feelings surface, "Now I can mourn my dear friend and fellow actor, Baek Young-hee-*ssi*, like everyone who loved her."

Fifty-Four: November 1ˢᵗ, 2018 — Seoul, South Korea

Black tree trunks emerge from the mist on this November morning at Bundang Memorial Park. Adam's father, mother and sister have joined him on All Souls' Day. He flew in the night before from Udo Island, where he spent the last two months re-learning how to live. He rented a modest house, did his own cooking and cleaning, and kept away from soju and StarCraft. He went for walks on the trails that crisscross both Udo and Jejudo, even made the day-long climb up Mount Hallasan and gazed at the world below. He tried to forgive himself as In-sung insists he must.

His friend means well, though Adam cannot help thinking that he should have given Baek Young-hee a warning. Three words, "Use with caution," and she would not be lying in a grave under a black marble slab with her name and two dates.

Her many supporters have installed plexiglass cases to display their messages of love. Adam's white chrysanthemums join their more exuberant roses, lilies and birds of paradise. His family performed the ritual prostrations, following his father's lead, and are now waiting. His father paces, hands joined behind his back, rather than joining the others in examining the testimonials left by visitors: "Farewell, First Lady of Korea." "Thank you for the light you brought into our lives." "My deepest sympathy to your father, mother and husband."

"They're coming." Adam's father surveys the bottom of the hill where three figures cross the cemetery from one end to the other and trudge up the slope, heads bent over their feet, delaying as long as possible to acknowledge the Ahn family. Baek Young-hee's husband is the first to make eye contact. Adam expected looks of blame and hatred. He sees a kernel of acceptance.

Adam's father steps forward and leads the family into a deep bow held for several seconds, staring at the three pairs of feet planted on the ground. As they rise Baek Young-hee's mother catches Adam's eyes and bursts into sobs that soon become wails. She breaks off and starts again, propped by her men in case her knees buckle under her.

Adam's father reaches for his son's hand and tugs him forward. He kneels on the cold ground, left hand over right, and bows his deepest apology. His family kneels behind him while wails continue to pierce the mist.

Adam's father clears his throat for them to rise. Had the timing been left to Adam, he would have remained prostrated much longer. They bow their heads again. "We are utterly sorry," they keep saying as Baek Young-hee's family members turn their backs on them and make their way downhill.

Fifty-Five: January to February, 2019 — Ithaca, New York

Snow falls in fluffy clumps outside the shoe repair shop. Cars hiss by on Oak Street as I duck inside Collegetown Bagel, relieved that the line is not too long. Students crowd around tables, talking, laughing, while taking hungry bites of their sandwiches.

After ordering, I wait by the window. Three inches of downy white already blanket the sidewalk, benches, trees, and branches. A red fire hydrant sports a new toque until someone brushes it away with a hand. He reminds me of Adam, although everything reminds me of Adam, tempting me to send a text saying that I saw his doppelganger—from the back, admittedly—sweeping snow with his bare hand as he did at the *hanok*.

He is staying on an island at the southern tip of Korea, I learned from Kang Min-chae. Last week, I received a text. *I went fishing today.* Yesterday I wrote, *I went skating with Sean.* I called on November 16th to wish him a happy birthday. I asked how he was doing. "Oh, you know…" he replied. I did not know what to say. The silence on the line stretched on. "I should let you go," he said.

For Christmas, I texted him a few emojis, nothing overly jolly, and on New Year's Eve, he texted me a calendar page with "31" flying away. His *annus horribilis* was finally over.

It is the mid-winter break, and Sean and I have delayed our grocery shopping trip until Monday. He is well past the age of sitting in the cart while I push him around. He steers us unerringly towards the ultra-sweet cereals and overly salty chips. A simple "no" is never enough. He wants to know why. I'm teaching him how to decode nutritional labels and lists of ingredients. Today he scrutinizes a box of soft ginger cookies. "What's benzoic acid?"

"It helps the food stay fresh. A preservative."

He puts the box in our cart.

"Not so fast. Do you realize there are only eight cookies in there? How much do they cost?"

He doubles back to the shelf and returns, saying two boxes cost $7.99 while one costs $4.99.

"We can make our own cookies for a lot less, and they'll taste even better."

"Aw." He sighs, still hanging on to the box as we enter the next aisle. "Can we add chocolate chips?"

I agree, provided he puts the cookies back and meets me at the far end of the aisle. I return to my list and hunt for the next item. Sean, as I discover next, stopped to talk to a man and now points at me; waves me over.

Adam bows in the formal way he did when he first came to the Center. "Good morning."

Am I dreaming? "Hello. I didn't know—I thought you were still—"

"I'm working with Jamie and Maria."

It takes me a moment to remember the two students who partnered with him for the film they shot outside my house. "That's great."

"Thank you." He bows again and turns his cart around.

Fifty-Six: February to June, 2019 — Ithaca, New York

If not for In-sung, Adam would still be on Udo Island, forcing himself to take long hikes or hiring a fishing boat rather than bingeing on American series streaming on television. The injunction that prevented him from starting post-production on *An Affair of the Heart* might have stayed uncontested indefinitely. And now that In-sung has cleared the way for him to resume that work, he would have chosen any corner of the earth other than where he may run into Joanne. He is nowhere near ready to face her. He may never be, In-sung's nagging notwithstanding.

His former schoolmates, Jamie and Maria, have agreed to help with editing the footage he brought to Ithaca. Time is limited. The submission deadlines for the major film festivals are soon. On the last Saturday in April, In-sung calls him with the news that Baek Young-hee's family has signed off on the trailer, and they can send their submission to the Busan International Film Festival.

"Will you come?" In-sung asks.

"No, you go, *Hyeong*. Assuming they accept the film."

"It would mean a lot for you to be there."

He takes a moment to reflect. "Too much, too soon. Sorry."

"Listen. I'll say it again until it sticks inside your thick skull. And stays there: you didn't sneak that pill into Baek Young-hee-*ssi*'s beer while she had her back turned. You didn't force her to swallow it."

"But I still gave her a pill that was too strong for her."

"You couldn't have predicted she would take the pill, run herself a bath, *then* slip on the wet floor."

"Mmm."

"Enough with looking back, OK?"

On Saturday afternoons, Adam carves time to go to the Unitarian Church to listen to the choir practice. He is not alone. Among the pews, in ones and twos, people let their thoughts wander while voices soar in the grand old church and light filters through the stained-glass windows, shifting and shimmering over their heads. The words float into Adam's soul: *Just as I am, though tossed about / With many a conflict, many a doubt / Fightings and fears, within, without / O Lamb of God, I come, I come.*

He walks back to his apartment, suffused with serenity. At the intersection of East Buffalo and Parker, the first butterfly of the year, yellow and delicate, circles around him. Cars zoom by as he waits for the traffic light to change. The butterfly flutters ahead. Stop! he shouts inwardly. The butterfly turns around and hovers at his side until it is safe to cross.

Adam was not going to take a detour via Joanne's street. He changes his mind.

The Redbud tree in front of her house is in full bloom. Two men with a dog on a leash have stopped to talk to a figure standing in the shade. He could turn away—the old instincts from when avoiding people was second nature—but he keeps going.

"Stunning." He bows a greeting.

The two men nod and move along.

"Happens every year," Joanne says. "Perfect strangers stop for pictures." Her eyes look like water on a shallow beach, more turquoise than blue. "How are you doing, Adam?"

"I'm well." He savours the way she says his name. "And you?"

He passes again the following week. The blooms are almost gone and leaves are emerging. Joanne works outside. He nods.

"Dandelions." She holds a plant. "Dig deep with trowel. Pull hard but slow. Make sure you have all the tap root." The specimen has an eight-inch carrot-like extension. "Throw into waste. Repeat."

"Looks like fun."

After a few weeks, their sidewalk encounters become less accidental and the topics less general. Adam greets her with a smile. He is still trying to join the dots in Yu-mi's story; it bleeds into their conversations. "Her father must have pulled strings with the head of the National Forensic Service. In-sung told me the two men play golf together. I can picture Han Do-ku dangling the threat of some scandal unless the director agreed to grant him that small favour."

Sean is playing across the street with his friend.

"I'm taking a dance class," Joanne says.

"Nice." He waves and walks away.

The following week she sits in a lawn chair, reading a book while Sean and his friend ride their bicycles.

"The film has been accepted at the Toronto festival," he says. "A world premiere." He is still digesting the news.

There is a second lawn chair, and she gestures for him to take it. She asks the same question as In-sung: "Will you go?"

"Jamie and Maria will go."

"You could wear dark glasses and sit at the back."

He smiles.

"We'll have to wait until it comes to the Ithaca Cineplex."

They laugh.

She said "we."

The sun dances on the gold in her hair. After a while, he says he has scenes to edit before the weekend is over.

He doesn't know how to move forward. Every plan he conceives—a weekday lunch near campus, a weekend outing with Sean, or without—is fraught with the danger of upsetting the fragile balance they have achieved. Maybe he should leave as soon as his work with Jamie and Maria is finished; if not for Korea, then for New York, where he might join an artist collective. He enquired, and the coordinator's response was more enthusiastic than he expected. He finds himself yet again in front of her house.

She is not outside. Should he knock on the door, or does it mean she has no time for him today?

Nothing ventured, nothing gained.

Sean answers through the screen door. "Oh, hi." He calls his mother and disappears, leaving Adam on the porch. He hears the boy playing inside with a friend. Across the street, someone is mowing a lawn. The purring sounds change as the person shifts directions. Adam sits on the top step, remembering Joanne telling him that the clover covering her lawn earned her nasty looks from a neighbour who spent the summers grooming his.

The lawnmower sounds cease, replaced by bumblebees buzzing. Joanne emerges, cheeks flushed and tendrils of hair escaping her ponytail. "I lost track of time." She sits beside him and they watch the dappled shade move at the whim of the wind.

"Sean's flight's tomorrow."

"Ah." He knew Sean would spend the summer with his father, though not when he would leave. He could say that her garden looks fantastic or comment on how peaceful it is now, without the lawnmower sounds, but why ruin the moment with trivialities? As if magnetized, his hand yearns to reach over and take hers. After a while he rises and dusts the seat of his pants. "See you next week?"

"Actually, do you have a bit of time?" She rises too.

He nods and she leads the way to her car, unlocks the driver's door and motions for him to get in.

He can't believe what is happening. Is she planning to leave Sean with his friend while they drive away?

She seems to read his mind and flashes him an *it's okay* look.

Maybe she wants to kiss him? But he is wrong. She sits on the passenger side, puts the key in the ignition, reaches over—her breasts brushing his thighs—and buckles him in. Tight.

"But, Sean—" He points to the bungalow.

"We're steps away." She leans over again. "I want to play something."

Play. His mind races to the obvious but all she does is pop a CD in the console.

Adam has not heard "The Fifth Season" for a long time, yet the notes flow exactly as he remembers, bars of flute weaving through guitars, lines of clarinet over a double bass, slides of organ, thunders of piano. Friends he has known all his life.

"Let yourself be the instrument," she says.

Actors are taught to be instruments, but here he doesn't have to give anything back, only receive. He takes her hand.

"Close your eyes. Feel." She gives his hand three squeezes and wraps his fingers around the steering wheel. The sounds glide. They soar. They leap. They resonate through his hands, his feet, his back, his thighs. They reverberate through his bones and amplify through his chest and abdomen, "The Isolation," "The Call," "The Encounter," familiar yet with new meanings, not the simple love story he imagined, but a real life story, with hardships and hard lessons in between.

"The Union" pulses back and forth. It gains momentum and sweeps the lovers along until they crash onto an imaginary shore. And now he feels it, the twang of the seatbelt against his heart, the jolt he felt the first time he heard this music, in this car, waiting for a traffic light to change.

"The Fifth Season" winds down with "The Great Ball," fast and lively. Hopeful.

-The End-

Acknowledgements

The novel's title draws from a 1975 album, *Si on avait besoin d'une cinquième saison* (*If We Needed a Fifth Season*), by Québécois progressive rock band, Harmonium. Fifty years on, this musical work continues to resonate deeply with me. In Chapters Eight and Nine, Joanne and Adam feel jolted through the heart while hearing an instrumental on the radio. They discover it is the aforementioned album's fifth track, "Histoires sans paroles" ("Stories Without Words"), better known as "La cinquième saison." In Chapter Twelve, Adam likens the five parts of the instrumental to his isolation as a superstar and his quest for a meaningful connection. In Chapter Fifty-six, he will revisit "La cinquième saison" and reach a startling new conclusion. *Mille mercis*, Serge Fiori, *Tes paroles, ta musique et ta poésie vivront dans mon coeur — et mes oreilles — pour toujours.*

My eternal gratitude goes to Marthe Dalpé-Scott, PhD, close friend since high school, for her thorough review of early drafts, and transformative advice on the forensic evidence, informed by her deep experience as Program Manager, Toxicology Services, Royal Canadian Mounted Police Forensic Laboratory Services, now retired, and her access to expert colleagues in the organization's Biology Services. Any forensic evidence error is solely mine.

To the talented and thoughtful members of the First Page writing group, Michelle Alfano, Arif Anwar, Michelle Boone, Justine Mazin, Liz Torlée, and Tina Tzatzanis: my deepest thanks for believing in my ability to tell this story and nudging me closer to publication. To my early readers, Dawn Chapman, Susan Doherty Hannaford, Iris Gershon, Camille Martin, Linda Muir, Candace Plattor, Lucie Sparham, and Catherine Szabo: thank you for making key suggestions to improve this story. To University of Toronto School of Continuing Studies faculty members, Ray Robertson, Dennis Bock, and the incomparable Kim Echlin: thank you for your judicious comments.

To the many friends who attended readings of early versions of these chapters and encouraged me along the way: I feel truly blessed.

Arigato gosaimasu to Serita Hiroko, who guided my visit to the Hamarikyu Gardens in Tokyo, which figured in a scene I later deleted – *gomen nasai*, Hiroko-*san*. To the tens of thousands of women from all over the world who gathered in Tokyo in 2009 to celebrate their friendship through learning about Korea: I bow to each of you in gratitude. Your hands-across-the-water love continues to give me hope despite how fractious our world is becoming. *Saranghae*.

My boundless gratitude goes to Shane Joseph, my editor at Blue Denim Press, who guided me unerringly through game-changing edits and designed a cover that vastly exceeded my expectations.

Both my parents left this world while I was writing *Our Fifth Season*. To my father, Roger Sigouin, I owe my love of reading. To my mother, Solange Levert, I owe self-esteem and belief in following my dreams.

Posthumously, as well, to my Chinese parents-in-law: thank you for welcoming me unconditionally into the Tong family. Your warmth and kindness made a huge difference in my life.

Helping my sons, Michael and Stephen Tong, with their high-school writing assignments taught me many lessons applicable to creative writing. Your unflagging support for "mom-GPT" means the world. Last, but not least, I wish to thank my husband, Jeff, to whom this novel is dedicated, for introducing South Korean stories in our lives and sharing this rich journey with me.

Author Bio

Josée Sigouin is French Canadian and lives in Toronto/Tkaronto with her Chinese Canadian husband and their two sons. Until 2021, she worked at the University of Toronto, where she specialized in telling stories with numbers.

Watching South Korean films and television series twenty years ago launched her on a quest to understand the fascinating culture in ever greater depth. She has learned the rudiments of the Korean language, visited the Land of the Morning Calm multiple times, and read extensively about its past and present. She also turned her attention to telling stories with words, mentored by award-winning authors Dennis Bock and Kim Echlin at the University of Toronto's School of Continuing Studies, and Giller Prize winner Omar El Akkad at a writing residency in Bangladesh.

Josée is a founding member of the Toronto-based writing group, First Page. An autobiographical piece about her creative writing journey appears in the Women Writing Letters series, Gailey Road Productions, 2016, and her literary blog. An early excerpt from *Our Fifth Season* (titled *Intersection*) was shortlisted for the 2011 Random House of Canada Student Award. In addition to travelling, Josée enjoys cycling, gardening, and welcoming birds to her tiny garden. *Our Fifth Season* is her first novel. She is currently working on a historical novel set in seventeenth-century Korea.